MOTOR MOUTH

MOTOR MOUTH

Janet Evanovich

ISIS

LARGE PRINT

Oxford

Copyright © Janet Evanovich, 2006

First published in Great Britain 2006
by HarperCollins*Publishers*

Published in Large Print 2007 by ISIS Publishing Ltd.,
7 Centremead, Osney Mead, Oxford OX2 0ES
by arrangement with HarperCollins*Publishers*

British Library Cataloguing in Publication Data
Evanovich, Janet
    Motor mouth. – Large print ed.
    1. NASCAR (Association) – Fiction
    2. Automobile racing – Florida – Miami – Fiction
    3. Automobile theft – Florida – Miami – Fiction
    4. Miami (Fla.) – Fiction
    5. Humorous stories
    6. Detective and mystery stories
    7. Large type books
    I. Title
    813.5'4 [F]

ISBN 978–0–7531–7846–1 (hb)
ISBN 978–0–7531–7847–8 (pb)

Printed and bound in Great Britain by
T. J. International Ltd., Padstow, Cornwall

CHAPTER
ONE

Sometimes there's a decision to be made between winning fairly and cheating for a good cause. And sometimes, in the heat of competition, I've slipped south of fair. So I understand the temptation. But here's the thing about cheating . . . don't cheat me. I take it personally.

And I was pretty sure I had my eye on a guy who was cheating at my expense. He was wearing a red suit. He was driving a flashy car with a big 69 painted on the side. And he was going too fast. I had my binoculars trained on him as he took a turn, his left-front tire tight to the curve.

I was standing on the flat roof of the Homestead-Miami Speedway grandstand, getting a bird's-eye view of the scrubby Florida landscape. Heat waves shimmered on the track below me, and the air was thick with fumes from scorched rubber, high-octane gas, and the euphoria NASCAR brings to a race. I was with forty-two guys on the roof. I was the only one on the roof wearing a pink lace thong. At least I was almost certain I was the only one in a thong since I was the only female, but hell, what do I know? I was wearing tight black jeans and a Stiller Racing shirt. The shirt had short sleeves, was white with black and gold trim, and the Stiller Racing logo was embroidered on the front. The embroidered name on the back was a garage joke: Motor Mouth. I'm Sam Hooker's race-day spotter. I'm the lip-glossed, bleached blonde who whispers into Hooker's ear while he sweats his brains out in a black-and-gold fire-resistant jumpsuit each week.

This week Hooker was running his black Metro-sponsored car around and around the Homestead 1.5-mile oval. It was the last race of the season and I was looking forward to a change of pace. I love my job, but there comes a time when a girl just wants to shimmy into a sexy little dress and sip a cosmo at a restaurant that doesn't feature barbecue. Not that I don't like barbecue, but I'd had a *lot* of it lately.

Hooker's voice was loud and clear in my headset. "Earth to Motor Mouth. Talk to me."

"I'm thinking thoughts that can't go public."

"Are these thoughts about getting naked?" Hooker asked.

"No, they're about getting even."

"Listen, it was an accident, I swear. I was drunk and I don't remember a thing. I don't know how I ended up in bed with that salesclerk. Darlin', you *know* I love you."

Mental head slap. "Not that, you moron. I'm talking about the race."

Hooker got his start on Texas dirt tracks. He's raced open-wheel karts, trucks, and everything in between. He's my age but he looks like a college kid. Sun-bleached blond hair, and a nice body that's got some muscle and stands a couple inches taller than me. The difference between Hooker and the college kid is in Hooker's eyes. There are lines at the corners that tell his age and grit. And there's a depth that comes from living hard and gaining something from it.

I'd done some racing when I was in high school. Strictly local amateur stuff. I'd wreck the cars, and then I'd fix them up in my dad's garage in Baltimore. Turned out I was a lot better at fixing them than racing them, so I bailed on the driving and got an engineering degree instead. Hooker isn't worth anything as a mechanic, but he can really run a car. I've worked as his spotter and also as part of his R & D team for an entire season, thirty-six Cup races, and I'm knocked out by his consistently aggressive attitude and his ability to drive.

There are those who question Hooker's balls-to-brain ratio. I've never seen an X-ray of his head, so I'm taking a winger on his brain, but I've seen the other equipment in question and I'm pretty confident the ratio is two to one.

I'd been involved in a romantic relationship with Hooker when I'd taken the job with Stiller. And I'd been idiot enough to think the relationship was serious. Hooker had proved me wrong at four months with a one-night stand that had gotten splashed onto every tabloid. I was now over Hooker . . . pretty much. The only thing I was currently serious about was my job. I was devoted to Stiller Racing.

"You've done two hundred and forty-four laps," I said. "You have twenty-three laps to go. The red sixty-nine car is four car lengths in front of you."

The 69 was sponsored by Lube-A-Lot and owned by Huevo Motor Sports, a Mexican powerhouse with money to burn on race cars. Huevo built good cars, but sometimes the 69 was *too* good, and I was willing to put money down that the 69 car was cheating, running with illegal technology.

"Four car lengths," Hooker said to me. "That's too much. *Do* something."

"I can tell you when it's safe to pass, and when it's okay to pit, and when there's trouble ahead. Being that I'm up here on the roof, and you're down there on the track, and I've left my magic voodoo dust back in the motor coach, it's going to be hard for me to *do* something."

And that was when the big one happened. The monster car crash that car owners dread and fans love. A Stiller car driven by Nick Shrin got loose, slid out of its groove, and the car following it made contact and punted Shrin into the wall. Six other cars got caught in the wreck and were instantly turned into twisted, shredded scrap metal. Fortunately, they were all behind Hooker.

When racing resumed and everyone lined up for the restart, the gap would be closed between the red 69 Lube-A-Lot car and Hooker's Metro car.

"Back her down," I told Hooker. "You just got lucky."

"What happened?"

"Shrin got loose and hit the wall, and after that he was hit by everyone except you and the pace car."

The caution flag was out and the field was frozen until the mess could be cleared. Stiller Racing runs three Cup cars. Hooker drives one. Larry Karna drives another. And Nick Shrin drives the yellow-and-red car sponsored by YumYum Snack Cakes. Nick's a good driver and a good person, and I was experiencing some anxiety about him right now. Stock cars are entered and exited via the driver's-side window, and Shrin hadn't yet climbed out. I had my binoculars trained on him, but I couldn't tell much. He was still in his restraint system, still had his helmet on, visor down. The car was surrounded by emergency workers. A bunch of cars were trashed in the crash, but Shrin was the only driver not yet out of his.

"What's going on?" Hooker wanted to know.

"Shrin's still in his car."

Shrin's spotter was standing next to me. His name is Jefferson Davis Warner, and everyone calls him Gobbles. He's in his early thirties, his ears stick out, his brown hair sticks up, and he has a nose that got smashed in a bar fight and was left slightly crooked. He's gangly legged and rail thin, and his hands and feet are too big for his body . . . sort of a cross between a fluffy-headed crane and a Great Dane puppy. He eats nonstop and never gains an ounce. I'm told he got the name Gobbles when he was in school and was always first in the lunch line. I guess it's ironically appropriate that he's now on the YumYum Snack Cake team. He has a good heart, and he's a good spotter. And like a lot of people in the program, when Gobbles got out of the NASCAR bubble, he wasn't the sharpest tack on the corkboard. He could calculate pit road speed from a tach reading, but he couldn't tell a con man from a cow flop. It all smelled the same to Gobbles. Right now his face was white, and he had the rail in a death grip.

"How is he?" I asked Gobbles. "Is he talking to you?"

"No. I heard him hit the wall, and since then there's been nothing but silence. He's not saying anything."

Every spotter was binoculars up on the YumYum car. Conversation on the roof was hushed. No one moved. If a driver was really in trouble, a tarp would be raised, shielding him from view. I had my teeth sunk into my lower lip, and my stomach clenched into a knot, praying not to see the tarp.

Rescue workers were at both side windows. The EMT at the driver's window backed out. He had Shrin in tow. They strapped Shrin onto a stretcher. I still couldn't see much. Too many people at the accident scene. NASCAR came on over their own frequency and announced that Shrin was conscious and going for tests. The PA system relayed it. An audible sigh of relief went up from the stands. Spotters backed off, using the break in action to scarf down junk food or smoke or rush to the men's room.

Gobbles was still attached to the rail, looking like he might keel over at any moment.

"He's conscious," I told Gobbles. "They're taking him for tests. Looks like you're done for the day."

Gobbles nodded but held tight to the rail.

"You don't look good," I told him. "You should go down and get out of the sun."

"It's not the sun," Gobbles said. "It's my life. My life sucks."

"It'll get better."

"Not likely," Gobbles said. "I'm a loser. I don't do nothin' right. Even my wife left me. I didn't do nothin' right there either. She took off six months ago with the kids and the dog. She said I didn't know nothin' about the man in the boat. The man in the boat don't like to be woke up in the middle of the night. And the man in the boat needs to have the oar in the water longer than thirty seconds. I tell you, there was a list a mile long about the man in the boat. Do this. Don't do that. Half the time I couldn't even *find* the man in the boat. It was just friggin' confusing. I mean, it wasn't like I didn't want to do right by the man in the boat, but golly jeez I couldn't get the hang of it. And if you ask me, the man in the boat is pretty fuckin' grumpy. I want to go back to the days when it was enough for a guy to take out the garbage. Whatever happened to those days? Those were simpler times. And now I'm making a mess of my job. I got my driver hurt."

"That wasn't your fault."

"It *was* my fault. Loser, loser, loser. That's me. I thought I was doing good, but it turned out bad. It's the man in the boat all over again."

"Maybe you should talk to Hooker. He knows a lot about the man in the boat."

Gobbles focused his binoculars on the infield and sucked in air. "And things aren't bad enough, the sonsabitches are talking to Ray Huevo. Lordy, what does that mean?"

The infield of a NASCAR track is a self-contained race city. The trucks that haul the cars are lined up across from the garages and serve as mobile command units. Beyond the trucks are the million-dollar-driver motor coaches. And if there's enough room, in a separate infield area, some lucky fans will get a campground space. I did a sweep, but I didn't know what I was looking for.

"I don't know Huevo by sight," I said to Gobbles. "Where is he?"

"There are three men standing alongside the sixty-nine car hauler. Ray Huevo's the one in the short-sleeved shirt. I only seen him a couple times. He don't usually show up at the races. He pretty much stays in Mexico. His brother Oscar is the head of Huevo Motor Sports, and it's usually him you see at the track. Ray is kind of the runt black sheep of the family. Anyhow, the little bald guy with Ray Huevo is the guy who run down Clay."

Clay Moogey worked in the engine department at Stiller. Three days ago he walked out of a bar, stepped off the curb to cross the street, and was killed by a hit-and-run driver.

"Are you sure?"

"That wasn't no accident what happened to Clay. I saw him run down," Gobbles said. "I was there. I seen Clay step off and then this guy come out of nowhere and aimed right for him."

"Did you tell the police?"

"I couldn't do that. I'm in a tight spot. I couldn't get myself involved. And it's not like I know a name or something. I'm just telling you now because . . . hell, I don't know why I'm telling you. I'm telling you everything. Cripes, I told you about the man in the boat. How embarrassing is that?"

In the distance, Ray Huevo was standing, hands on hips, leaning forward to better hear over the track noise. He suddenly straightened, turned, and looked directly at us. He pointed with his finger, and Gobbles shrieked and jumped back.

"He's far away," I said to Gobbles. "He could be pointing at anyone."

Gobbles's voice was up an octave. "He was pointing at me! I know he was pointing at me. I saw him."

Ray Huevo pivoted on his heel and stalked off. The two men in suits followed a few feet behind him. They all disappeared behind another hauler, and I was pulled back to the track by Hooker's voice in my ear.

"There must be something wrong with my radio," he said. "I'm not *hearing* anything."

"That's because I'm not *saying* anything," I told him.

"How much are we paying you?"

"Not nearly enough. Anyway, I only have one piece of advice. I think you should pass the sixty-nine."

"Yeah, that sounds like a good idea. Gee, why didn't *I* think of that?"

If the 69 car stayed in front, we'd come in second for the season. And in my book, second didn't count. Dickie Bonnano, also known as Dickwad, Banana Dick, Dickhead, and sometimes just plain Asshole, was driving the 69. Bonnano was an arrogant jerk. He was a mediocre driver. And he had a girlfriend who was equally disliked. She towered over Bonnano, had a preference for leather, lined her eyes to look like Catwoman, and she'd bought herself a pair of double-D boobs that didn't jiggle, droop, or have peripheral vision. The guys in the garage called her Delores Dominatrix. So when Bonnano wasn't being called Dickwad, Banana Dick, Dickhead, or Asshole, he was called Spanky.

Hooker had Bonnano by a few points, but Bonnano would win the series if he won this race. And unless God stepped in and blew Bonnano's engine, Bonnano was going to win.

There were thirty-two cars left in the race. They were lined up in running order behind the pace car, and they were circling the track at forty miles per hour, waiting for the signal that the track was clean and ready for racing. They approached turn number four, the pace car exited onto pit road, and the flag went green.

"The pace car's off," I said to Hooker. "Green, green."

The cars roared past me, all of them hard on the gas. Bonnano took the lead and kept it, gaining inches each time he came out of a turn. Hooker was silent on his radio.

"Steady," I told Hooker. "Drive smart. You have no one close behind you and only one guy in front of you."

"This is a nightmare," Hooker said. "A friggin' nightmare."

"Second isn't so bad. There are good points to second."

"I can hardly wait to hear."

"If you don't win the Cup, you don't have to sit on the stage and look like a moron at the awards banquet. Spanky and Delores will have to do the stage thing."

"You should be happy for that, too," Hooker said. "You would have been on the stage with me."

"No way."

"You would have been my date."

"I don't think so."

"You should check your contract. There's a clause in there about dating the driver under emergency conditions."

"What about the salesclerk?"

"Can't hear you," he yelled. "Too much static."

I had my binoculars still trained on Hooker, and I watched him sail under the checkered flag, a car length behind Bonnano.

"Wahoo, lookit me," Hooker sang out. "I'm second. I came in second."

"Very funny," I told him. "Just try to control yourself and don't hit anyone in the face when you get out of the car."

The radio went dead, so I packed up and turned to leave and realized Gobbles was still at the rail.

"You don't mind if I walk down with you, do you?" Gobbles asked. "I don't want to go down alone."

We took the elevator to ground level, and we fought our way through the crowd exiting the stands. Ordinarily I'd cut across the track, but Gobbles wasn't looking great, so I hitched us a ride on a golf cart that was going back to the infield. I squished Gobbles in as the third man on a two-man rear seat and kept watch to see that he didn't faint and fall out of the cart.

The track has golf carts, the teams have golf carts, the sponsors have golf carts, and the drivers have golf carts. Sometimes the golf carts are generic little white jobs and sometimes the golf carts are souped up and custom painted. Hooker's golf cart matched his motor coach and traveled to each race with the coach. At the start of the season, when I was involved with Hooker, I had had the use of his golf cart. After the salesclerk incident, I didn't feel comfortable using the cart and gave Hooker back his keys. Looking at it in retrospect, I probably should have kept the keys. Just because you're no longer sleeping with a guy doesn't mean you can't use his golf cart, right?

We took the tunnel under the track and came out into the infield. The deep rumble of stock cars had been replaced with the *wup wup wup* of helicopters passing overhead, transporting people back to Miami. On race day, helicopters start arriving early in the morning, a new bird touching down every few minutes, dumping celebrities, captains of industry, NASCAR family members, and sometimes sponsors into the infield, repeating the drill throughout the day and reversing the operation late into the night.

"Where are you going now?" Gobbles asked me. "Are you going to Hooker's hauler?"

"No. I want to watch the sixty-nine go through inspection."

12

"You think there's something fishy about the sixty-nine?"

"Yes. Don't you?"

"I surely do," Gobbles said. "And this isn't the only race where I thought that. And now that I seen them two guys talkin' to Ray Huevo, I'm getting real bad vibes. I can't tell you more than that on account of like I said before, I'm in a tight spot. Problem is, they inspected that sixty-nine car before and never found anything."

The drill was that Spanky would do a burnout for the fans and then drive the 69 into Victory Lane for pictures. When the photo op was over, NASCAR would commandeer the car for inspection and testing, along with the other top five cars and a couple more chosen at random. By the time the 69 got to the garage, NASCAR would already have rolled it through the scales and measured its height and weight. Once it was in the garage, fuel would be drawn, ignition boxes taken out and cut apart, the engine heads removed, gears checked, cylinders measured, and shocks examined.

When you watch a car get stripped down and tested, it's hard to believe anyone would try to cheat. And even harder to believe they'd get away with it. And yet almost everyone tries at one time or another.

If you've got an experienced crew, the entire exercise takes about ninety minutes. The carcass of the car after it's been picked clean is then loaded into the hauler, along with the backup car, and brought back to the shop in North Carolina where it'll get rebuilt for another race.

13

Gobbles stayed glued to my side while I stood at a distance and watched the 69 get taken apart.

"I never watched this whole inspection thing," Gobbles said. "The team's always in a hurry to leave. I never got a chance to do this."

I looked back at the line of haulers. The YumYum car hauler was ready to go, motor running. I didn't see any of Gobbles's team.

"You're looking like a man without a country," I said to him.

"Yeah, I should have met up with everybody at the van a while ago, but I got business to do. Not that I really want to do it. Anyways, I was hoping to take care of it here, only it don't seem to be happening. I guess I need to take off." Gobbles gave me a hug. "I appreciate your being a friend and all."

"Be careful."

"I'm trying," Gobbles said, walking off toward media parking.

Fifteen minutes later, when it was obvious nothing illegal was going to turn up on the 69, I headed for the drivers' lot.

I found Hooker's motor coach, opened the door, and yelled to Hooker, "Are you decent?"

"Guess that's a matter of opinion," Hooker said.

Hooker was showered and dressed in jeans and a ratty T-shirt and was watching cartoons with Beans, his newly adopted Saint Bernard. Beans gave an excited *woof* when he saw me, launched himself off the couch, and caught me midchest with his two massive front

14

paws. I went flat on my back with Beans on top, giving me lots of slurpy Saint Bernard kisses.

Hooker pulled Beans off and looked down at me. "Wish I'd had the guts to do that."

"Don't start. I'm not in a good mood."

Hooker yanked me to my feet, I went straight to the refrigerator, and I got a Bud. I put it to my forehead and then I took a long pull. Every driver's fridge is filled with Bud because first thing in the morning, the Bud beer fairy arrives and leaves a fresh delivery on the motor coach doorstep. I stayed in an economy hotel six miles away with the rest of the crew and the Bud beer fairy didn't go there.

"So," Hooker said. "What's up?"

"As far as I could see, they didn't find anything illegal on the sixty-nine car."

"And?"

"I don't believe it. You can drive rings around Spanky, and you had a great car, and he got time on you in every corner."

"Which would mean?"

"Traction control."

In street cars, traction control is done by a computer that detects slip and then directs power to the appropriate wheel. In a race car, traction control really means speed control. A race-car driver learns to sense his wheels slipping and then gets off the gas to control engine power, which in turn slows the wheels and controls the slip. Computer-based electronic traction control duplicates this throttle management but much more efficiently and effectively. NASCAR thinks it takes some of the fun out of racing and has ruled it illegal. Still, if you want to take the risk, an average driver can pick up to a fifth of a second per lap using electronic traction control. And that could be enough to win a race.

Beans was sprawled in the middle of the floor, his head next to Hooker's sneakered foot. Beans was white with a black face mask, floppy black ears, and a brown patch on his back that was shaped like a saddle. At 140 pounds, he sort of looked like a small hairy cow. He was a sweetie pie, but he wasn't going to win any dog-show prizes. Maybe for drooling. He was a really good drooler. He opened a droopy Saint Bernard eye and gave me one of those looks, like *what?*

Hooker was giving me the exact same look. "Traction control is easy to spot," he said. "You need a power source, wires, a switch."

"I could put traction control on your car and no one would find it."

Now I had Hooker's attention. Hooker would use illegal technology on his car in a heartbeat if he thought he could get away with it. And the possibility of being able to efficiently power down to gain more control in a turn was driver mind candy.

"Then why don't I have it on my car?" Hooker asked.

"For starters, I don't like you enough to risk it."

"Darlin', that's cold."

"Plus, there are too many people around the cars when they're being built. It's the sort of thing that would need a closed shop. And a closed shop would attract attention. And then there's the power source . . ."

Hooker raised an eyebrow.

"I've never actually put this on a car, but I think I could use a lithium watch battery as a power source and run the wires inside the frame. Maybe put the battery-powered computer chip in the roll bar. NASCAR wouldn't tamper with the roll bar. Even better would be to use wireless technology and place the chip directly on the engine. It could be made to look like a flaw in the housing and would be so small it wouldn't be noticed."

"How small?"

"Smaller than a contact lens. And if this was the case, you wouldn't need a closed shop. You'd just need a cooperative engine builder."

"What about the off/on switch?"

"Pocket-size remote control that could be hidden in a fire suit."

Hooker drained his beer can, crushed it, and pitched it into the sink. "Barney girl, you're damn sneaky. I respect that in a mechanic."

"Have you heard anything about Shrin?"

"Yeah, he's okay. He got rattled around pretty good, and it knocked the wind out of him. I guess he was disoriented when they first got to him, but he's back to his normal stupid self now."

I could hear the car haulers rumbling out of the adjoining lot. They were loaded and on their way back to the garages in North Carolina. Forty-three haulers. Each hauler containing more than a million dollars' worth of cars and equipment. Two race cars ride end to end in the top half of the hauler. The bottom half contains a lounge, a bathroom, a kitchenette of sorts, a small office area with a computer, closets for the crew's uniforms, plus all the spare parts and tools needed to keep the cars racing. Large rolling toolboxes were secured in the aisle and filled most of the space from the rear door to the side door.

Only the hauler drivers rode in the haulers. Crew members and race-car drivers traveled in private planes. Stiller owned an Embraer that it used to fly team members. Hooker and Beans flew in Hooker's Citation Excel. And I usually bummed a ride with Hooker. Most drivers were helicoptered from the track to the airport, but Beans didn't like helicopters, so we were forced to drive. Fine by me. I didn't like helicopters either.

We snapped a leash on Beans and took him out for a walk. Most of the motor coaches were still in place but were empty, abandoned by their owners. Tomorrow morning the motor coach drivers would come onboard and maneuver the coaches out of the infield and onto the open road. Beans wandered out of the drivers' lot and into the garage area. Only one hauler was still parked across from its garage. The 69. The hauler driver and a couple of guys from the 69 team were huddled around the cab.

"Got a problem?" Hooker asked.

"Fuel pump. We're waiting on a part."

We went back to the motor coach, made some sandwiches, and zapped on the television. No point sitting in traffic. In another half hour it would thin out, and we could pack off for the airport.

My phone rang, and I wasn't surprised when I saw the readout. Gobbles. Probably missed the team plane and wanted a ride home.

"I need help," Gobbles said.

He was whispering, and he was hard to hear, but the desperation in his voice was clear.

"Sure," I said. "Do you need a ride?"

"No. And I can't talk. I'm afraid someone will hear me. I'm trapped in the sixty-nine hauler. I crawled in here to hide, but now I'm sealed up and can't get out. I can't even get the floor hatch open. You have to help me."

"You're not serious."

"You're going to have to sneak me out somehow. You can't let the drivers know I'm here. I'm already in enough trouble. And Ray Huevo is involved in this, so you have to be real careful."

"Involved in *what*?"

"I can't tell you, but it's serious shit. Oh fuck! They're pulling out. Sweet Jesus, I'm gonna die. I'm on the second deck with the cars, and the truck's moving. You and Hooker are the only ones I can ask for help. I trust you. You have to get me out of here."

"Okay, don't panic. We'll come up with something."

I disconnected and looked over at Hooker.

"Gobbles is trapped on the second deck of the sixty-nine hauler and wants us to rescue him."

"Darlin', you've had too much beer."

"I'm serious! He's involved in something bad. It has to do with Ray Huevo and two guys who look like goons-in-suits. He said he crawled into the truck to hide and got locked in."

"And he didn't bang on the side of the truck and yell because . . ."

"He's scared."

We both turned at the sound of the hauler slowly rumbling down the road past the motor coach.

"We have to get him out," I said to Hooker. "I don't know what this is about, but he really sounded panicked. And he said something weird on the roof. He said Clay was intentionally run down."

"Sounds to me like Gobbles has been watching too many *Sopranos* reruns."

"I had the same thought, but it doesn't matter because the problem at hand is that he's trapped in Spanky's hauler."

"Never let it be said I walked away from a friend in need," Hooker said. He shoved off the couch, crossed to the little built-in desk on the other side of the room, and took a gun out of the desk drawer.

"I'm a rootin', tootin', shootin' Texan," he said. "And I'm going to rescue my good buddy Gobbles."

"Oh boy."

"Not to worry. I know what I'm doing."

"I've heard that before."

"If you're referring to that incident with the condom, it wasn't my fault. It was too small, and it was a slippery little devil. And anyway, it was defective. It had a big hole in it."

20

"You did that with your thumb."

Hooker grinned at me. "I was in a hurry."

"I remember."

"Anyway, I knew what I was doing *most* of the time."

"I remember that, too. How are we going to manage this?"

"I guess the easiest way is to follow the truck and wait for the drivers to take a rest break. We only need five minutes to plug in the remote and open the back enough for Gobbles to get out."

"It's too bad we don't have ski masks or something. Just in case."

"I haven't got any ski masks, but we can put my Calvin briefs over our heads and cut eyeholes in the ass."

"Yeah," I said. "I'll look forward to that."

I changed into a T-shirt, we shut off the coach lights, loaded Beans into the back of Hooker's rental SUV, and took off after the number 69 Lube-A-Lot car hauler.

CHAPTER
TWO

Traffic wasn't gridlock, but it wasn't good either. The track glowed bright white behind us and in front of us was a line of red brake lights stretching clear to Miami. The hauler was out of sight, up the road, but it was in traffic, too. There were two drivers, and they'd most likely drive through the night. With any luck, they'd stop to eat and stretch their legs, and we could accomplish our rescue.

The traffic began to open up as cars peeled off onto side roads. Hard to tell exactly what was in front of us, but there appeared to be a couple trucks ahead, their roof running lights visible above the stream of SUVs and sedans.

An hour later, we'd made enough progress at working our way up to the trucks to see that one of them was the 69 hauler. We were a bunch of cars back, but we had it in sight.

I called Gobbles on his cell.

"We're a couple cars behind you," I told him. "We're going to get you out when they stop to take a break. Are you okay?"

"Yeah. I'm cramped, but I'm okay."

I disconnected.

"Do you know the hauler driver?" I asked Hooker.

He shook his head. "Only superficially. The Huevo people keep to themselves. Not a real friendly group."

We were about ten miles north of Miami when the hauler took an exit. My heart did a little tap dance in my chest, and I momentarily stopped breathing. The smart, sane part of my brain had been hoping I'd get a call from Gobbles saying he'd found an unlocked escape hatch in the roof, and he didn't need our help. The stupid, crazy part of my brain was flirting with the fantasy that I was about to have a James Bond experience and perform a kick-ass rescue. And the chickenshit part of my brain was running down black roads of terror.

The truck stopped at the end of the off-ramp and turned left. A half mile down the road, it pulled into the lot for a large truck-stop-type diner and drove to the truck and bus parking at the rear. Three other haulers were already parked there. Hooker circled the lot and waited at idle toward the front. The two hauler drivers came from behind the building and went into the diner.

The back lot where the trucks were parked was lit by a single overhead halogen. The 69 hauler had running lights on and the engine at idle. Standard procedure. It was a natural assumption that no one would be insane enough to try to steal a hauler. No point in shutting down the systems. Hooker cut his lights, eased up to the 69, and parked. All haulers have exterior cargo bays that are used for storing cartons of soda, automotive equipment, barbecue grills, and whatever else. The cargo bay closest to the left-rear door usually contains the remote used to operate the back-panel hydraulics. I ran to the hauler and attempted to open the rear-bay door. Locked. Hooker tried the bay on the other side. Also locked. We tried the side door. Locked.

"Find something to jimmie the bay door," I told Hooker. "We're going to have to break him out."

Hooker searched the rental for a tire iron or screwdriver, and I searched the truck cab for a key. We both came up empty.

I glanced at my watch. We'd gone through fifteen minutes. "We can't get the door open without the remote," I said to Hooker. "And he's going to be in there for a long time if we miss this opportunity. I'm at a loss. Do you have any ideas?"

Hooker sucked in some air and blew it out. "Yeah. We could steal the hauler."

"Get serious."

"I am serious. It's all I can come up with. We drive the hauler down the road, park it behind a Wal-Mart or something, buy a can opener, get Gobbles out, and take off. Some of the trucks are equipped with a GPS tracker. If Huevo has a tracker on this hauler, they can find it immediately. If not, we can go to a pay phone and tell them where the hauler is located."

"This hauler has a tracker. I saw the antenna when I was crawling around, looking for a way to break in. So we wouldn't really be stealing. It would be more like borrowing."

"Whatever."

I gnawed on my lower lip. The very thought of "borrowing" the hauler gave me stomach cramps.

24

"We're running out of time," Hooker said. "What's it going to be? Are we doing this?"

I punched Gobbles's number into my cell. "Are you still okay?"

"It's really stuffy in here. Are you going to get me out soon? I'm not feeling good."

"We can't get the door open. We're going to drive you down the road and get some tools. Hang in there."

Hooker hauled himself up into the truck cab and angled behind the wheel.

"Hey, wait a minute," I said. "Why do you get to drive the big truck?"

"I'm the driver. I always drive. It's what I do. Anyway, have you ever driven an eighteen-wheeler?"

"Yes. Have you?" I asked him.

"Yep," Hooker said.

"Liar, liar, pants on fire."

"You don't know that for sure."

"I do. Your mouth gets this little crook in it when you lie."

"Give me a break here. I'm a testosterone-crazed race-car driver. I've gotta drive the boat."

"This is a truck."

"Truck, boat . . . it's all the same. Look at it. It's big. It's a guy toy."

"You know about the air brakes, right?" I asked Hooker.

"Yeah. Air brakes."

"And you know how to turn the headlights on? You've only got running lights right now."

"Yeah. Lights."

"This truck has approximately five hundred and fifty horses and an eighteen-speed transmission."

"Yep."

"The trailer's fifty-three feet long, so you have to watch the turning radius —"

"I've got it under control," Hooker said. "Get in the car and follow me out."

Beans was sitting up, looking out the window at me when I returned to the SUV. He was doing heavy-duty panting and his forehead was wrinkled.

"Don't worry," I said to him. "He'll be fine. He knows what he's doing."

Beans looked like that registered a seven on his bullshit-o-meter. I'd actually placed it a couple points higher on mine. I buckled myself in, cranked the engine over, and waited for Hooker to roll. I gripped the wheel and whispered under my breath, "Take it slow." When the hauler crept forward, my grip went white knuckled and my breath caught in my chest.

Hooker was smoothly moving the truck across the back lot, toward the front of the building, inching along without lights. He eased the hauler into the exit lane, and I fell in line behind him. This was the moment of no return. In minutes he'd be on the highway in a hijacked truck. Time for honesty. If we got caught, we'd be out of NASCAR and into Florida penal.

My heart was pounding so hard it was blurring my vision. Even Beans was instinctively alert, no longer panting. I checked him out in my rearview mirror to make sure he was okay and we locked eyes. Probably it

26

was my spooked imagination, but I swear he looked as terrified as I felt.

Hooker left-turned the hauler off the diner property and his rear tires ran over the curb and took out a four-foot-tall pygmy date palm and an entire flower bed. I looked around in panic, but didn't see anyone rushing out of the diner after him.

"I didn't see that," I said to Beans. "You didn't see it either, right?"

Hooker maneuvered the truck out of the flower bed, onto the feeder road and then onto the highway, heading south. He turned his lights on, brought the rig up to speed, and we both went into cruising mode. After a few minutes, I realized cars were pulling up to the truck to get a better look. Every inch of a car hauler is a rolling advertisement for the car and the sponsor. They're works of art. The 69 was decorated in Spanky's colors with a bigger-than-life-size picture of Spanky and his race car.

I called Hooker on his cell phone. "We have a problem," I told him. "Everyone's interested in the hauler. Some people are taking pictures. You should have brought the briefs to put over your head."

"Hard to feel righteous when you've got your underwear on your head," Hooker said. "Anyway, I'm taking the next exit. I saw a sign for services. I'll find a dark place to hide, and you can go to a gas station and steal something helpful."

Hooker crawled off the exit, turned right, and rolled down the road. After about a half mile, he came to a small strip mall that was lights off for the night. His turn signal went on, he slipped into the lot, and he disappeared behind the buildings. I made a U-turn and drove back to a gas station and convenience store.

Ten minutes later, I pulled around the end of the strip mall and caught Hooker in my headlights. The hauler was at idle. The headlights and running lights were off. Hooker was lounging against the hauler.

I parked and ran over with a small screwdriver I'd bought at the convenience store. I ripped the packaging apart and gave Hooker the screwdriver.

"This was the best I could do. The garage was closed."

Hooker rammed the screwdriver between the bay door and the outside rim of the truck and leaned into it. The metal bent and the lock gave. We searched the bay. No remote.

"Try forcing the side door," I said to Hooker. "We can't get to the ceiling hatch or the back door because the aisle will be filled with the tool carts, but I can get to the lounge and maybe find a key for the other locker. Or maybe they left the remote in the lounge."

Hooker popped the side door, and I jumped inside and flipped on a light. I rapped on the ceiling and yelled up to Gobbles, "Are you okay?"

"Yeah," Gobbles yelled back, his voice muffled by the sheet-metal slab under him. "What's going on?"

"We can't find the remote to open the back door."

I searched all the drawers and cabinets. No remote. No key. No helpful crowbars lying around. No power equipment that would slice through metal.

Hooker appeared in the doorway. "I broke the screwdriver trying to get the second bay open. Did you find anything in here?"

"No."

Hooker looked at his watch. "The drivers are probably out of the diner by now, calling the police."

"They won't call the police," Gobbles yelled down. "There's something in here that's worth a billion dollars, and they don't want anyone to find it."

Hooker looked up at the ceiling. "Are you fucking kidding me?"

"I wish," Gobbles said. "I heard them talking outside the hauler. They were taking this truck to Mexico. You've got to get me out. They'll kill me if they find me in here."

"We need a little more time and a lot bigger screwdriver," Hooker said.

"Okay, let's not panic. We need time and tools and a better place to hide this thing," I said. "Who do we know?"

"Has to be someone we trust," Hooker said. "Someone close. Someone with a garage or an airplane hangar or an empty warehouse. It would be good to get under cover for a couple minutes in case we have to cut Gobbles out."

"Felicia Ibarra," I said. "We can use that abandoned warehouse behind her fruit stand."

Felicia Ibarra was a chunky little Cuban immigrant lady who was in her early sixties. She was surprisingly wealthy, owning an entire block of real estate in Little Havana that was just short of prime. And she was frighteningly kick-ass, having once shot a guy on my behalf.

Hooker locked eyes with me for a beat. "Our motives might be good, but no matter how you spin it, this is grand-theft auto, big-time. If I get caught on the road in this rig, my career will be over."

"If you get caught, you'll be dead," Gobbles yelled down.

Hooker was hands on hips. "That makes me feel a lot better."

"Let me drive," I said to Hooker. "I could do grand-theft auto better than you. You'd just have to promise to come visit me once in a while."

"Yeah, right. I could almost live with that. See if you can disable the GPS. I'm going to try to rip some of this shrink-wrap off the outside so we're not so recognizable."

I was able to squeeze my arm in far enough to reach a roll of aluminum foil sitting on the kitchenette counter. I ripped a couple chunks off the roll, swung out of the hauler, and climbed onto the back of the cab. The antenna had been placed in the usual location, between the exhaust pipes. I wrapped the antenna in aluminum foil and jumped off. Turns out it's pretty easy to screw up a GPS system.

Ten minutes later we'd done enough slash and peel that we were able to get rolling.

I followed Hooker back out to the highway and trailed behind him. The truck was for the most part white now and didn't attract a lot of attention. We took 95 South to Flagler and went straight into Little

Havana. We passed the Ibarras' fruit stand, turned left at the next street, and rolled to a stop in front of the warehouse.

I'd called Felicia, and she said the warehouse was ours to use, and she'd leave one of the garage doors open. Hooker lined himself up in front of the open door, pulled the truck into the dark warehouse, and I scooted in around him. I got out of the SUV, ran back to the warehouse door, and pushed the button to close it. When the door shut, I hit the button for the lights and overhead fluorescents flickered on.

Felicia and her husband had bought blocks of real estate around their fruit stand at a time when real estate was cheap. Some of the properties were now leased to other businesses, and some of the properties lay fallow. This warehouse was one of the fallow properties, used occasionally for the storage of seasonal fruit. It was cinder-block construction, with three garage bays and enough room to hold six eighteen-wheelers or a kajillion oranges. The ceiling was high enough to accommodate the hauler. The lighting was adequate. The ambience left something to be desired, but then, we weren't here for ambience.

Hooker cut the engine, swung down from behind the wheel, and jogged over to some empty fruit crates stacked against the rear wall. A couple crowbars and a mallet lay on the floor by the fruit crates. He grabbed a crowbar and in seconds had the remaining storage-locker door open. The remote plus a bunch of power cords were in the locker. I plugged the truck into a 220-volt outlet so we didn't have to run on generator.

And then I plugged the cord with the remote into its receptacle. I pushed the control button, and like magic the entire back panel of the truck slid to horizontal and became a ramp. I used the remote to raise the ramp to the second deck, and Gobbles inched his way around the primary car and crawled onto the ramp. He lay there spread-eagled, hand to his heart.

"I thought I was going to fucking die," he said. "Swear to God."

I powered us down, and when we reached the cement floor, Hooker grabbed Gobbles and dragged him up to his feet.

"We need to talk," Hooker said. "I want to know what's going on."

Gobbles shook his head. "You don't want to know. It isn't good."

"I just hijacked a hauler because of you. Talk to me."

Gobbles blew out a sigh. "I'm in a mess. A couple weeks ago this guy come to me and said he represented a company that was working on this new traction-control technology that they needed to test. He said it was a big secret, and they needed someone who could keep his mouth shut. They were going to pay in cash, and I needed cash real bad. I've got two kids I love, and a wife who wants to suck every last cent out of me, and wicked-bad lawyer bills. They said all I had to do was push a button on a remote when the car was going into a corner. Last week it was your car, and this week it was Shrin's. You got loose last week and tore up a fender, but this week . . . I almost killed him. I swear, I never thought it would cause a crash like that."

I cut my eyes to Hooker and saw his face flush, and I was pretty sure he had some steam coming off the top of his head. "You aren't going to hit him, are you?" I asked Hooker.

"I'm thinking about it."

"We don't actually have time for that."

"Just one good shot," Hooker said.

"I didn't have it figured out," Gobbles said. "I thought it would give us an advantage. Everybody wants traction control on their car, right? I thought it was a fluke that Hooker spun out on it. When it made Shrin's car go loose today, I knew there was something else going on. As soon as I pushed the button, both cars spun out."

"What about Clay? Why did you think Clay was involved and deliberately run down?"

"They had someone on the inside, doing whatever they needed to do to the engine. I didn't know who it was. Didn't *want* to know. The night I saw Clay get run over, I said to myself Clay was the one fixin' the engine. I don't know why they run him over. Maybe he wanted more money. Or maybe they didn't need him anymore and were cleaning up. But I'll bet you anything Clay was the one on the inside."

"And you didn't say anything to the police."

"I didn't want to drag us all into a big cheating scandal," Gobbles said. "I still thought I was doing a good thing for the team. I thought Shrin's car had something on it that would help us. Now you see why I was in a tight spot there. It's not like I didn't want to do what was right. I just couldn't decide what was more right than the other. And I didn't even know any names. The big guy and the little guy always come to me. They just show up. I've been calling them Horse and Baldy."

"To their face?"

"Hell, no. They're friggin' scary. I yessir them to their face."

"You're talking about the two men you pointed out to me when we were on the roof? The two men with Huevo."

"Yeah."

"Why Horse?"

"I met them in a men's room once, and I, you know, looked. And the other one, the smaller guy, is obvious. He's bald as could be.

"Anyway, after the race I was supposed to give Horse and Baldy the remote, and they were supposed to give me my money, but I was worried about what happened to Clay. And I didn't know if the traction control just worked wrong or if they intentionally wrecked our cars. I thought I'd play it safe, and I'd stay someplace where there were lots of people, like the garage area. I hoped they could find me and get the remote, and I'd be done with it, and nothing bad would happen.

"I hung with you in the garage for as long as I could, but they didn't show, and I was afraid I was going to miss the plane, so I started walking back to the rental van. They came from out of nowhere in the parking lot, and Baldy had a gun, and I freaked. I took off and ran back to the garage. I don't think they ran after me, but I didn't care. I didn't stop running until I was back in the garage area. Only thing, the haulers were all leaving and there weren't a whole lot of people there anymore. The sixty-nine was still open, and there wasn't anyone around, so I climbed in and hid behind the backup car. It seemed like a smart thing to do at the time. Hard to think good when you're running from someone who wants to shoot you."

"You said Ray Huevo was involved."

"They were standing alongside the truck, and I was trapped inside, and I could hear everything they said."

"Who's they?"

"It sounded like Horse and Baldy and someone else. The third guy was pissed because I got away. He said it was Horse and Baldy's responsibility to clean up after themselves. Then he said there was a billion dollars' worth of trouble that had to be shipped out, and Huevo wanted to make sure it got to Mexico.

"Horse said arrangements were complete. He said the item was in the hauler, and the drivers had instructions to take the hauler to Mexico."

I was an engineer, and a spotter for a race team. I'd toyed with the idea of being James Bond for a moment back there, but the moment had passed and I didn't really want be involved in this . . . whatever it was.

"I think we should turn this hauler over to the police," I said. "Let them go through it and solve the mystery."

"Don't they need to have a reason to do a search?" Gobbles asked. "Do you think they'd have enough cause to search it from what I'd tell them?"

Hooker and I looked at each other and shrugged. We didn't know.

"I watch *CSI: Miami* all the time," Hooker said, "but they haven't covered this."

"They're going to hunt me down and kill me," Gobbles said. "My kids won't have a daddy. They'll be left with my money-grabbing ex-wife. And she'll get married to some asshole who knows all about the stupid man in the freakin' stupid boat, and he'll probably have a lot of money and take them all to Disney World. And my kids will forget all about me."

Hooker looked at me. Confused. "Man in the boat?"

"It's complicated," I said.

"I was thinking while I was locked up," Gobbles said. "We could search the hauler, and we could find the billion-dollar thing. Then maybe we can go to the police with our evidence and get the bad guys arrested. Then they'll be in jail, and they won't be able to kill me. I came up with an alternate plan, but I don't like it as well. It involves kidnapping my kids and moving to Australia."

"I can't wrap my mind around this," Hooker said. "I don't think it's a sure thing that we can send the bad guys to jail. And I'm having a hard time imagining a billion dollars' worth of technology."

"I think it's on the car," Gobbles said. "I think they fixed it so my car would spin out, and Dickie's car would win. I think NASCAR just isn't looking in the right spot."

"Why would they want to take the hauler to Mexico?" I asked.

"Huevo's R and D team is in Mexico," Hooker said. "He has a shop in Concord, but all research and development is done in Mexico. It's on a separate campus a couple miles from Huevo corporate headquarters. If the sixty-nine had some incredible technology installed on it, they might want it taken back to R and D. Oscar Huevo is chairman of the board of Huevo Industries and the driving force behind Huevo Motor Sports. His little brother Ray runs R and D."

"And Ray was at the race today," Gobbles said. "Barney and me saw him talking to Horse and Baldy."

I have to admit I could feel my curiosity ratchet up. Gobbles was suggesting there was a billion dollars' worth of illegal technology on a race car that was at my disposal. As a member of the racing community, I was incensed that the technology might have been used to cause a crash. And as a car junkie and engineer, I was dying to get my hands on it.

Hooker glanced over at me. "You're looking like Beans when he sees a thirty-two-ounce steak left unattended on a kitchen counter."

"At least I'm not panting and drooling."

"Not yet," Hooker said, "but I know you're capable."

"We're sort of safe here in the warehouse," I said to Hooker. "Maybe we should roll the sixty-nine out and take a peek."

Hooker smiled. "I knew you wouldn't be able to resist."

I entered the trailer through the rear-pocket doors. Hooker, Gobbles, and I pulled the two large toolboxes out of the aisle, onto the ramp, and rolled them out to the warehouse floor.

We all got on the ramp, I powered us up to the second deck, we rolled the primary car out, set chocks to keep it stable, and I powered the ramp back down. We rolled the car off the ramp and onto the floor, and I got ready to go to work, helping myself to some disposable gloves, opening the toolboxes, releasing the hood latches.

We'd let Beans out to stretch his legs, and he was running around, acting goofy, looking to play. Hooker took a hand towel from the tool chest, tossed it to Beans, and Beans caught it and tore it to shreds.

"He's just a big puppy," Hooker said.

"Keep your eye on him so he doesn't eat a wrench or a lug nut. I'm going to borrow a jumpsuit from the Huevo hauler."

The first locker I tried was empty. I opened the door to the second locker and a shrink-wrapped body fell out. It was folded up, knees to chest. It was male. It was buck naked. It was completely encased in layers and layers of plastic wrap. With the exception of the gruesomely distorted face and open, unseeing eyes, the shrink-wrapped corpse looked a lot like 180 pounds of expired raw chicken parts packaged for supermarket bulk sales.

I jumped back and slammed into the locker on the opposite side of the narrow aisle. A wave of nausea slid through my stomach, and the room dimmed for a moment. In my mind I was screaming, but I think the reality was that my mouth was open and no sound was emerging.

Hooker looked in at me. "See a spider?" His eyes focused on the plastic-wrapped chunk of body parts on the floor. "What the hell is that?"

I was breathless and too horrified to move. "I think it's a d-d-dead guy. I opened the cabinet, and he fell out."

"Yeah, right."

"You need to come take a look, because I seriously think it's a dead guy, and I'd like to get out of here, but my feet won't go anywhere."

Hooker moved next to me, and we both stared down at the body. The eyes were open in a look of unblinking surprise, and there was a big bullet hole in the middle of the forehead. He was maybe in his fifties with a stocky build, and dark brown hair cut short. He was naked and bloody and grotesque. In fact, he was grotesque beyond seeming human, so that after the first shock wore off, it was like looking at a movie prop.

"Shit," Hooker said. "This really is a dead guy. I hate dead guys. Especially when they've got a bullet hole in their forehead, and they're in a hauler I just stole."

I glanced at Hooker and saw that he'd broken out in a sweat. "You aren't going to get sick, or faint, or something, are you?"

"Race-car drivers don't faint. We're manly men. I'm pretty close to blowing chow, though. Manly men are allowed to do that."

"Maybe you should sit down."

"That sounds like a good idea, but I'm too freaked to move. And here's more bad news. Do you know who this is?"

"No. Do you?"

"The plastic wrap has his face sort of distorted, but I think this is Oscar Huevo."

I clapped my hands over my ears. "I didn't hear that."

Gobbles wandered in. "Holy fuck," Gobbles said. "That looks like Oscar Huevo. *Holy fucking fuck.*"

"Someone has to get me out of here," I said. "I'm going to be sick."

Hooker gave me a shove, and we all rushed out and stood gulping air in the middle of the warehouse. Gobbles had started shivering. He was shivering so much I could hear his teeth chattering.

"This is b-b-bad," he said.

Hooker and I nodded agreement. It was bad.

"Who would want to kill Oscar Huevo?" I asked Hooker.

"The list is probably in the tens of thousands. He was a brilliant businessman, but I'm told he was a ruthless competitor. He had a lot of enemies," Hooker said.

"We need to call the police."

"Darlin', we're standing in front of a hauler we just hijacked and vandalized. And the dead guy on the floor owns the car that just beat me out of the championship. And if that isn't bad enough, two Stiller employees are involved in some really bad shit."

40

"Do you think Oscar Huevo is the billion-dollar cargo that was going to Mexico?"

"I think it's a good possibility."

We fell silent for a couple minutes, all of us absorbing the extent of the disaster.

"I got the icky c-c-creepy c-c-crawlies," Gobbles said. "M-m-maybe we could just p-p-put Oscar back in the l-l-locker."

CHAPTER
THREE

A car door slammed outside the warehouse and Hooker, Gobbles, and I went rigid. A beat later the lock tumbled on the side door and Felicia Ibarra and her pal Rosa Florez walked in. Rosa works in one of the cigar factories on Fifteenth Street. She's in her forties. She's half a head shorter than me and twenty pounds heavier. And while I like to think of myself as having an okay shape, I'm built like a boy compared with Rosa.

Beans gave a happy *woof* and took off at a gallop, chugging across the room like a freight train. He skidded to a stop in front of Felicia, put his two front paws on her chest, and she went down to the floor with Beans on top of her.

Hooker gave a whistle, pulled a dog biscuit out of his pocket, and tossed it across the room. Beans's head snapped around, his eyes opened wide, and he abandoned Felicia like she was yesterday's news, thundering off in search of the biscuit.

"He likes you," Hooker said to Felicia, helping her get to her feet.

"Lucky me," Felicia said. "It's a dog, right?"

Rosa hugged Hooker and me. "We just came to say hello. We never see you anymore." She looked over

Hooker's shoulder and went wide-eyed at the hauler. "Omigod, this is one of those NASCAR trucks, isn't it? It's the thing the car goes in. How does it work? Where do you put the car?"

"The car goes in the top," I told her. "The ramp is on hydraulics. It lifts the car and the car gets rolled into the bay on the top."

"And who's this?" she said, eyeing Gobbles.

"This is Gobbles. He also works for Stiller Racing."

"Ladies," Gobbles said, bobbing his head.

"Are you a driver?" Rosa wanted to know.

"No, ma'am," Gobbles said. "I'm a spotter like Barney. And during the week I do some detailing."

Felicia swept past me to the hauler. "What's in the downstairs? I always wanted to see this. I just want to look in the door," she said. "Just take a little peek."

"No!" Hooker and I said in unison, blocking the way.

Rosa tried to see around Hooker. "Does this truck have one of those lounges with black leather couches where all the drivers have sex?"

"We don't *all* have sex there," Hooker said.

"Is there someone back there now?" Rosa asked. "Someone famous?"

"No," Hooker said. "No one's back there."

"Your mouth is crooked," Rosa said. "Your mouth always gets that little crook in it when you tell a fib. Who's back there? It's not a movie star, is it? I'm not giving up until I find out."

There was a loud *woof* and then a *thud* from inside the hauler. We all turned and looked and saw that Beans had gone into the hauler through the side door and was trying to get Oscar Huevo to play. He'd managed to knock Huevo over, and now he was jumping on him, making growly dog sounds. Huevo didn't move or squeak, so Beans straddled him and sunk his teeth into what I suspected was Huevo's shoulder.

"Holy crap!" Hooker said.

He threw a biscuit at Beans, and Beans snapped it up in midair. The next biscuit fell short, and Beans had to jump over Huevo to get it.

I ran to the SUV and opened the back hatch. "Get him to jump in," I yelled to Hooker. "Throw some biscuits in here."

Hooker whistled and tossed the biscuits, and Beans galloped across the floor and sailed into the SUV. I slammed the hatch closed and leaned against the car, my hand over my heart.

"What is that?" Felicia wanted to know, looking into the hauler. "It looks like a big bag of chicken parts. No wonder the doggie wanted to chew it. What are you doing with chicken parts? Are you having a barbecue party?" She elbowed Hooker out of her way and stepped into the hauler. "It smells funny in here," she said, bending for a closer look. "I think these chicken parts are rotten." She suddenly straightened and made the sign of the cross. "This isn't chicken parts."

Hooker blew out a sigh. "It's a dead guy."

"Holy mother," Rosa said. "What are you doing with a dead guy?"

I gave Rosa and Felicia an abbreviated version of the last six hours. Felicia made the sign of the cross at least ten times, and Rosa listened with her mouth open and her eyes half popped out of her head.

"I gotta see this," Rosa said when I was done. "I gotta see the dead guy."

We all returned to the hauler and gaped at Huevo.

"He doesn't look real," Rosa said. "He looks like one of those wax people. Like he was made for a horror movie."

Especially now that he had big tooth marks in his shoulder.

"What are you going to do with him?" Rosa wanted to know.

Hooker and I looked at each other, sharing the same thought. We now had a dead man with holes in him that perfectly fit Beans's canines. We couldn't just put Huevo back in the locker like Gobbles had suggested. Sooner or later it would occur to people that there's only one dog on the circuit with teeth that big . . . and Hooker would be dragged into the murder mess. Even without that, I couldn't put Huevo back in the locker. It felt disrespectful to dismiss him that easily.

"I think he looks like fish food," Rosa said.

Felicia did another sign of the cross. "You better hope God wasn't listening to that. Suppose this man is Catholic? It would be our fault he doesn't get a prayer over his body. It would be a black mark on our soul."

Rosa cut her eyes to me. "Can't afford to get too many more of those."

"Yeah," Hooker said. "I'm standing in a hot hauler, staring down at a Mexican with a hole in his head. Wouldn't want to push my luck by pissing God off."

"We should take him to his relatives," Felicia said. "It's what God would want."

"His relatives are in Mexico," I said. "What would God's second choice be?"

"He must have somebody here," Felicia said. "He wouldn't be traveling alone. Where is he staying?"

We all shrugged. It wasn't as if we could go through his pockets and find a matchbook.

"Not in a motor coach," Hooker said. "Probably in one of the big hotels on Brickell Avenue."

"We need to put him someplace where he's going to be discovered," I said. "If we leave him in the hauler, he might be taken to Mexico and disposed of and his family would never know what happened to him. Hard to know the killer's plans. We could leave him in the hauler and make sure the police find him, but it'll be even more of a scandal for NASCAR. And chances are good that Hooker and Beans will be brought into the investigation. Hooker might even become a suspect. So I think we need to find neutral ground. We need to leave Huevo someplace not associated with NASCAR and someplace where he'll be found and recognized."

"The Huevo corporate yacht is tied up in South Beach," Gobbles said. "We could put him on the yacht."

"That would be nice," Felicia said. "We could take him for a ride. I bet he'd like that."

"He's *dead*," Hooker said. "He doesn't like anything. And that's a terrible idea. We'll get caught and arrested and spend the rest of our lives in jail. We'll never get him on the yacht without being seen."

"Then maybe someplace *close* to the yacht," Felicia said. "God likes the yacht idea."

"What, do you have a direct line?" Rosa wanted to know.

"I got a feeling."

"Uh-oh, is it just a feeling feeling? Or is it one of those Miguel Cruz feelings?"

"I think it might be a Miguel Cruz feeling."

Rosa looked at me. "That's a serious feeling. Felicia had a feeling Miguel Cruz was in trouble, and an hour later he fell into a sinkhole on Route One, car and all, and broke his back. And another time Felicia told Theresa Bell she should light a candle. And Theresa didn't do it, and she came down with shingles."

Hooker looked pained. He drove race cars. The only vision he really related to was a back bumper.

"How about this," Hooker said. "In the interest of moving on with our lives, let's put Oscar in the SUV and drive him to South Beach. We can go to the marina and look around for a nice final resting place for him. Then we can check into a hotel for the night, and we'll figure the rest out in the morning when we're not so creeped out."

I nodded agreement. I was hoping I'd go to sleep and wake up and find out none of this had ever happened.

"We gonna have to scootch him to the door," Felicia said. She looked at Huevo through the plastic wrap. "Okay, mister, we gonna move you now. You gonna be home soon." She looked over at Gobbles. "You and

Hooker gotta grab hold of Mr. Dead Guy's behind, or something."

Gobbles clapped a hand over his mouth and ran for the bathroom.

"Gobbles got a weak stomach," Felicia said. "He'd never make it in wholesale fruit."

"If we scootch him along, we'll rip the plastic," Rosa said. "I think we gotta carry him. I'll get one side and Hooker can get the other side."

I got disposable gloves from the box in the tool chest and gave them to Hooker and Rosa. They took opposite sides of Huevo. Hooker got his hands under Huevo, then turned white and started to sweat again.

"I can do this," Hooker said. "No problem. I'm a big, tough guy, right? I don't go all pukey just because I'm carrying a dead guy around, right? It's not like I'm gonna get cooties, right?"

"Right," I said. Trying to be supportive. Glad I wasn't the one with my hands under Huevo's dead ass.

Hooker and Rosa got Huevo out the hauler door, down the ramp, and set him on the cement floor. We all took a couple steps back and fanned the air.

"We gotta rewrap Mr. Dead Guy if we're taking him for a ride," Felicia said. "Mr. Dead Guy don't smell good."

I ran to the hauler and came back with boxes of plastic wrap, some duct tape, and a can of room freshener I'd snitched from the bathroom. We sprayed Huevo with Tropical Breeze, rewrapped him in plastic, and secured him with duct tape.

48

"I think he looks good," Felicia said. "You can hardly see where he got chewed on. He looks like a big present."

"Yeah, but some of the smell is still leaking through," Rosa said. "We're gonna have to strap him to the roof rack."

I hustled back to the hauler and returned with three air fresheners shaped like pine trees and designed to hang in a car. I tore their cellophane wrappers off and taped them to Huevo.

"That's better," Felicia said. "Now he smells like a pine tree. It's like being in the forest."

"Good enough for me," Hooker said. "Let's get him in the car."

Hooker and Rosa picked Huevo up and walked him to the SUV. A big shaggy head appeared in the back window, nose pressed against the glass.

"*WOOF!*" Beans said, eyes riveted on Huevo.

"You got a real sicko dog," Rosa said to Hooker. "You're not gonna be able to put Mr. Dead Guy back there with Cujo. Mr. Dead Guy's gonna have to go in the front seat."

I moved the front seat back as far as it would go, and Hooker wedged Huevo in and closed the door. Huevo looked like he was intent on the road ahead, knees bent and pressed against the dash, feet on the edge of his seat, arms tucked in at odd angles. Probably best not to dwell on how his arms got to look like that.

Felicia and Rosa slid onto the backseat, and Beans snuffled them from the cargo area at the rear of the

SUV. Gobbles, fresh from the bathroom, climbed in with Beans.

Hooker stared in at Felicia and Rosa. "You don't have to go with us to South Beach. It's late. You probably want to get home. Barney and Gobbles and I can handle this."

"That's okay," Rosa said. "We're gonna help you."

Hooker draped an arm around my shoulders and whispered into my ear, "We have a problem, darlin'. I was going to leave Huevo sitting in front of a Dumpster. Taking him to the marina is a stupid idea."

"I heard that," Felicia said. "And you're not leaving that poor Mr. Dead Guy sitting by a Dumpster. Shame on you."

Hooker did an eye roll and took the wheel, and I squeezed in next to Rosa. Hooker drove north to First Street and headed east. He wound his way through downtown Miami and picked up the MacArthur Causeway bridge to South Beach. It was after midnight and there weren't a lot of people on the roads. Hooker turned south onto Alton and pulled into the lot by Monty's Restaurant. Miami Beach Marina and Huevo's yacht were just beyond a fringe of trees. And the entire marina was lit up like daylight.

"I wasn't counting on so much light," Felicia said.

"Maybe we could steal a car and leave him in valet parking," Rosa said.

"What's to the side, past those trees?" Felicia wanted to know. "Looks like there's a driveway going somewhere."

"It's for deliveries to Monty's," Hooker said.

50

"I think we got a delivery," Felicia said.

Hooker cut his eyes to her. "You sure it's okay with God?"

"I'm not getting any messages," Felicia said. "So I'm thinking it's okay."

Hooker dimmed his lights and pulled into the driveway, close to the delivery door. We wrangled Huevo out of the front seat and set him on the little cement pad in front of the door.

"How they going to know what to do with him?" Felicia asked. "Maybe no one recognize Mr. Dead Guy."

I went to my bag and returned with a black Magic Marker and wrote OSCAR HUEVO in big letters on the top of Huevo's head. We all got back into the SUV, Hooker cranked the motor over, and Beans started barking. He was doing his bird-dog impersonation, his attention riveted on Huevo.

"What's wrong with him?" Rosa asked. "Maybe he thinks we leave his chew toy behind?"

And then we saw it. The dog. It was a big scruffy mutt, and it was creeping in on Huevo. Huevo was a dog magnet.

"This won't work," Felicia said. "God won't like it if Mr. Dead Guy turns into dog food."

We got out of the SUV, picked Huevo up, and put him back into the passenger seat, next to Hooker.

"Now what?" Hooker asked. "Does God have a plan B?"

"Go back to the parking lot," I told him. "We'll just put Huevo on top of a car. The dog won't be able to reach him there."

"What about cats?" Felicia asked. "Suppose some kitties find Mr. Dead Guy?"

I cut a death glare at Felicia. "God's just going to have to deal with it."

"Yeah," Rosa said, "if it's all so big-deal important to God, let *him* keep the cats away."

We returned to the lot and slowly drove around. Hooker stopped at the end of the second line of parked cars. He was looking at one of the cars and grinning. "This is the car," he said.

I looked past Hooker. It was Spanky's gift car from Huevo. It was a brand-new, shiny red Avalanche LTZ sport utility truck. The vanity license plate read DICK69. Most likely sounded good on paper.

"What's Spanky's truck doing here?" I asked.

"Huevo probably invited him to spend a couple days on the boat," Hooker said.

We hauled Huevo out of our SUV and put him into the back of Spanky's truck. We sat him with his knees tucked up, facing the road behind him, looking like he was waiting to go for a ride.

"There's something funny about the dead guy," Rosa said. "From this angle, I could swear he got a stiffy."

"Have some respect," Felicia said. "You're not supposed to look there."

"I can't help it. It's right in front of me. He got a big boner."

"Maybe it's just rigor mortis," Felicia said.

Hooker and Gobbles went over and took a look.

"Died in the saddle, all right," Hooker said. "I hope I don't go blind from seeing this."

Felicia made the sign of the cross, twice.

A half hour later we were back in Little Havana. We dropped Rosa off, Hooker hung a right at the next cross street, drove one block, and pulled to the curb in front of Felicia's house. It was a two-story stucco deal, crammed into a block of identical two-story stucco deals. Hard to tell the color in the dark, but peach was a good guess. No yard. Broad sidewalk. Busy street.

"Where are you going now?" Felicia asked Hooker. "Are you going back to your condo or your boat?"

"Sold them both. Didn't get enough chances to enjoy them here in Miami. We'll check into one of the hotels on Brickell."

"You don't need to do that. You can stay with me tonight. I've got extra room. And everybody would like to meet you in the morning. My grandson is here. He's a big fan. Just pull around to the alley in the back where you can park."

Minutes later, Gobbles was tucked into a bunk bed above Felicia's grandson, and we were standing in a bedroom that was charming but roughly the size of a double-wide bathtub. It contained a chair and a twin bed . . . and now two adults and a Saint Bernard. The curtains on the single window were mint green and matched the comforter on the bed. A crucifix hung on the wall over the headboard. We had the door closed, and we were whispering so our voices didn't carry through the house.

"This isn't going to work!" I said to Hooker.

Hooker kicked his shoes off and tested the bed. "I think it'll work just fine."

Beans looked around the tiny room and settled onto the floor with a sigh. It was way past his bedtime.

"I like it," Hooker said. "It's homey."

"That's not why you like it," I said. "You like it because there's only a twin bed in here, and I'm going to have to sleep on top of you."

"Yeah," Hooker said. "Life is good."

I unlaced my sneakers. "You make a move on me and life as you know it will be nonexistent."

"Boy, that really hurts. Have I ever forced myself on you?"

"I'm talking about wandering hands."

"Jeez," Hooker said. "You're a real spoilsport." He unzipped his jeans and had them halfway off his ass.

"What are you doing?" I whisper-shouted.

"I'm getting undressed."

"No way!"

Hooker was down to his T-shirt and Calvins. "Darlin', I've had a long day. I lost a race, I stole a truck, and I left Oscar Huevo DOA in an Avalanche. I'm going to bed. And I don't think you have anything to worry about. I've had just about all the excitement I could handle in one day."

He was right. What was I thinking? I wriggled out of my jeans and cleverly removed my bra without removing my T-shirt. I carefully stepped over Beans, crawled in next to Hooker, and tried to find a place in the bed. He was against the wall on his side, and I was plastered against him spoon fashion, my back to his front, wrapped in his arms, his hand cupping my breast.

"Damn it, Hooker," I said. "You've got your hand on my breast."

"Just holding on to you so you don't fall out of bed."

"And I'd better be wrong about the thing poking me in my back."

"Turns out I have a little energy left for some more excitement."

"No."

"Are you sure? Did you ask the man in the boat?"

"Do not even *think* about the man in the boat. The man in the boat isn't interested. And you're going to be sleeping on the floor with the dog if you don't get a grip on yourself."

I opened my eyes to sunlight pouring in through the pretty mint green curtains. I was partially on top of Hooker, his arm draped around me. And I hate to admit it, but he felt nice. He was still asleep. His eyes were closed, and a fringe of blond lash lay against his suntanned, stubbled face. His mouth was soft, and his body was warm and snuggly. It would be easy to forget he was a jerk.

Barney, Barney, Barney! Pull yourself together, the sensible inner Barney yelled. *The guy slept with a salesclerk.*

Yes, but it wasn't as if we were married, or even engaged. We weren't even living together, Barney the slut answered.

You were dating . . . regularly. You were sleeping together . . . a lot!

I blew out a sigh and eased off Hooker. I slipped out from under the quilt, stood, and stepped over Beans and into my jeans.

Hooker half-opened his eyes. "Hey," he said, his voice soft and still husky from sleep. "Where are you going?"

"Time to get up and go to work."

"It doesn't feel like time to go to work. It feels like time to be asleep." He looked around the room. "Where are we?"

"Felicia's house."

Hooker flopped over onto his back and put his hands over his face. "Omigod, did we really steal a hauler?"

"Yep."

"I was hoping it was a dream." He propped himself up on one elbow. "And Oscar Huevo?"

"Dead." I had my shoes on and my bra in my hand. "I'm going to the bathroom and then I'm going downstairs. I smell coffee brewing. I'll meet you in the kitchen."

Ten minutes later, I was across from Hooker at Felicia's kitchen table. I had a mug of coffee and a plate heaped with French toast and sausage. Felicia and her daughter were at the stove, cooking for what seemed like an endless supply of grandchildren and assorted other relatives.

"This is Sister Marie Elena," Felicia said, introducing a bent little old lady dressed in black. "She come from the church on the corner when she hear Hooker is visiting. She's a big fan. And this guy behind her is my husband's brother Luis."

Hooker was shaking hands and signing autographs and trying to eat. A kid climbed onto Hooker's lap and scarfed down one of Hooker's sausages.

"Who are you?" Hooker asked.

"Billy."

"My grandnephew," Felicia said, putting four more sausages on Hooker's plate. "Lily's youngest boy. Lily is my sister's middle child. They're living with me while they look for a place. They just came here from Orlando. Lily's husband got transferred."

Everyone was talking at once, Beans was barking at Felicia's cat, and the television was blaring from the kitchen counter.

"I have to go," I shouted at Hooker. "I want to get to the car. I've been thinking about it, and I've decided to take a look. Just in case."

Hooker stood up at the table. "I'll go with you."

"When Gobbles gets up, tell him to stay in the house," I told Felicia. "Tell him we'll be back later."

"Dinner at six o'clock," Felicia said. "I'm cooking special Cuban for you. And my friend Marjorie and her husband are coming. They want to meet you. They're big fans."

"Sure," Hooker said.

"But then we have to leave," I said to Felicia. "We need to get back to North Carolina."

"I'm in no rush to get back to North Carolina," Hooker said, grinning down at me. "Maybe we should stay another night."

"Maybe you should take out more health insurance," I said to Hooker.

CHAPTER
FOUR

It was early morning and the sky over Miami was a brilliant azure. Not a cloud visible, and already the sun was heating things up. It was the first day of the workweek in a neighborhood of hardworking people. Clumps of Cuban immigrants and first-generation Americans stood waiting at bus stops. Not far off, in South Beach, the traffic was light and the gleaming and immaculate pricey cars of the rich and famous were cooling off in air-conditioned garages after a night on the town. In Little Havana, dusty trucks and workhorse family sedans hustled down streets, carrying kids to relatives' houses for day care and adults to jobs citywide.

Hooker drove past the front of the warehouse and turned at the corner. He circled the block and we looked for cars occupied by cops, Huevo henchmen, or crazed fans. There were no occupied cars that we could see, and the traffic was minimal, so Hooker found a parking spot on the street and we unloaded Beans. Felicia had given us a key to the side door. We let ourselves in, switched the lights on, and closed and locked the door behind us.

Everything was just as we'd left it. I found a jumpsuit, pulled on a pair of gloves, and went to work on the car.

"What can I do?" Hooker asked.

"You can go through the hauler and make sure there aren't any more dead people in there."

Hooker prowled through the hauler and cleaned up after me as I methodically examined the car.

"Find anything interesting?" he asked.

"No. But that doesn't mean it isn't here. It just means I haven't found it yet."

Hooker looked inside the car. "I have to give Huevo credit. They take every opportunity to make the car better. Right down to the gearshift knob."

"Yeah, I'm taking the knob with me. It's aluminum and super light. They've even used a carved design to shave an ounce off it. I thought we might adapt it for your cars. Steal the concept but change the design."

The side door opened and Felicia and Rosa bustled in.

"It's all over the television," Rosa said. "It's a big hoohah." She looked at Beans, sprawled on a blanket we'd lifted out of the hauler. "What's with him? Why isn't he trying to knock us over?"

"He's got a stomach full of French toast and sausage. He's sleeping it off."

"Good to remember," Rosa said.

"We saw pictures of Mr. Dead Guy," Felicia said. "He was on the news. They have a television at the cigar factory and Rosa saw it and called me so I could put the television on at the fruit stand. First they had pictures of Mr. Dead Guy getting taken away in the truck thing . . . what's it called?"

"Meat wagon," Rosa said.

Felicia shook her finger at Rosa. "Don't stand near me if you're going to disrespect the dead. I don't want God to get confused when he sends the lightning bolt down."

"You worry too much," Rosa told Felicia. "God's a busy guy. He don't have time to micromanage. What are the chances he heard that? It's early in the morning. He's probably having breakfast with Mrs. God."

Felicia made the sign of the cross two times.

"Anyway, they had him covered up with a blanket in those pictures," Felicia said. "You couldn't actually see him. But then they interviewed the restaurant worker who found Mr. Dead Guy, and this is the good part . . . the worker said this was the work of some kind of monster killer who eats dead flesh. He said Mr. Dead Guy was all wrapped up like a mummy, but that he could see through the plastic wrap that he was shot in the head and that someone ate part of Mr. Dead Guy's shoulder. And it was someone with real big teeth."

"And then there was a press conference and the police person said it was true that someone or some*thing* had eaten part of the deceased. And they think the fact he was all wrapped up might be part of some devil ritual," Rosa said.

"They didn't say devil," Felicia said. "They just said ritual."

"They didn't have to say devil," Rosa said. "What other kind of ritual could it be? You think they used him for shrink-wrap practice at butcher school? Of course it would be a devil ritual."

"Then they showed some pictures of him before he got wrapped up," Felicia said. "Pictures of him with his wife. And a picture of him with his race driver."

"What about the hauler?" Hooker asked Rosa and Felicia. "Did anyone say anything about the missing sixty-nine car hauler?"

"No," Rosa said. "Nobody said anything about that. And I got a theory. You ever see the girlfriend that goes along with the Mr. Dead Guy race driver? I bet she's the one ate Mr. Dead Guy."

"Beans ate Mr. Dead Guy," Felicia said. "We saw it."

"Oh yeah," Rosa said. "I forgot."

"We gotta get back to work," Felicia said, heading for the door. "We just wanted to tell you."

"We need to talk," Hooker said to me. "Let's take a break here and find a diner. I didn't get a chance to eat at Felicia's house. And after the diner, I need to go shopping. You took your bag with you, but I've just got the clothes on my back. I thought I'd be home by now."

I pulled my gloves off and peeled myself out of the jumpsuit. Hooker snapped the leash on Beans and we locked up and loaded ourselves into the SUV. It was a couple blocks to a bunch of coffee houses and small restaurants on Calle Ocho. Hooker chose a restaurant that advertised breakfast and had a shaded parking lot attached. We cracked the window for Beans and told him to hang tight and promised to bring him a muffin.

It was a medium-size restaurant with booths against the wall and tables in the middle of the floor. No breakfast bar. Lots of signed photographs on the wall of people I didn't recognize. Most of the booths were filled. The tables were empty. Hooker and I slid into one of the two empty booths, and Hooker studied the menu.

"Do you think the fact that Oscar was shot while naked and flying his colors would suggest angry husband?" I asked Hooker.

"It's possible. What I don't get is the shrink-wrap, hide him in the hauler, and ship him to Mexico thing. Wouldn't it have been easier and safer to dump him in the ocean? Or turn him over to an undertaker for transport? Why would someone want to smuggle him across the border?"

The waitress brought coffee and gave Hooker the once-over. Even if you didn't recognize Hooker, he was worth a second look. Hooker ordered eggs, sausage, a short stack of pancakes with extra syrup, home fries, a blueberry muffin for Beans, and juice. I stayed with my coffee. I figured I wasn't going to look great in prison clothes. Best not to compound it by getting fat.

Hooker had his cell phone in his hand. "I have a friend who works for Huevo. He should be at the shop by now. I want to see what the guys know."

Five minutes later, Hooker disconnected and the waitress showed up with his food. She gave him extra syrup, a complimentary second muffin, more juice, and she topped off his coffee.

"I'd like more coffee," I said.

"Sure," she said. "Let me get a fresh pot." And she left.

I looked over at Hooker. "She's not coming back."

"Darlin', you've gotta have more faith in people. Of course she'll come back."

"Yeah, she'll come back when *your* coffee cup is empty."

Hooker dug into his eggs. "Butch says everyone's in shock over Oscar Huevo. He said a lot of people weren't all that surprised to hear Huevo was shot, but everyone's having a cow over the shrink-wrap and the biting thing. Butch said half the garage thinks it's the work of a werewolf, and the other half thinks it's a contract hit. And the half that thinks it's a hit thinks it was bought by Huevo's wife. Apparently Huevo was getting ready to trade up, and Mrs. Huevo was mucho unhappy with Mr. Huevo."

I looked into my coffee cup. Empty. I looked for our waitress. Nowhere to be seen.

"Anything about the hauler?" I asked Hooker.

"No. Apparently word hasn't gotten out that the hauler's missing."

I saw the waitress appear on the other side of the room but couldn't catch her attention.

"NASCAR has to know," I said to Hooker. "They track those haulers. They'd know when it went off their screen."

Hooker shrugged. "Season's over. Maybe they weren't paying attention. Or maybe the driver called in and said the GPS was broken so NASCAR wouldn't get involved."

I clanked my teaspoon on my coffee cup and waved my hand at the waitress, but she had her back to me and didn't turn around.

"Darlin', that's just so sad," Hooker said, trading coffee cups with me.

I took a sip of coffee. "There are some worried people out there. They're scrambling to find the hauler, and they're going to want to find the idiots who stole it because those idiots know Huevo was stuffed into the locker."

"Good thing we're the only ones who know we're the idiots," Hooker said.

The waitress stopped at our table and filled Hooker's empty cup. "Anything else, sweetheart?" she asked Hooker. "Everything okay with your breakfast?"

"Everything's great," Hooker said. "Thanks."

She turned and sashayed off, and I gave Hooker a raised eyebrow.

"Sometimes it's good to be me," Hooker said, finishing his pancakes.

"So we're sticking to our plan to check out the car and leave the hauler on the side of the road somewhere."

"Yeah, except I don't know what to do about Gobbles. No one knows we're involved, so we can go home and get on with our lives. Gobbles has a major problem. Gobbles's life expectancy isn't good. I have no idea how to fix that."

Hooker signaled for the check, and the waitress hustled over with it. "Are you sure you wouldn't like another cup of coffee?" she asked Hooker.

"No," Hooker said. "We're good."

"I hope she gets a melanoma," I said to Hooker.

Hooker pulled out a wad of cash and left it on the table with the check. "Let's roll. I need clothes. We're going to take ten minutes out to shop."

Miami weather is gorgeous in November, as long as there's not a hurricane blowing through. It was shirt-sleeve, ride-with-the-top-down weather. Bright sun and no clouds.

The top didn't go down on the SUV, but we opened the windows and tuned the radio to salsa music. We were relatively mellow, all things considered. Beans was happy with his muffin. Hooker took off in search of a mall, and Beans stuck his head out the driver's-side back window and his tail out the window on the opposite side of the car. His soft, floppy Saint Bernard ears flapped in the wind, and his big loose Saint Bernard lips ruffled as they caught air. Hooker drove out of Little Havana and headed southwest.

Forty-five minutes later, Hooker had a bag of clothes. One-stop shopping for jeans, T-shirts, underwear, and socks, plus a canvas duffel bag. Life is simple when you're a guy. We hit a drugstore and Hooker got a toothbrush, a razor, and deodorant.

"That's it?" I asked him. "Don't you need shampoo, body wash, shaving gel, toothpaste?"

"I thought I'd use yours. I'd use your razor, but it's pink."

"A Texas tough guy can't shave with a pink razor?"

"Hell, no. I'd get kicked out of the club."

"What club is that?" I asked him.

Hooker grinned at me. "I don't know. I made that up. There isn't any club. I'd just feel silly if I used a pink razor. I'd feel like I had to shave my legs."

We returned to the warehouse, I zipped myself into the borrowed jumpsuit, and I got back to work attacking those areas where I would have hidden a wire and microprocessor. I cut through the roll bar and every other piece of the frame where it could possibly run. I searched through the entire wiring harness. I disassembled the tach. NASCAR had already cut into the ignition box, so I didn't have to check that. I pulled the engine out with the help of an engine hoist, and started going over it inch by inch with a flashlight and my bare hand, skimming the surface with my fingertips.

"What are you looking for?" Hooker wanted to know.

"If Huevo found a way to go wireless, he could stick the microprocessor directly onto the engine block. These things are so small, he could make it look like a casting flaw."

I very carefully explored two burrs in the surface. Neither proved to be anything. I found a third and eventually got it to lift off. I was pretty sure it was a chip, but it was too small to see any detail, and I'd partially mangled it trying to get it unstuck from the engine.

"Is that it?" Hooker asked.

"I'm not sure. It's even smaller than I thought it would be, and it's not in perfect shape. I need magnification to see it." I dropped it into a plastic sandwich bag and sealed it. "If this isn't it, then I'm stumped. I've looked everywhere I could think to look. I want to roll the second car out so I can check the engine for a similar chip."

A half hour later, I was convinced a second chip didn't exist. I'd carefully examined every inch of the engine but hadn't found anything.

Hooker had his hands in his pants pockets, and he was rocked back on his heels. "Okay, Ms. Criminal Mastermind . . . now what?"

"The Huevo people will take one look at the sixty-nine primary and know someone associated with racing hijacked the truck," I told him. "I wouldn't care about that except it now involves us in a murder. So I don't think we can return the hauler with the car in it. My suggestion is to unload the second car and make this look like someone took the truck because they wanted to steal the cars. It could be any car thief. Or some insane Spanky fan. And that would go along with Oscar getting dumped into Spanky's truck like a drunken joke."

"I think we should make *everything* disappear *permanently*," Hooker said.

"It's not that easy. We could drive the hauler to North Dakota but I'm afraid we'd be spotted. If we drive the whole truck into the ocean, it'll still be sitting there at low tide. If we torch it, we'll be left with a bunch of burned-out carcasses. I could dismantle the hauler piece by piece but that would take time . . . lots of time and hard work. The cars would go a lot faster. Give me an acetylene torch and a power saw and by the end of the day I can have the two cars reduced to unrecognizable junk that could be tossed off a bridge. Then we just leave the hauler on the side of the road somewhere, far away from Little Havana. And we can remove the aluminum foil from the GPS so the Huevo people can recover their truck."

"I like it."

"We don't want to attract attention with the truck," I said. "We don't want to drive it around in daylight. And it would look suspicious if we took it out at two in the morning. Although in this neighborhood it might just be one more hijacked truck moving through its paces. I think we should take it out at four thirty in the morning, while it's still dark, and it'll look like some driver's getting an early start." I pulled a pair of gloves on and got back into the jumpsuit. "I'm going to chop up Huevo's cars, and I could use a helper."

"I guess that would be me," Hooker said.

I checked my watch. Five forty-five. Felicia was expecting us for dinner at six.

"We're almost done," I said to Hooker. "Another hour of work and we can start carting this junk out of here. Let's break for dinner and come back to finish up later tonight."

Hooker stood looking at the mound of hacked-up car parts. "There's a lot of shit here. And it's heavy. We're going to need a dump truck to get rid of this."

"Forget it," I told him. "I'm not stealing a dump truck. I'll take it out piece by piece in the SUV."

"Okay by me," Hooker said. "It'll take us days to do it that way and in the meantime I get to snuggle with you in Felicia's little guest bed."

I felt a dull ache start to throb behind my left eye. I was going to steal a dump truck, no doubt about it. As I saw it, my life was now divided into two parts. Before Hooker and After Hooker. The Before Hooker half had been a lot more sane than the After Hooker half. Hooker brought out the crazy part of me.

"If I get arrested and sent to prison, I'm never talking to you again," I said to Hooker. "Not ever!"

We drove the short distance to Felicia's house, and Beans got excited the instant we opened Felicia's front door. His eyes got bright, his nose lifted and twitched, and drool pooled in his mouth and oozed over loose lips.

Hooker leaned into me. "This house reeks of pork barbecue and fried bread. Beans probably thinks he's arrived at the all-you-can-eat buffet in dog heaven."

Felicia rushed over to us. "Just in time," she said. "Everyone's waiting to meet you. Let me introduce you. This is my cousin Maria. And this is my other cousin Maria. And these are Maria's two girls. And this is my good neighbor Eddie. And his boy. And my sister Loretta. And this is Joe and Joe's wife, Lucille. And over there is Marjorie and her husband. They're big fans. And you already know my daughter and Sister Marie Elena and Lily."

Beans was jumping around like a rabbit, going nuts over the food smells and the mix of people. I had the leash shortened and wrapped around my wrist, and he was yanking me forward, gaining inches in his quest to get to the pork.

Hooker was chatting and signing autographs. No help there. I dug my heels in and leaned back, but Beans had me outweighed, dragging me toward the dining room in unrelenting determination. I reached out, snagged Hooker by the waistband on his jeans, and held tight.

"Darlin'," Hooker said, wrapping an arm around me. "You're gonna have to wait your turn."

"It's your darn dog!"

Beans made a lunge at a round little lady carrying a bowl of beans and sausage, planting his two front feet squarely on her back. They went down to the ground with a *woof* from Beans and an *oouf* from the woman, food flying everywhere. Beans flopped on top of the woman and snarfed up the sausage that had landed in her hair.

Hooker muscled Beans off the woman, grabbed her under the armpits, and dragged her to her feet. "Sorry," he said to the woman. "He gets playful."

"He should be in a zoo," she said, brushing at the sauce on her shirt. "What is he? He looks like a Yak dog. Like a Chewbacca." She felt on top of her head. "What's this goo in my hair?"

It was a glob of dog drool.

"Must be from the casserole," I told her, luring Beans away with a roll.

"Everybody come eat before the food gets cold," Felicia said.

70

Felicia had her table extended to maximum capacity, and we fit around it cheek by jowl, with a couple kids sitting on parents' laps. Every inch of table was covered with bowls of food . . . rice, beans, fried bread, pork barbecue, sweet potatoes, fruit casseroles, chicken, and who-knows-what.

Maria passed a platter of fried sweet-potato cakes. "How about that Mexican race-car man who got killed? It's all that's on the news." She turned to Hooker. "Did you know him?"

"Only in passing."

"I heard he was ripped apart by a man-eating swamp monster."

Hooker and I glanced under the table at Beans. He was making sloppy wet *snorking* sounds, licking his privates.

"Lucky bastard," Hooker whispered. "Every time I try to do that, I throw my back out."

"I don't know how that swamp monster got to South Beach," Loretta said. "I get goose bumps thinking about it."

"Yeah, and how'd the swamp monster get all that plastic wrap? What'd he do, go rob a Winn-Dixie? Personally, I don't think it was a swamp monster," Maria said.

"So what do you think?" Loretta asked.

"Werewolf."

"How's the werewolf gonna get the plastic wrap?"

"Simple," Maria said. "He eats the guy, only the guy's too big to finish up in one meal. There's a lot left over, right? So when the sun comes up, the werewolf turns into a human, and the human goes to the store and buys the plastic wrap and wraps the guy so he stays fresh."

"That makes a lot of sense," Loretta said.

Felicia made the sign of the cross and passed the fried bread.

"If he wrapped him up to keep him fresh, then why did he leave him at the restaurant?" Lily asked.

"Changed his mind," Maria said. "Maybe the werewolf got indigestion. Like when I eat too many chiles and I get heartburn."

Felicia's husband opened another bottle of wine. "It wasn't a werewolf. There wasn't a full moon. Werewolves need a full moon."

"Are you sure they need a full moon?" Maria asked. "I thought they only needed a piece of the moon. How much of the moon was showing when this guy was killed? Anybody know?"

"I'll show you a moon," Luis said. "Anybody want to see a moon?"

"No," everyone said. No one wanted to see Luis's moon.

Two hours later we were still at the table, and Hooker and I were antsy to get back to the warehouse. Hard to relax when the hauler was sitting there beside a mound of scrap metal that used to be two race cars.

"This has been great," I said to Felicia, "but Hooker and I need to get back to work."

"What about dessert?" Felicia wanted to know. "I haven't brought dessert out yet."

"We'll be back later for dessert." A lot later.

72

"Should I come with you?" Gobbles asked.

Gobbles had been tending bar and looked like he'd been drinking more than serving.

"Going to leave you here, buddy," Hooker said. "Some body needs to stick around and protect the homestead."

"That's me," Gobbles said. "I'm the homestead protectorer."

Turns out you work a lot slower when you're full of pork and fried bread. It was close to ten o'clock and I was struggling with the last large piece of metal when Felicia opened the side door and peeked in at us.

"It's me," she said. "I brought you dessert, but I'm afraid to come in and get jumped on by the doggie."

"It's okay," Hooker said. "He's sleeping in the lounge in the hauler. It's past his bedtime."

It was past my bedtime, too. Taking a car apart is hard physical labor, and I was exhausted.

Hooker closed the door to the lounge and went to help Felicia. She was carrying two grocery bags and had a newspaper tucked under her arm.

"I brought the paper," she said. "It has a big story about the dead guy. I didn't know if you saw it."

"Does it say he was killed by a swamp monster?" Hooker asked.

"No. It says the medical examiner believes the man was attacked by a large dog. And that he was already dead when the dog attacked him."

"Time to get out of Dodge," Hooker said.

I agreed, but we couldn't leave before cleaning house.

"What's this?" Felicia said. "What's this pile of stuff?"

"Car parts," Hooker told her.

"Are you making a car?"

"No," he said. "We unmade a car. Now we have to get rid of the parts."

Felicia was pulling containers out of the bag and setting them on a toolbox. "That's a lot of parts. How are you going to get rid of them?"

"Dump truck," Hooker said.

"You got one?"

"Not yet."

The last thing to come out of the bag was a thermos of coffee and two cups. "I know someone who has a dump truck," Felicia said. "Rosa's uncle owns a junkyard. Sells scrap metal. He's got a nice big dump truck." Felicia had her purse on her arm. She took her cell phone out of her purse and punched in a number. "You eat your dessert, and I'll get the dump truck," Felicia said.

"We can't have anyone else involved in this," Hooker said.

"Don't worry. We keep it nice and quiet."

I poured the coffee and Hooker and I laid waste to the dessert. Bananas drenched in rum, some kind of fruitcake smothered in whipped cream, fried dough balls coated with cinnamon sugar, a chocolate cake that had obviously been soaked in booze, an assortment of little cookies, and some sort of parfait that was crumble cake, fruit, whipped cream, and liquor.

"This is the first time I've ever gotten buzzed from dessert," I told Hooker. "My life is dirt, but I'm suddenly feeling very happy."

Hooker gave me a sideways glance. "How happy are you?"

"Not *that* happy," I told him.

Hooker blew out a sigh.

"You wouldn't take advantage of me in a drunken state, would you?" I asked him.

"Darlin', I drive stock cars. Of course I'd take advantage of your drunken state. It's practically required."

A truck engine rumbled outside the warehouse, and there was a short blast from an air horn.

"That's Rosa," Felicia said, going to the bay doors. "I'll let her in."

"Tell her to back in," Hooker said. "I'm going to cut some of the lights."

The door to the middle bay rolled up, and we could see red brake lights attached to a massive industrial-grade dump truck.

"You're clear," Felicia yelled. "Back it up."

The truck inched into the warehouse, stopping a couple feet short of the pile of scrap metal. Felicia hit the button that rolled the bay door back down. The driver's-side door to the truck opened, and Rosa swung out, wearing four-inch heels that were clear plastic and rhinestones, a tight black spandex skirt, and a red sweater with a low scoop neck that showed a *lot* of cleavage.

"I was on a date when you called," she said to Felicia. "You guys owe me big-time for ruining my love life."

Hooker was smiling, hands in pockets, rocked back on his heels. "Where'd you learn to drive a dump truck?" he asked Rosa.

"My first husband was a truck driver. I used to go on the road with him sometimes. And sometimes I helped my uncle in the junkyard. You gotta know how to do a lot of different things in my family."

A car horn beeped outside the warehouse.

"That's probably my uncle," Rosa said. "I told him you'd autograph his hat if he loaned us the truck."

I sensed Hooker do a mental grimace.

"You didn't tell him about the hauler, did you?" Hooker asked.

"No. I told him there was a big secret in here and he couldn't come in. So he's waiting outside for you."

Rosa, Felicia, and I started throwing pieces onto the dump truck, and Hooker trotted to the door with a pen. He opened the door and took a step back.

"Rosa, there must be fifteen people out here!"

"Yeah," Rosa said. "You're such a popular guy. Everybody loves you. Just hurry up because we're saving the big, heavy pieces for you to put in the truck."

Twenty minutes later Rosa went to the door, opened it, and stuck her head out. "Hey, Mr. Rock Star, you want to stop signing autographs and help us out here?"

I could hear Hooker yelling though the open door. "This crowd keeps growing! Where are these people coming from?"

"All you people," Rosa shouted. "You gotta go home and let Hooker come in here now. We got some bimbos in here for him."

Felicia giggled. "I guess that's us!"

I didn't think it was all that funny. I'd actually *been* his bimbo.

Some laughing and clapping drifted through the open door. Hooker swooped in, and Rosa closed and locked the door behind him. We wrestled the heavy pieces onto the truck, cleaned up the stray nuts and bolts, swept the floor, and dumped the sweepings into the back with the rest of the criminal evidence.

Rosa climbed into the cab and cranked the engine over. "I'll take this to the junkyard and tomorrow it'll get compacted into a chunk the size of a loaf of bread."

"We'll follow you," I said.

"You don't need to do that," Rosa said. "My cousin Jimmy is going to tie up the dogs and let me in."

We killed the lights in the warehouse and Felicia opened the bay door. Rosa popped her headlights, the dump truck rumbled out of the warehouse, into the street, and turned left. Felicia rolled the bay door closed, and we put the lights back on in the warehouse. I put the thermos and cake containers back into the bags and walked Felicia out to her car.

"Thanks," I said. "I really appreciate the help. This didn't work out exactly as planned."

"You mean with the dead guy? That's okay. We're in the wholesale fruit business. It's not the first time I had to do cleanup after a dead guy. See you at breakfast."

I nodded numbly and looked at my watch. Breakfast wasn't all that far away. Hooker and I put the tools back in the carts and pushed the carts onto the lift. I powered the lift up to the bottom deck and rolled the carts off, into the narrow hauler aisle. We secured the carts and then we secured the pocket doors. I pressed the button that magically turned the lift into the hauler back door and watched it slide into place. We secured the two top-to-bottom corner pieces that held the back panel firmly in place. And then I disconnected the power cord and control and stowed it in the outside compartment. Then we walked through the warehouse, making sure it was exactly as we'd found it. No spare parts or tools left behind for Police Squad to find.

Hooker looked at his watch. "Four o'clock," he said. "Let's get the hauler out of here and wrap this up. I'm dead on my feet, excuse the expression."

"Do you need help backing out of the warehouse?" I asked him.

"I'm cool. Kill the lights."

"You won't be able to see the door."

"I have eyes like a cat."

I shut the lights off in the warehouse and stood to the side, watching Hooker move the hauler. He misjudged the door by about six inches and bashed in the left-rear corner of the trailer.

"Maybe you're right about the lights," Hooker said, taking the truck forward.

I switched the lights on and Hooker made another try, this time succeeding in getting everything out the door and into the street. He pulled forward and sat there at idle. I made sure the warehouse was locked, and then I ran to the SUV and fell in line behind Hooker. Any halfway intelligent person would have had heart palpitations and a sick stomach at this point. I was too tired to be weirded out. I had a backache and very little going on in my head. I followed after Hooker on autopilot, just wanting it all to be over.

Hooker drove out of Little Havana and took Route 95, heading north to the interstate that stretched, dark and endless, in front of him. Trucks sporadically cruised by in the blackness, only headlights and running lights visible, moving in caravans, looking like highway ghost trains.

After ten miles Hooker pulled off the interstate, found a strip mall, and parked the truck. I parked behind him, and jumped out of the SUV with the motor still running. I peeled the aluminum wrap off the GPS, gave Hooker a weary thumbs-up, and we climbed into the SUV and hauled ass back to the highway.

I was behind the wheel, and Hooker was eyes closed, slumped in the seat next to me.

"Are we the good guys or the bad guys?" he asked me.

"That's a tough one. We started out as the good guys. We rescued Gobbles. After that it goes into the gray zone."

"At least it's done, and we got rid of all the evidence without getting caught. We were careful. We used gloves. We wiped everything down. We compacted the cars. No one will tie us to any of this."

I pulled into a space behind Felicia's house, and Hooker and I staggered across the small yard, through the door, and up the stairs to our guest room. Hooker flopped onto the bed and I flopped on top of him.

"I'm too tired to get undressed," I said. "I can barely breathe."

"I've got you beat," Hooker said. "I'm too tired to *get* you undressed."

CHAPTER
FIVE

I was tangled together with Hooker when I woke up, our legs intertwined, my nose tucked under his chin. He was still asleep, his breathing deep and regular. I looked at my watch. It was almost nine.

"Hey," I said to Hooker. "Wake up. It's almost nine and Beans should go out to tinkle."

Hooker half-opened an eye. "Okay. Just give me a minute."

"Don't you dare close your eyes," I said. "I know you. You're going to close your eyes and instantly fall asleep again. And Beans should have gone out an hour ago."

"He's not complaining," Hooker said.

I looked around the room. "That's because he isn't here."

"Maybe Felicia came to get him."

A tiny, horrible tendril of panic curled in my stomach. "Hooker, do you remember Beans coming into the house with us?"

Hooker opened both eyes. "No."

"Do you remember him being in the SUV with us?"

"No."

Our eyes locked. "Did you ever take him out of the hauler?" I asked Hooker. "He was sleeping in the lounge. You locked him in when Felicia came to help us."

"Don't tell me I left him in the hauler," Hooker said, hands over his eyes. "I'm still sleeping and this is a nightmare, right? Jesus, pinch me or something."

I bit into my lower lip. "I'm going to throw up."

"*Shit*," Hooker said, on his feet, hunting down his shoes. "I don't fucking believe this. We were so careful not to leave prints, and then we leave the dog."

I had the SUV keys in my hand and my other hand on the doorknob. "Maybe we can get to him before Huevo's people."

I drove because Hooker couldn't afford to lose his license by doing a hundred on the interstate. I took the off-ramp on two wheels and laid four feet of rubber when I jumped on the brakes in the strip-mall lot where we'd parked the Huevo hauler.

The SUV rocked to a stop, and Hooker and I sat in frozen silence. No hauler.

Hooker cut his eyes to me. "You aren't going to cry, are you?"

I blinked tears away. "No. Are you?"

"I hope not. I'd feel like a real pussy."

"We need to get Beans back."

"Yeah, and Beans isn't our only problem. We just told the Huevo team we stole their hauler and made off with their cars. And we told the guy who killed Oscar Huevo that we found Huevo wrapped up like a Christmas ham."

82

"You're in big trouble," I said. "They're going to come looking for you. Good thing I'm not involved."

"I'm going to tell them it was all your idea."

I smiled over at Hooker. He might be a jerk when it came to fidelity, but he'd protect me with his last breath. "What do we do now?"

"They might not be too far in front of us. We could cruise north and try to catch them. They might not even know Beans is in the lounge. Maybe we could sneak in and get Beans when they stop for lunch."

I wheeled the car out of the lot and was turning toward the interstate entrance when Hooker's cell phone rang.

"Yeah?" Hooker said. "Uh-huh. Uh-huh. Uh-huh." And he disconnected.

"Who was that?"

"I don't know. He didn't give me his name. He said I was a rotten bastard for abandoning my dog. That I didn't deserve to have a great dog like Beans. And that he was going to kill me." Hooker slouched in his seat. "I can't believe I left Beans in the hauler."

"We were exhausted. We just weren't thinking."

"That's no excuse. This is Beans we're talking about. Beans is . . . family. He's special. And he's kind of dumb. How's he going to get by without me?"

"Well, at least the killer likes Beans; that's a good thing, right?"

"Of course he likes Beans. How could anyone *not* like Beans? I tell you, this is war. No more Mr. Nice Guy. I'm getting my damn dog back. I'm going to find this Beans snatcher, and I'm going to get medieval on his ass. Oscar Huevo won't be the only one with bullet holes and tooth marks in him. This piece-of-shit Beans snatcher is going down."

"You're sounding a little on the edge here," I said to Hooker. "We need to get Beans back, but maybe you want to chill. You wouldn't want to do anything rash, right?"

"When have I ever done anything rash?" Hooker yelled, cords standing out in his neck. "Do I look like I'm going to do something rash?"

"Yeah. Your face is real red, and your eyes are crazy man. How about we think this out over breakfast. And maybe I can find a diner that has a defibrillator just in case you have a heart attack."

"I'm not hungry," Hooker said. "I just want my goddamn dog back."

"Sure. I know that, but we need a plan. And you could think better if your eyes weren't so popped out of their sockets, right?"

"Are my eyes popped out of their sockets?"

"If they popped out any more, they'd be rolling around on the floor."

I pulled into the first diner I saw, and I got Hooker settled into a booth. Hooker ordered a ham-and-cheese omelet, bacon, pancakes, home fries, juice, coffee, and a side of biscuits with white gravy. Good thing he was too upset to be hungry, otherwise he might have cleaned out the kitchen and the diner would have had to close.

Hooker's eyes were narrowed, his mouth was tight, and he angrily tapped his fork on the table.

84

I firmly removed the fork from Hooker's hand. "Did the killer guy have an accent? Did he sound Mexican?"

"No. No accent."

"Did he say when he was going to kill you?"

"He didn't go into detail."

"Were there noises in the background? Could you tell where he was?"

"It sounded like he was driving. I could hear Beans panting."

"Did he give any indication of where he was going?"

"No. Nothing."

The food arrived, and Hooker forked in some omelet. I drank my coffee and stared into my empty cup. I looked around for the waitress but couldn't find her.

"Have you always had this waitress problem?" Hooker asked.

"Only when I'm with you."

Hooker swapped coffee cups with me. The waitress appeared and gave him a refill.

I ate the cereal I'd ordered and drank some more coffee. A tear slid down my cheek and plopped onto the Formica tabletop.

"Oh crap," Hooker said, reaching over, cradling my face in his hands, using his thumb to swipe the tears from my cheek. "I hate when you cry."

"I'm worried about Beans. I'm trying not to be crazy, but I feel terrible. I bet he misses us."

"I'm worried about him, too," Hooker said. "And now some guy wants to kill me."

I snuffled the tears back. "Yes, but you deserve to die."

"Jeez," Hooker said. "You really know how to hold a grudge."

"A woman scorned."

"Darlin', I didn't scorn you. I just boinked a salesclerk."

"There were pictures on the Internet!"

Hooker's cell phone rang.

"'Lo," Hooker said. "Uh-huh. Uh-huh. Uh-huh."

He disconnected, and I gave him raised eyebrows. "Well?"

"That was Ray Huevo . . . the grieving younger brother of the deceased Oscar. You remember Ray, the brother not eaten by the swamp monster, the brother you saw at the track with Horse and Baldy, the brother who undoubtedly knows the spawn of Satan who has my dog. He wants his cars back."

"That could be a problem. Does he care if they're the size of a loaf of bread?"

"Let's walk through this," Hooker said. "Someone killed Oscar Huevo, shrink-wrapped him, and stuffed him into a locker in the hauler. We're assuming it was an inside job, but the truth is, those haulers aren't locked and anyone could get in and dump a body."

"Not entirely true. You need a garage pass to get to the hauler area."

"That narrows it down to a couple thousand."

"Okay, so a lot of people had access. It's still not that easy. They had to bring the body in somehow. And we know he was brought in, because there wasn't any blood in the hauler. Even if they'd scrubbed it down, I think we would have seen some blood or signs of a struggle. Even if they shot him outside the hauler and dragged him in, we'd see blood. And he was naked, with a boner . . . okay, I guess that could happen in the hauler."

"No way," Hooker said. "He didn't have socks on. Nobody bothers to take their socks off to have sex in the hauler."

I cut my eyes at him.

"Not that I would know from personal experience," Hooker said.

"The paper said Oscar Huevo was last seen having dinner with Ray. That was Saturday night. Both brothers were planning on attending the race, but only one showed up. No one saw Oscar at the track. A doorman remembers Oscar going out for a walk after dinner. No one remembers seeing Oscar return from the walk."

Hooker finished his pancakes and started on the biscuit. "So how did they get the body into the hauler without being seen? There's always activity around the hauler. Plus, they couldn't drive him in on a golf cart. The carts are stopped at the gate."

"Maybe they brought him in after the race. Remember, the sixty-nine hauler was last to leave because they were waiting for a part. Maybe somehow they smuggled the body in then. At a certain point, all the rules are relaxed and carts and vans can move into the garage area.

"And the back of the hauler was still open when we walked Beans. They had the tool cart out so they could work on the truck."

"Seems like a stretch," Hooker said, "but I guess it's possible. Here's question number two. Ray Huevo just called and said all's forgiven if he just gets his cars back. Why would he say that? If he knows I stole his hauler, why wouldn't he go to the police? Why didn't he go to the police in the first place?"

"Because Huevo knows Oscar was stashed in the hauler? And he knows you know that he knows?" I said.

"That's a lot of 'knows'." Hooker forked in some more omelet. "And why does Ray care about the cars? It was my understanding that he wasn't enamored of racing."

"They're still Huevo property."

Hooker shook his head. "It feels too weird to promise forgiveness if I return the cars. I can understand trying to kill me. And I could understand trying to buy me off or blackmailing me into keeping quiet."

"Be hard to blackmail you. The press hangs all your dirty laundry out to dry in public."

"Yeah," Hooker said. "And I have too much money for them to be able to buy me."

"Let's face it," I said to Hooker. "He's not going to forgive you. He's just saying that to give you a false sense of security. He's going to kill you. His goon already tipped his hand."

"Actually, the Beans snatcher didn't say *why* he wanted to kill me. He could be acting independently of Ray Huevo. Like, maybe he just goes around killing people who leave their Saint Bernard's in hauler lounges."

Hooker ate his last piece of bacon and pushed back from the table.

"You don't seem too worried," I said to him.

"If I could just get my heart rate to drop below stroke level, I'd look even less worried."

"We should tell someone at NASCAR."

"Can't do that," Hooker said. "I'd be done as a driver. And driving's all I know."

"It's not *all* you know," I said.

Hooker grinned. "Darlin', you're flirting with me."

"Trying to cheer you up."

He signaled for the check. "It's working."

I was never the nut in my family. My younger brother, Bill, had that honor. I was the kid who graduated from college with an engineering degree and then took a safe, steady job with a boring insurance company. I was the reliable kid who showed up on time for Sunday dinner and remembered birthdays. Until Hooker. Now I'm working for Stiller Racing and running neck and neck with my brother for loose cannon of the year.

Hooker was driving, and I was riding shotgun, watching the world fly by. Breakfast was a half hour behind us. Miami was in front of us.

"So," I said. "Now what?"

Hooker swung off the turnpike onto the east-west expressway. "I want my dog back."

"Looks to me like you're heading for South Beach."

"Ray Huevo said he's on the corporate yacht. I figure that's a good place to start looking for Beans. It's one thing to steal a man's car. It's an entirely different category of stealing when you're talking about a man's dog. And this isn't even a normal dog. This is Beans."

"He didn't say anything about the fact that the holes in his brother's shoulder matched your dog's fangs?"

"He didn't mention his brother or my dog. He just wanted his cars back."

"Don't you think that's odd?"

"I think it's scary cold."

"Has it occurred to you that there's an outside chance Ray won't be cordial?"

"Spanky and his girlfriend are on that boat celebrating his win. And there's a full crew. I don't expect to be offered lunch, but I also don't think I'll get shot. I'm not sure what I'll accomplish, but I don't know where else to start."

Twenty minutes later the SUV was parked in the lot by Monty's, and I was shoulder to shoulder with Hooker, standing on the cement walkway that ran the length of South Beach Harbor.

Hooker was grinning, looking down at me. "I thought you were going to wait in the car."

"Someone has to watch out for your sorry ass."

"I thought you didn't care about my ass anymore."

I narrowed my eyes at him. "Don't push it."

Hooker pulled me to him and kissed me. It wasn't a sexy, passionate kiss. It was a smiling kiss. I'd made him happy. Hooker wasn't a guy who hid thoughts and emotions. You always pretty much knew what was in

Hooker's head. And, I knew from experience, if I let the kiss linger it would turn sexy. What Hooker lacked in guile he made up for in testosterone.

"Stop that," I said, breaking from the kiss and jumping away.

"You liked it."

"I didn't!"

"Okay," Hooker said. "Let me try again. I can do better."

"No!" I turned and shaded my eyes with my hand, searching the harbor. "Which boat belongs to Huevo?"

"It's the big one at the end of the pier, one pier past the dockmaster's office."

"The one with the triple deck?"

"Yep."

"No helicopter," I said. "Huevo cheaped out."

"It's probably just not on deck. Huevo has a fleet of planes and helicopters."

"He also has security. Are you sure you don't want to phone this in?"

Hooker took my hand and pulled me forward. "Sweetie, I *never* phone it in."

I don't know a lot about boats, so my opinion of Huevo's yacht was that it was big and it was pretty. It was three decks of pristine white fiberglass with a single blue stripe running the length of the first deck, the windows all black glass. A ramp led from the boat to the dock and there was a uniformed crew member standing watch at the top of the ramp.

I followed Hooker up the ramp and tried to look calm when he told the crew member we were there to see Ray Huevo. At the very least, I feared this would be mortally embarrassing. And at the most, I worried it would be fatally final.

This morning, wearing the same clothes I'd slept in, I'd jumped out of bed and rushed to the car. I'd clamped a hat on my head and never given makeup a second thought. I don't think I'm any more shallow than the next person, but I suspected I'd be feeling a lot braver right now if I was fresh out of the shower and wearing clean jeans.

Ray had an office on the second deck. He was at his desk and glanced up when we entered. Didn't seem surprised. Annoyed, maybe. Like Ricky Ricardo when Lucy did something stupid. In fact, he looked a *lot* like Ricky Ricardo. Same coloring. Thick, dark hair. Stocky build. Hard to judge his height. He motioned for us to sit, but Hooker and I remained standing.

"I'm looking for my dog," Hooker said. "Have you seen him?"

"I'm looking for something, too," Huevo said. "Perhaps it would be best if the young lady waited outside for a moment."

Hooker looked around at me and smiled. Pleasantly calm. No problemos. "Would you mind?"

I left the office, shutting the door behind me, and I stood close on the other side, trying to listen but not hearing much. After a couple minutes, four large crew members marched past me and into the office. A moment later the crew members escorted Hooker out, lifted him off his feet, and pitched him over the side of the boat, into the water. He hit with a splash and disappeared below the surface.

A hand clamped on to the back of my neck and squeezed. I yelped and was brought face-to-face with Horse. His eyes were narrowed, and his mouth was twisted into a scary, gap-toothed smile. He was in his late forties and he looked like he shopped in the Big and Tall store. He was thick-lipped and had close-set eyes. His dark hair was cut short. Because I'd seen him through binoculars at the track, I knew he had a tattoo on the back of his neck. It had looked like a snake, but it was hard to tell for sure at that distance.

"Well, look who we have here," he said. "I was supposed to go out and find you, but you came onboard with your boyfriend. The pretty little fly walked right into the spider's web."

I tried backing away, and his hand tightened.

"What's the matter?" he asked. "Thinking about leaving? Don't you like me? Maybe you just have to get to know me. Maybe we should go belowdecks and get acquainted."

I heard Hooker surface and flounder beside the boat. I turned my head to see him, and Horse fisted his hand in my hair and yanked my head back.

"Pay attention when I'm talking to you," he said. "Didn't anyone ever teach you manners?"

"Let go of me."

"Maybe I should be the one to teach you manners. It wouldn't be the first time I had to teach a woman to pay attention. In fact, it's one of my specialties. That's why I got the job of talking to you. Everyone knows I have a way with women. I can make women beg. Of course, there's some pain in the beginning. Do you like pain?"

I opened my mouth to scream, and he yanked my head again.

"Nobody's gonna care if you scream," he said. "There's only crew on the boat right now. All the guests are off in the launch taking a harbor tour. So this is how it works. I'm gonna hurt you pretty bad, and you're going to spill your guts to me. You're going to tell me everything I need to know. And if you're real nice to me after that, I'll let you go when I'm done with you."

I broke into an instant violently-sick-stomach cold sweat, and I threw up on Horse. The only time in my life I've ever done projectile vomiting.

"Oh shit," I said. "I'm really sorry."

Horse jumped back and looked down at himself. "What the fuck is this?"

"Cereal and bananas."

"Fucking bitch. You're gonna pay for this."

My heart stuttered in my chest, and then terror-driven instinct took over, and without giving it a second thought, I turned, scrambled over the rail, and jumped. I went under and took in some water before I pushed myself to the surface and bobbed up next to Hooker.

I was wearing jeans and sneakers and they were weighing me down. "Help!" I gasped, spitting out seawater. "Sinking!"

Hooker grabbed me by the front of my shirt and towed me around the side of the boat. We struggled to get past the prow and latched on to the dock while we caught our breath. We went partway down the finger pier, until we came to a ladder and were able to climb out of the water.

My hair and clothes were plastered to me. My sunglasses and hat were riding on the tide. My cell phone was still clipped to my belt and was oozing water.

"I *hated that*," I yelled at Hooker. "I don't know why I went with you. I knew something like that was going to happen. I was almost tortured by the monster with the horse dick. My phone is ruined. And I lost my hat and my sunglasses. And my sneakers are soaked. And they were my favorite sneakers. It's not like great sneakers grow on trees, you know. And I could have drowned."

Hooker was staring at my soaked T-shirt and smiling. "Nice," he said.

Life is simple when you're a guy. All the world's problems can be at least momentarily forgotten when in the presence of a wet T-shirt and cold nipples. I blew out a sigh and squished my way to the SUV. I stopped when I got to the car and stared into the empty back window, my teeth clamped into my bottom lip.

Hooker put an arm around me and cuddled me against him. "I miss him, too," Hooker said. He gave me a brotherly kiss on the top of my head. "Don't worry. We'll get him back."

"I didn't actually like him all that much when he was around. But now I feel terrible."

"Sometimes you don't know what you've got until you lose it," Hooker said.

Everyone in the Ibarra house was off working at the fruit stand, including Gobbles. Hooker and I were alone at the Ibarras' kitchen table, eating leftovers from the night before. I was showered and dressed in my only clean outfit: khaki shorts, a white T-shirt, and white sneakers.

Hooker was in shorts, T-shirt, and borrowed flip-flops. "I didn't count on wet shoes," he said. "I need to stop someplace and get something to wear besides flip-flops. Hard to kick ass in flip-flops."

"You never told me what went on in Huevo's office."

"He asked me why I stole his cars. I said I didn't steal his cars. He asked me how my dog came to be in the lounge if I didn't steal his cars. I said someone stole my dog and planted him in the lounge. He said he wanted his cars back. I said I wanted my dog back. He said if he didn't get his cars back by the end of the day, he was going to cut off my balls and feed them to my dog. I said at least I *had* balls. And then he had me thrown overboard."

"Good thinking."

"When in doubt, deny everything."

I paused with my fork halfway to my mouth and stared at him.

"I never denied sleeping with that salesclerk," he said. "I just don't remember it."

"Do you have any plans for keeping your anatomy intact?"

96

"I'm not too worried. I figure he'll beat the crap out of me, but he probably won't cut my balls off, because then I'd most likely die and he'd never find his cars. He wants those cars back bad."

"Here's a thought — why don't you offer to *pay* Huevo for the cars in exchange for Beans?"

"Yeah, that sounds fair. A million plus for a Saint Bernard whose only talent is drooling."

"It's not his only talent. He says hello by knocking people down to the ground. And he can stand on three legs and scratch his ear with his foot. And he has pretty brown eyes."

"Like me," Hooker said. "Except I can't scratch my ear with my foot."

"Yep. You and Beans are the perfect pair."

Hooker grinned at me and reached for his cell phone. He went to punch in Huevo's number and water leaked out. "It's dead," Hooker said. "Drowned."

"Can you get Huevo's number off it?"

"No, but I can probably get a number from Butch."

Ten minutes later, Hooker put the Ibarra phone back in its cradle on the kitchen counter.

"Well?" I asked.

"Huevo said he doesn't want the money. He wants the cars."

"Maybe it's the chip that he wants. Maybe you should call him back and offer him the chip."

Hooker was fidgeting with the gearshift knob we'd lifted off the 69 car. He was turning it upside down and right side up, examining it. "This is a work of art," he said. "Huevo's machine shop has designed this knob so it's strong and comfortable in your hand with minimum weight."

He set it on the table with the threaded side down and there was a barely perceptible *plink*. He picked the knob up and a tiny metal disk was left lying on the table.

I pushed the disk around with my finger. It was silver and slightly smaller than a contact lens.

"It looks like a watch battery, but it doesn't have any markings," I said to Hooker. "And I don't know what the heck it was doing inside the gearshift knob."

"Maybe this is the traction-control thingy."

"Impossible. It doesn't connect to anything. I cut the shifter in half. No wires. The microprocessor has to send electricity to a mechanical part to get the engine to slow down. We only know two ways to send electricity. One is over a wire. The other is a lightning bolt."

"Then what is it?"

I turned it over in the palm of my hand. "I don't know. I'd like to see inside, but I'm afraid I'll destroy it if I try to open it. It wouldn't be a problem if we were in Concord."

"I don't want to go to Concord. I think Beans is in Miami, and I'm not leaving until I get him back."

"Then let's find a jeweler."

A half hour later, Hooker stood over a case filled with diamond bracelets. "Most women would forgive me if I bought them one of these bracelets."

"Don't kid yourself. A woman might take the bracelet, but she wouldn't forgive you."

98

"That explains a lot," Hooker said.

"Wasted your money on a bunch of diamond bracelets?"

He smiled sheepishly. "I've bought a few."

I was with the jeweler who was laboring over the little metal button. He had it in a miniature vice, and he was trying a variety of things, none of which was working. Finally he took it out of the vice, put his tiny tools away, held the button between his thumb and forefinger and whacked it with a hammer. The metal shell cracked open and the inside of the button was exposed.

We all stared down at it.

"What is it?" Hooker asked.

I borrowed the jeweler's loop and examined the button. "It looks like a circuit board. And it's welded onto something that might be a miniaturized battery."

"So, this could be it," Hooker said. "Except it's not attached to anything."

"Yeah. But maybe it talks to the chip that was stuck on the engine."

I pulled the plastic bag out of my pocket, put the damaged piece-of-something on the counter, and looked at it under the loop. It was for sure a chip. I could see the circuits.

"It's a chip," I said to Hooker. "I don't know why you would need two, though. I'd think the chip on the engine would do it all."

I put the two chips back into the plastic bag, slipped the bag into my pocket, and we left the jewelry store and walked out into the mall. We were at a touristy waterside section of Miami with shops and food courts opening to a marina. It was tropical and colorful and the stores featured ashtrays that were decorated with flamingos, rubber alligators made in China, beach towels, T-shirts, lamps shaped like palm trees, sunglasses, sunscreen, sun visors, and bags of shells that had probably been collected in China. We bypassed the trinket shops and bought new cell phones, running shoes for Hooker, and binoculars.

By the time we left the mall, it was late afternoon. Our plan was to park our butts on bar stools at Monty's outdoor tiki bar and watch Huevo's yacht. The bar was nice and public, and we thought chances were slim that Hooker's gonads would get lopped off from the rest of his body while at Monty's.

We ordered nachos and beer and broke out the binoculars. We'd each gotten one of those mini things. Not as much power as what I was used to but easier to carry. We had a good view of the boat without the binoculars, but the binoculars would let us see faces better.

"To Beans," Hooker said. And we clinked our beer glasses together.

I put my binoculars to my eyes for a test, focused on the pier leading to the Huevo boat, and then a woman walked into the picture. "Hello," I said. "Who's this?"

The woman looked like Blond Bitch Bimbo. A platinum-haired Cruella DeVil. She was wearing four-inch heels and a designer suit that fit her like skin. She had enough diamonds on her watch and in her ears to give me cataracts from the sun reflection. Her hair

100

was knotted at the nape of her neck and her face was frozen in a look of perpetual open-eyed awe. She had a long-legged, ass-swinging stride that carried her down the pier to the yacht gangplank. The uniformed guard onboard ship snapped to attention when he saw her and rushed forward to help her with her single bag, but she waved the help away. A small, tufted dog head popped out of the bag.

I glanced at Hooker and found him readjusting his binoculars.

"Focusing on her ass?" I asked.

"It's a pretty decent ass. Looks to me like a StairMaster ass. Man, her ass is so tight, you could bounce a quarter off it."

"You like that?"

Hooker had his binoculars to his eyes. "I like any ass that . . ." He froze in midsentence. He was having a mental headslap moment. A deer-in-headlights moment. He lowered the binoculars and looked at me. "I like *your* ass."

Okay, so he wasn't perfect, but he was trying.

I had my binoculars back up, watching the woman go into the main salon and disappear from sight. "Do you know who she is?"

"Darlin', that's the newly widowed Mrs. Oscar Huevo."

"Zowie."

"Exactly. She's wife numero uno, and she's out for bear."

Ten minutes later numero uno marched out of the salon door, crossed the deck, and swung her ass down the gangplank. She adjusted her sunglasses, tucked her dog back into the bag, and power-walked the length of the pier.

I dropped my binoculars into my new tote bag. "You stay here and watch the boat," I said to Hooker. "I'm going to follow her, see where she goes."

Hooker handed me the keys to the SUV. "In a small, dark corner of my brain there's a fear that once you're out of my sight you're going to get on a plane and go home without me," he said.

CHAPTER
SIX

I ran to the SUV and slid behind the wheel just as the widow Huevo strode into the parking lot and got into a waiting limo. I cranked the engine over and followed at a distance. The driver took Fifth Street and then went north on Collins. Several blocks later, the driver turned into the elaborate entrance to the Loews Miami Beach Hotel. Mrs. Huevo disembarked, still carrying her doggie bag. The limo trunk popped open and bellmen scrambled to unload luggage. The luggage was put on a cart and whisked away into the hotel, following the swinging ass of Mrs. Huevo.

I had Hooker on the phone. "She's checking into Loews, and she's got a lot of luggage."

"She looks like she'd take three steamer trunks for an overnight."

"I'm going to hang out here for a while and see if anything interesting happens," I told Hooker.

"Ten-four."

Loews is a spectacular hotel with acres of marble, pretty couches, and potted palms. It has outdoor areas that look like a cross between a Fred Astaire movie and King Tut's tomb. And it all leads to the glorious wide white sands of South Beach and the rolling Atlantic. I valet-parked the SUV and walked into the super-air-conditioned lobby. It was so cold my nipples got hard and my fingertips turned purple. I'm not one to make frivolous purchases, but in the interest of nipple well-being I forked over thirty dollars to the hotel gift shop and bought a sweatshirt.

I took a position on one of the couches and watched the elevator. Widow Huevo looked to me like a woman who needed a drink, and I was guessing she'd settle into her room then waste no time hitting the bar. My plan was to wait around for an hour. If nothing happened, I'd go back to Hooker. Turned out an hour was overkill because the widow emerged from the elevator after ten minutes and went straight to the bar. Since South Beach doesn't actually cook until midnight, the bar was empty. Mrs. Huevo took one of the little tables and looked around for a waitress. Impatient. *Really* needed the drink. She still had the doggie bag with her, but the dog was deep inside. Probably freezing. As soon as the dog head popped out, I was going to make my move.

Not a bartender or waitress in sight. No one in the area but me and Mrs. Huevo. I cracked my knuckles and zipped the sweatshirt. Mrs. Huevo removed her suit jacket. Obviously having a hot flash. Or maybe she just liked hard nipples. Probably the latter. I saw the dog stick his head out and look around and instantly disappear back into the bag. Good enough for me.

I approached Mrs. Huevo and bent down a little by the bag. "I'm sorry to bother you," I said, "but I had to

104

come see your dog. He just popped his head out, and he looked so adorable."

Here's the thing about people who carry their dogs everywhere with them. They love their dogs. And they love talking about their dogs. So it's possible to approach a total stranger, coo over the dog, and become instant best friends.

The widow Huevo looked at me hopefully. "You wouldn't happen to work here, would you? Christ, who do I have to fuck to get a drink in this place?"

"This bar doesn't look like it's operating right now," I said. "I was going to try one of the tables on the porch. People seem to be sitting there."

Widow Huevo craned her neck to take it in. "You're right!"

She was on her feet and moving, her long legs gobbling up the Loews art nouveau patterned carpet. I was taking two steps to her one, trying to keep pace.

"Jeez," I said, "how can you walk so fast?"

"Anger."

I tried not to smile too much. Oh yeah, I thought, this was going to work out just great.

We pushed through the doors and found a table on the patio that overlooked the pool and the ocean. Probably the dog wasn't allowed here, but no one was going to tell that to the bitch Huevo. She put the dog bag on her lap and swiveled in my direction, opening the bag a little. "This is Itsy Poo," she said. "She's three years old, and she's the best little girl."

Itsy Poo popped up and looked at her mistress, and Huevo made an instant transformation from bitch woman to gaga googoo dog mommy.

"Isn't she the best?" Huevo asked Itsy Poo. "Isn't she the cutest? The sweetest? Isn't she mommy's darling?"

Itsy Poo's eyes bugged out of her tiny head and she vibrated with excitement. She was a miniature something, small enough to sit in a woman's hand. Sort of rat size but not that much muscle. Her mousy brown hair was long but not especially full. If Itsy Poo were a woman, she'd be on Rogaine. The hair on her head was pulled into a topknot and tied with a tiny pink satin ribbon.

I tentatively stuck my hand into the bag, and Itsy Poo cuddled into it. She was in a nest made from a cashmere shawl. She was warm, and her scraggly hair was as soft as a baby's breath.

"Wow," I whispered, genuinely taken with the dog. "She's so silky. So pretty."

"She's mommy's baby. Isn't she? Isn't she?" Huevo gurgled at the dog.

A waiter approached the table, Mommy Huevo partially closed the bag, and Itsy Poo settled herself into her cashmere.

"Martini, dry," Huevo told the waiter. "Three of them."

"Iced tea," I said.

The widow Huevo's unblinking eyes fixed on me. "Get serious."

"I have to drive."

"I can't sit here drinking martinis with someone nursing an iced tea. How about a margarita? It's got fruit juice in it. It hardly counts. You can pretend it's breakfast." Huevo flicked a glance at the waiter. "Give her a margarita. Cabo Wabo, on the rocks, float the Cointreau."

A handful of very tan people lounged by the pool. No kids. No one actually *in* the pool. There was a slight breeze, but the sun was still hot and the temperature was about forty degrees higher than the hotel lobby. I felt the blood pulsing back into my fingertips, felt my nipples relaxing. I removed the sweatshirt and slouched back in my chair. The widow Huevo didn't slouch. She was at rigid attention, hands clenched on the tabletop.

"So," I said, "what brings you to South Beach?"

"Business."

Our drinks arrived, and Huevo belted the first martini back, exhaling when the alcohol hit her stomach.

I extended my hand. "Alexandra Barnaby."

"Suzanne Huevo."

Her handshake was firm. Her hands were like ice. Definitely needed another martini.

I raised my margarita glass. "To Itsy Poo."

"I'll drink to that," Suzanne said. And she downed the second martini.

I gave the new blast of alcohol a minute to register, and then I got right to the meat of the matter, because at the rate Suzanne Huevo was slurping martinis, I worried she wasn't far from incoherent. "Did you happen to know the man who was murdered? I think his name was Huevo."

"Oscar Huevo. My asshole husband."

"Omigod, I'm so sorry."

"Me, too. Someone killed the bastard before I could get to him. I had it all planned out, too. I was going to poison him. It was going to be nice and painful."

"You're kidding."

"Do I look like I'm kidding? I was married to that jerk for twenty-two miserable years. I gave him two sons. And I sacrificed and suffered for him. I logged enough hours on the StairMaster to go to the moon twice. I've had my thighs sucked out and my lips plumped up. I've got enough Botox injected in my face to kill a horse. I've got double-D implants and full-mouth veneers. And how does he thank me for my effort? He trades me in for a newer model."

"No!"

She ate a couple olives. "He was going to. Served me with divorce papers. And then he died before I signed them. How's that for justice?"

"Do you know who killed him?"

"No. Unfortunately. I'd send him a fruit basket. And then I'd beat the crap out of him for robbing me of the pleasure of seeing Oscar die in front of me." She looked around for a menu. "I'm starved. We should order something to eat. French fries. I haven't had a French fry since 1986."

"Wasn't Oscar Huevo Mexican? You don't look Mexican."

108

"I'm from Detroit. I met Oscar in Vegas back when Vegas was Vegas. I was a showgirl."

I reached for my margarita and was shocked to find it was empty.

"Hey!" Suzanne yelled to a passing waiter. "Another margarita and bring me more martinis, and we want French fries and onion rings and macaroni and cheese."

"I'm not really a two-drink person," I said to Suzanne.

Suzanne made a dismissive gesture. "It's just fruit juice."

I licked a few grains of leftover salt from the rim of my glass. "Are you here for the funeral?"

"No. The funeral will be held in Mexico next week. They haven't released the body yet. I came to harass Ray. He's sitting out there in that yacht like he owns it."

"He doesn't own it?"

"Huevo Enterprises owns it. Oscar was Huevo Enterprises, and when the estate is settled, that boat will belong to my two sons."

"How old are your sons? They must be in shock over this."

"They're both in college, and they're dealing with it."

"Let me guess. You're here to guarantee no one screws your kids out of their inheritance."

"Ray is slime. I wanted to make sure the yacht didn't mysteriously disappear. I want to make sure *nothing* disappears."

The food was delivered, along with the drinks. Suzanne polished off the third martini and dug into the onion rings. Her right eye was drooped half closed. I was trying not to stare, but it was a complete car crash.

"What?" she asked.

"Uh, nothing."

"It's my eye, isn't it? It's drooping, right? Goddamn freaking Botox. Can't even get hammered without something going all to hell."

"Maybe you need a patch. Like a pirate."

Suzanne stopped eating and drinking and gaped at me. She burst out laughing, and the laughter rocketed around the patio. It was deep and straight from her belly and gave an insight into a happier, less angry, less Botoxed Suzanne.

"Oh jeez," she said, dabbing at her eyes with her napkin. "Is my mascara running?"

It was hard for me to tell if her mascara was running, because somehow I'd managed to slurp up the second margarita, and Suzanne had gotten extremely fuzzy.

"This is sort of embarrassing," I said, "but I seem to be drunk, and you're a big blurry blob. Nothing personal."

"S'all right," she said. "You're blobby, too. Doncha love when that happens?" She ate some fries. She ate some more onion rings. And then she slumped in her seat and fell asleep.

I dialed Hooker.

"I've got a problem," I told him. "I'm at the patio restaurant at Loews, and I'm too drunk to move. And even worse, I'm with Suzanne Huevo, and she's passed

110

out. I was hoping you could ride your white horse over here and rescue me."

I ate the macaroni and cheese, finished off the French fries, and drank a pot of coffee. People came and went in the restaurant and pool area, and Suzanne and Itsy Poo peacefully snoozed.

I was about to order more coffee when Hooker showed up. He sauntered across the room and slouched into the seat next to me. "What's her problem?" he asked.

"Four martinis. Maybe five. I lost count. How'd you get here? I have the car in valet parking."

"Took a cab." Hooker turned his attention to me, grinning. "Darlin', you're snockered."

"What gave me away?"

"For starters, you've got your hand on my leg."

I looked down. Sure enough, my hand was on his leg. "I don't know how that happened. Don't get any ideas," I told him.

"Too late. I have *lots* of ideas."

"I hope one of those ideas is about getting Suzanne back to her room."

Hooker ate a cold onion ring. "Why can't we just leave her here?"

"We can't do that. She'd be a spectacle."

"And?"

"I like her. We've sort of bonded."

"Have you tried waking her?" he asked.

"Yeah. She's out for the count."

"Okay, sit tight. I'll be right back."

A couple minutes later Hooker returned with a wheelchair.

"That's genius," I told him.

"Sometimes this is the only way I can get my team back to their rooms at night. The luggage cart works good, too."

We got Suzanne into the wheelchair, placed her jacket and the doggie bag on her lap, and Hooker started rolling her toward the door. I followed behind Hooker, took a misstep, and crashed into an empty table. I grabbed at the white linen cloth in an effort to find my balance and took the entire table setting down to the floor with me. Cups, saucers, plates, silverware, napkins, and the little flower vase all slid off the table with the cloth. I was on my back, spread-eagled with the cloth and the crockery around me, and Hooker's face swam into view.

"Are you okay?" Hooker asked.

"I'm having a hard time focusing. I have the whirlies. You aren't laughing at me, are you?"

"Maybe a little."

"I look silly."

"Yeah," Hooker said, a smile in his voice. "But I don't mind. I like when you're on your back."

He reached down and scooped me up, setting me on my feet, holding me close to him, picking smashed crockery out of my hair. I could hear waiters scrambling around, setting things right. "Is she all right?" the waiters were asking. "Is there anything we can do? Does she need a doctor?"

"Just lost her balance," Hooker said, positioning me behind the wheelchair, my hands on the handles. "Inner-ear problem. Ménière's disease. Can't let her drive. Very sad case." He had his hand on my back. "Just push the wheelchair, darlin'. We need to take the nice sleepy lady back to her room."

Hooker scrounged in Suzanne's bag when we got to the elevator and found her room key still in the envelope marked with her room number. He maneuvered us into the elevator, pushed the button, herded us out at the appropriate floor, and walked us down the hall to Suzanne's suite.

The suite looked out at the ocean. The décor was South Beach modern, Loews style. Pale pastel fabrics and light woods. Gauzy curtains at the balcony window. Her luggage was in the middle of the living room, still unpacked.

I hung the doggie bag on my shoulder, and Hooker pulled the widow Huevo out of the wheelchair and flopped her onto the bed.

"Mission accomplished," Hooker said. "Hop into the wheelchair, and I'll push you out of here."

"What about Itsy Poo?"

"What's an Itsy Poo?"

I opened the bag and the tiny dog head popped out.

"What is it?" Hooker wanted to know.

"It's a dog."

Hooker looked at the tufted head with the little pink bow. "Darlin', that's not a dog. *Beans* is a dog. This is . . . what the heck *is* this? Beans would think this was a snack."

"It's a miniature something." I put the bag on the floor and Itsy Poo jumped out and started investigating.

Loews had set out a doggy welcome center complete with place mat, dog bowls, treats, a chew bone, and a map to the dog park. Hooker filled one of the bowls with water and put a couple treats in the other. "That should hold whatever it is until its owner wakes up," he said.

"Stick a fork in me," I told Hooker. "I'm not too far behind Suzanne Huevo."

"I don't want to drive all the way back to Little Havana," Hooker said. "The action seems to be here in South Beach. I'm going to check you into the hotel and take the car back to the marina so I can watch the boat."

Even before I opened my eyes, I felt disoriented. Too many room changes. The motel at Homestead, Felicia's guest room, and now I sensed something different again. Big bed; very comfy, warm body next to me; heavy arm across my chest. I looked down at the arm. Tan. Blond hair on the arm. Damn. I was in bed with Hooker. I peeked under the covers. I was wearing my T-shirt and panties. Hooker was in boxers. The boxers were blue with pink flamingoes. Cute.

"Morning," Hooker said.

"What are you doing in my bed?"

"Sleeping?"

"Why don't you have your own bed?"

Hooker eased his hand up under my breast. "You don't remember?"

I pushed the hand down. "No."

"You begged me to sleep with you."

I rolled out of bed and collected my clothes. "I don't think so. I was *drunk*. I wasn't *insane*."

"I watched the boat until midnight and didn't see Beans. I don't think he's on the boat. Did you learn anything good from the grieving widow?"

"The only thing she's mourning is the fact that she didn't get to kill Oscar herself. And she doesn't think a lot of Ray. Turns out he's squatting in a boat her sons are due to inherit. She said Huevo Enterprises owns the boat, and Oscar *was* Huevo Enterprises."

"I talked to some people last night while I was hanging out at the marina. Word on the street is that the lion's share of everything goes to the two boys, but Ray is executor until they reach thirty. And that's ten years down the pike."

"Anybody know what Suzanne's going to get?"

"Speculation is . . . not much. Couple million maybe. The bulk of the assets are in Mexico. No joint property."

"I'm taking a shower and then I'm going downstairs for breakfast."

"I'll go to breakfast with you," Hooker said. "Just in case you need coffee."

An hour and lots of pancakes later, Hooker and I were in the lobby, waiting for the elevator, wishing we knew what to do next. The elevator doors opened, and two men stepped out. They were Hispanic. They were wearing dark suits. One was maybe five nine, slim build, bald, pockmarked face, sharp features, bright bird eyes. The other was huge and frighteningly familiar. Horse and Baldy. They didn't look our way. They were in a hurry, moving toward the hotel's main entrance.

"It's them," I said to Hooker. "It's Horse and Baldy."

"Are you sure?"

My stomach was clenched into a painful knot. "I'm sure."

We trailed behind Horse and Baldy and watched them get into a black BMW. Hooker grabbed a cab and told the driver to follow the Beemer. It wasn't a long drive. Horse and Baldy parked in the lot at the marina.

"Wow, big surprise," Hooker said.

It was too early for the tiki bar at Monty's, so we sat on one of the benches that lined the marina walkway. Horse and Baldy approached the Huevo gangplank and were waved onboard. They went straight to the first-deck salon and disappeared.

We hadn't been prepared to leave the hotel. No hats. No sunglasses. No binoculars. After a half hour, Hooker was fidgeting.

"I hate sitting around like this," Hooker said. "It's boring."

"I agree. Let's take turns. I'll take the first watch, and you can go back to the hotel and get our stuff. We need a car, anyway, in case we want to follow somebody. Maybe one of these guys is the Beans snatcher."

The sun was just beginning to warm Miami. The water in the marina was as smooth as glass. The air was still. No breeze to rustle palm fronds. The boats were leisurely coming to life. The morning aroma of coffee brewing in galleys mingled with the sharper scent of ocean brine.

I watched Hooker head for the parking lot, and I stretched on the bench and thought this would all be incredibly nice . . . if only Beans was here. And if only I wasn't being hunted down by a sadistic maniac with an oversized johnson. It seemed to me that Ray Huevo would get over the loss of his cars. He was bent over about it now, but he had a lot on his mind and a business to run, and I suspected if we just weathered this, we'd be off the hook in a day or two. Ray Huevo had never before cared about the car side of the business. And God knows, Huevo could afford to build two more cars. Even if he had illegal technology on the 69, he should be realizing he wasn't going to get busted on it.

You would think a more worrisome issue would be Oscar Huevo packaged up and rammed into a storage locker. Someone out there knew the body was discovered and moved. If that person was inner circle to Ray Huevo, he knew Hooker was the one who moved the body. But then, maybe the murderer wasn't inner circle.

A man and a woman in brilliant white uniforms trimmed with blue were moving around on the second deck, setting up for breakfast. Two women strolled out, the world seemingly a better place for their perfect blondness. They were wearing floaty caftan-type things that are worn only by the very fat and the very onboard-ship. They were followed by four men in

117

casual shirts and slacks. The men were power breakfasting. Spanky and Delores followed the power breakfasters. Good thing my stomach was full of pancakes or I might be feeling left out.

Everyone milled around for a few minutes until Ray Huevo appeared. He took his seat and everyone followed his lead. Horse and Baldy weren't among the invited breakfast guests.

Halfway through breakfast, Spanky glanced my way, and I could see recognition register. He leaned left to catch Ray Huevo's attention and words were exchanged. Huevo looked in my direction, and I felt the roots of my hair get hot. The meeting of eyes was brief. Huevo barely acknowledged me, immediately dismissing my presence, returning to his role of genial host, eating his omelet, smiling at the blonde at his side.

The white-uniformed waiters poured more coffee and juice. The chef served crepes from a rolling cart. The sun climbed higher in the sky. The breakfast felt endless.

I called Hooker. "Where the heck are you?"

"I'm at Felicia's. I went back to get our things. I think we're better off staying in South Beach."

"What about Gobbles? What's Gobbles doing?"

"Gobbles is watching television. I told him to stay with Felicia."

"I'm dying here. I need my iPod. I need sunglasses and sunscreen."

"I hear you," Hooker said. And he hung up.

I blew out a sigh and slouched a little lower on the bench.

Baldy appeared on deck and my breath caught in my chest. Baldy bent to speak to Huevo. He was nodding his head. Yes, yes, yes. He looked my way. Damn.

Huevo returned his attention to his breakfast party and Baldy left the boat and walked toward me. He stopped when he got to my bench.

"Miss Barnaby?"

"Yes."

"Mr. Huevo would like me to take you to breakfast."

"Thanks, but I've already had breakfast."

"Then I'll escort you to your car."

"I don't have a car."

He shifted foot to foot. I was being difficult.

"I've been asked to remove you from this bench. I'd prefer to keep this civil."

"Me, too," I said. And I for sure meant it. I wasn't exactly Batman. I wasn't even Bruce Willis. I was a little bleached-blond coward.

Baldy reached out for me, and I batted his hand away. "Don't touch me," I said.

"I thought you might need some help getting off the bench."

"News flash. I'm not leaving this bench. I'm meeting a friend here. And he's real big and mean. And he has a vicious dog."

"Come on, lady, give me a break. If you don't cooperate, I'm going to have to pick you up and take you away and shoot you."

"Touch me and I'll scream," I said.

"Goddamn it," Baldy said. "I hate when my day starts like this." He grabbed my arm and pulled me to my feet, and I let out a shriek. He was trying to wrestle me away from the bench, and I was struggling and screaming. A flock of gulls and two pelicans took to the air. A plate dropped and smashed on the deck of the Huevo boat.

"*Help! Rape!*" I yelled.

A red scald rose from Baldy's collar and colored his face. People were emerging from inside their boats. A security guard appeared outside the dockmaster's office. Baldy let go of me and took a step back.

"Okay already. Jesus, just shut up," he said. "I'm only doing my job."

"You should get a new job," I told him, "because this one sucks."

I sat down on the bench and crossed my legs. Very ladylike. I was there to stay. I was calm. Unperturbed. I looked down at my chest. I could see my heart beating. *Baboom, baboom, baboom.* Everyone on the boat was looking at me. I gave them a little finger wave and smiled. The people on the boat went back to breakfast. Except for Spanky. Spanky kept staring at me. Finally Delores gave him an elbow and Spanky stopped staring.

I took a couple deep breaths and checked around the bench. Baldy was nowhere to be seen. I sat for about a half hour and Hooker showed up.

"So," he said. "How's it going?"

"Baldy stopped by and tried to evict me, but I told him I was waiting for you."

Hooker put my hat on my head and slid my sunglasses onto the bridge of my nose. "And he wanted to evict you why?"

"Ray was having a breakfast party and thought I detracted from the scenery."

"That man has no taste," Hooker said. "You always pretty things up." He handed me my iPod and a tube of sunscreen. He took some lip balm out of his pocket and added it to the iPod and the sunscreen. "Want to keep your lips soft . . . just in case."

"Always thinking," I said to Hooker.

He tapped his head with his forefinger. "No grass growing here."

I stood and stretched. "I need a break. I'm going for a walk."

"If you're walking in the direction of the deli, you could bring me a soda. Maybe a sandwich. And some cookies."

CHAPTER
SEVEN

I had a six-pack of diet soda in cans, a bag of cookies, and two ham-and-cheese subs. I was in front of the bench and there was no Hooker. I looked to the boat. No one on deck. Two possibilities. Hooker went looking for a bathroom or he decided to follow someone. Either way, I was surprised he hadn't called to tell me. I took the walkway to the parking lot and looked for the SUV. The lot was pretty much filled for the day. No one going in or out. I could hear conversation behind a green panel van. It sounded like Hooker. I rounded the van and found Hooker on the ground with Horse and Baldy over him. Horse and Baldy were concentrating on kicking Hooker and weren't looking in my direction. Baldy was to the side. Horse had his back to me.

"*Hey!*" I shouted, coming up on Horse.

Horse turned toward me, and I roundhoused him in the face with the six-pack of soda. There was a satisfying crunch and blood spurted out of Horse's nose. He stood there, stunned for a moment, and I clocked him again in the side of the head. Then I jumped away before either of them could catch me. I ran to the front of the lot screaming, "Fire! Fire!"

I heard car doors open and slam shut and an engine catch. I ran back to Hooker and saw the goon car wheel around and speed out of the lot. Hooker was on his hands and knees. He dragged himself to his feet and gave his head a shake to clear the cobwebs.

"Well, that was friggin' embarrassing," Hooker said. "I just got my ass saved by a woman with a six-pack of soda."

"What were you doing back here with them?"

"They said they wanted to talk to me."

"And they couldn't do it by the bench?"

"Looking at it in retrospect . . ."

I broke a can of soda off from the six-pack and handed it to Hooker. "Boy, you don't know much. You wouldn't last ten minutes as a woman. I guess Huevo really doesn't want anyone sitting on that bench."

"It's the cars. He wants his cars. All the while they were kicking me they wanted to know where I'd stashed the cars."

"Did you tell them?"

"Of course I told them. They were kicking me!"

"Did they do any damage? Are you okay?"

"Remember when I hit the wall at Talladega and flipped four times? I'm a shade past that."

"Cracked ribs?"

"Don't think so."

"Internal bleeding?"

"Hard to tell, but I'm not coughing up blood, so that's a good sign. They could have kicked a lot harder. They didn't want to kill me. They just wanted to get my attention and tell me Huevo was serious."

"We should leave. I wouldn't want them to think things over and come back to take a shot at seeing what *I* know." Been there, done that.

Hooker limped to the SUV and gingerly eased himself onto the passenger seat. I got behind the wheel, hit the door locks and took off.

"I think we should return to the hotel and regroup," I told Hooker. "And I've been thinking about the chip. There might be people who could back their way through the circuits and find out exactly what it does."

"I thought we knew what it did."

"I'd like it to turn out to be some kind of illegal technology, possibly traction control, but I can't say that I *know* what it does. I'm thrown by the fact that it was just sitting in the knob without a connection to an electronic system. And I don't know why there were two chips."

"Do you know anyone who could find out?"

"Yes, but no one in Miami."

I'd just turned onto Fourth, heading for Collins. I was driving on autopilot, trying not to let Hooker see how rattled I was, trying not to burst into tears because he was hurt. I stopped at a cross street and looked right. A car moved through the intersection. Hooker and I vacantly stared ahead at the car. It was another black BMW. Absolutely unremarkable . . . except for the big dog nose pressed to a rear side window.

"Beans!" Hooker shouted.

I was already on it. I had my left-turn signal blinking and a white-knuckle grip on the wheel. I had to let two cars go through before I could move. I took the corner, and we were both sitting forward, our eyes glued to the BMW. I followed for three blocks, keeping the BMW in sight. The BMW sailed through a yellow light, the car in front of me stopped for the red, and the BMW disappeared from view.

I did my best to run the BMW down when the light changed, but had no luck. The BMW was gone, last seen heading north.

"At least we know Beans is okay," Hooker said.

More than could be said for Hooker. His eye was getting puffy and a brilliant magenta bruise was flowering on his cheek. I gave up on the search for Beans and headed back to the hotel.

"You could use some ice," I told him.

"Yeah, and it wouldn't hurt to have some Jack Daniel's swirling around it," Hooker said, eyes closed, head back on the headrest.

I drove to the hotel with my heart aching and my mind working hard to sort through the jumble of bad luck and terrible events that had occurred in the last four days. I needed to make some sense of it all. And I needed to find a way to fix it.

I found my way to Loews, handed the SUV over to the valet, and helped Hooker get to the room. We didn't have a suite like Suzanne, but the room was nice, with a king-size bed, a writing desk and chair, and two club chairs with a small table between them.

Hooker hunkered down in one of the two club chairs. I gave him a ham-and-cheese sub and fashioned an ice pack for his eye. I sat in the other chair and started working my way through an identical sub.

"Do you think Ray Huevo knows his brother was stashed in the hauler?" I asked Hooker.

"He gave no indication that he knew, but I wouldn't be surprised. He didn't look too broken up by the death."

I was standing at the window, looking out at the pool, and my attention was caught by a flash of white and black and brown.

"Omigod," I said. "Beans."

Hooker slumped back in his chair. "I know. I feel terrible about Beans. I don't know where to look."

"How about the pool?"

"The pool?"

"Yeah, I think that's Beans down by the pool."

Hooker came to the window and looked out. "That's my dog!" He ran to his newly acquired duffel bag and started rummaging around in it.

"What are you doing?"

"I'm looking for my gun," he said. "I'm getting my dog back."

"You can't go down there with a gun! We have to be sneaky about this. It looks to me as if they're passing by the pool area to get to the little dog park. I'll go down to the lobby and follow them back to their room. Then we just wait for the guy to leave, and we go in and rescue Beans."

"I'll go with you."

"You can't go with me. Everybody knows you. You'll spook the Beans-napper. Just sit tight and keep the ice on your eye."

I ran down the hall, punched the elevator button, and seconds later I was in the lobby, hiding out behind a potted palm. I called Hooker on my cell phone.

"Do you see them?" I asked Hooker.

"No. They walked past the pool and disappeared. Wait a minute, here they are. They're walking back the same way they left. They're about to come into the hotel."

I heard Beans panting before I saw him. He wasn't a hot-weather dog. He was walking beside a guy wearing khaki cargo shorts and a collared knit shirt. In his late thirties. Soft in the middle. They stopped in front of the elevator and the guy pushed the button. When the doors opened, I hurried over and slipped into the elevator with them. Two more people followed.

Beans's ears instantly went up, his eyes got bright, and he started jumping around doing his happy dance. The guy was trying to control Beans, but Beans was having none of it. He pushed against me, snuffling my leg, leaving a wake of dog slobber from my knee to my crotch.

"He's usually so well behaved," the guy said. "I don't know what's gotten into him."

"Dogs like me," I said. "Must be something about the way I smell. Eau de pot roast."

The elevator stopped at the sixth floor and the guy got out, but Beans wouldn't leave my side. Beans had his four feet planted and his toenails dug into the elevator floor. The guy pulled at the leash, and Beans sat down. Hard to move Beans when he's got his mind made up not to move. The two remaining people were nervously crowded into a corner.

"Maybe I should adopt him," I said. "Want me to take him off your hands?"

"Lady, I lose this dog and my life isn't worth dirt."

I stepped out of the elevator, and Beans got up and moved to my side. "This isn't my floor, but I'll walk you to your room," I told the dognapper. "Your dog seems to have attached himself to me."

"I've never seen anything like it. It's like he knows you."

"Yeah, it's weird. I have this happen all the time."

We walked down the hall to the dognapper's room, he inserted his key card, then he opened the door.

I pointed to the sign dangling from the doorknob. "I see you have a DO NOT DISTURB sign on the door."

"Yeah, I keep it there so the maid doesn't come in. I can't take a chance on someone accidentally letting the dog out." He stepped inside and tugged on the leash. "Come on, big guy. Be a good dog."

Beans pressed himself against me, and I fondled his head. "I don't think he wants to go into the room."

"He's got to. I got things to do, and I can't take him with me."

"I could take him for a walk for you."

"Thanks for the offer, but he was just out for a walk, and he did everything, if you know what I mean." He searched through his pockets and came up with a dog biscuit. "I save these for emergencies," he said. "I don't give him too many because I don't want him to get fat."

He threw the dog biscuit into the room, Beans bounded in after it, and the door was slammed shut.

I stood outside, waiting and listening, and a moment later I heard Beans give a *woof*. There was the sound of a body getting knocked to the floor, and there was some swearing.

I got back into the elevator, returned to the lobby, and called Hooker. "I have a plan. Meet me in the lobby. And try not to be conspicuous."

A half hour later, Hooker and I were on a couch, our noses buried in a paper, our eyes trained on the elevator. We watched a lot of people go up and come down, but none of them was the Beans-napper. And then, there he was, stepping out of the elevator. He punched a number into his cell phone, talking as he walked to the door. He exited the hotel and got into a car that had just come up from valet parking.

"Do you know him?" I asked Hooker.

"Roger Estero. He works for Huevo. His official position is public relations, but he's really a babysitter for Spanky. He tries to keep Spanky from punching out photographers, and he makes late-night pizza and Pepto-Bismol runs. I think he's related to Huevo. A nephew or something. Not real bright. If you were even a little smart, you wouldn't take a job babysitting Spanky."

We waited until Estero drove away, and then we hustled up to the seventh floor. I found Beans's room and removed the DO NOT DISTURB sign.

"Okay," I said to Hooker. "You call room service and tell them you want the room made up. Then as soon as

129

the maid appears and puts the key in the door, you distract her and I'll sneak in."

Hooker made the call, and we positioned ourselves at opposite ends of the hall. The door leading to the service elevator opened, and I hid around the corner. Hooker was down the hall fumbling with his key card. I heard the maid's cart roll out. I heard her at Estero's door. I heard Hooker approach her.

"Hey there, darlin'," he said. And much as I hate to admit it, if I'd been the maid, I would have given him my full attention.

Hooker handed the maid a line about not being able to get his door open. He switched to speaking Spanish and I was lost. I peeked around the corner and saw that the door was ajar and the maid was down the hall with her back to me, giggling at something Hooker had said.

I pushed open Estero's door and slipped inside. Beans was on the bed, ready to pounce, giving me his devil dog look. It was the look he always got just before he knocked me to the ground. I jumped into the bathroom and closed the door.

Moments later, the maid returned. I heard her open the door, heard Beans leap off the bed and gallop across the room. There was an audible gasp and the door to the room slammed shut.

Hooker knocked three times and then two. Our signal. I opened the bathroom doors and looked out at Beans. He was standing, nose pressed to the bottom of the entrance door, sniffing for Hooker. He was drooling and whining. I left the bathroom, opened the door to Hooker, Hooker stepped into the room and Beans

130

knocked him to the ground and sat on him. Happy dog. Happy Hooker.

"Guess the maid decided Estero's room didn't need cleaning," I said to Hooker.

"I'd tell you what she said, going down the hall, but it was in Spanish, and I'm not sure of the translation. I think it had to do with private parts and ravenous rodents."

We called down to have the car brought around, clipped the leash onto Beans's collar and walked him straight out the door of Loews Hotel and into the waiting SUV.

"I'll find a place to hide," Hooker said. "You get everything from the room and check us out, and I'll meet you here in thirty minutes."

The SUV pulled away and a black stretch limo pulled in. The bellman snapped to attention and Suzanne Huevo swung her ass out of the hotel. She was wearing a black suit and black stiletto heels. Her skirt hem came to just above her knees and the front slit went a lot higher. She had a leopard Itsy Poo bag on her shoulder and a no-shit diamond pin on her lapel.

"Omigod," she said when she saw me. "You're what's-her-name!"

"Barney."

"Yeah, Barney. Last time I was with you, I was facedown in my macaroni and cheese. How did you get me to my room?"

"Wheelchair."

"Clever. Was I a spectacle?"

"My friend rescued us. The wheelchair was his idea. And I took an entire table down with me when I stood up. No one noticed you in the wheelchair."

"Very nice. If you're here around six o'clock, we can get shit-faced again. As you can see, I'm the grieving widow today. Got a lawyer meeting, a fucking memorial service, and then I'm heading for a bar."

"Sorry, I'm on my way to check out. How much longer are you going to be here in Miami?"

"As long as it takes. At least through the weekend. They still have Oscar on ice."

I raced up to the room, gathered our belongings and put them into our two travel bags, and settled our bill. I left the lobby and took a position in the porte cochere, just to the side of the hotel entrance. I had our bags in hand. I was mentally cracking my knuckles, praying that Hooker didn't drive up simultaneously with Roger Estero. I blew out a sigh of relief when I saw the SUV cruise down the street and turn onto hotel grounds. Hooker stopped in front of me, and Beans stared out at me. He gave a loud *woof* and the car rocked.

I opened the side door and tossed the bags onto the backseat. I closed the door and was about to get in next to Hooker when I was brought up short by my purse strap. It was Estero, and he wasn't happy.

"I should have known there was something fishy about the way the dog was acting with you," Estero said.

I tugged at the strap. "Let go of my bag."

"I want the dog."

132

"It's Hooker's dog. If you don't let go, I'm going to start screaming."

"Hooker's a dead man as soon as I get the word. And I don't care how loud you scream, I'm gonna get that dog back." He dug his fingers into my arm and dragged me to the rear of the SUV. "Open the door."

I started shrieking, and Estero clamped a hand over my mouth. I bit him, and he jerked his hand away, taking my bag with him.

I heard someone calling for security. Beans was barking. Hooker was yelling for me to get in the SUV. Estero was screaming threats, trying to get a handhold on my shirt. A bellman wedged himself between Estero and me, I rammed myself into the SUV, and Hooker took off while my door was still open.

I pulled the door shut and turned in my seat to look back at the hotel. "He's got my purse."

"Do you want me to go back and get it?"

"No! I want you to go far away from here."

"How do you feel about North Carolina?"

"North Carolina would be good."

"Do you have plans for Thanksgiving?"

I had a mental head-slap moment. Tomorrow was Thanksgiving. I'd completely forgotten.

"No," I said. "I usually go home to my parents' for Thanksgiving, but they're going on a cruise this year. My dad won it in a raffle at his lodge. How about you?"

"My parents are divorced and holidays are always a tug of war. I avoid them when I can. I was planning on defrosting a Thanksgiving pizza and watching a ball game with Beans. You're welcome to join me."

"I can't believe I forgot Thanksgiving."

"When I went back to get our stuff from Felicia, her kitchen was filled with women making pies. She invited us to stay, but Gobbles needs to get home. He gets to see his kids on Thanksgiving. It's a big deal for him."

"It must be hard to be separated from your kids."

"Like losing Beans," Hooker said.

Traveling by private jet is painless. No waiting in line. No security hassles. No kids kicking the back of your chair. Hooker's Citation is white with a narrow black-and-gold stripe running the length of the plane, and HOOKER written on the tail. Very sleek. The interior is cream leather and beige carpeting, with a small refreshment center in the front, by the door, and a small but comfortable lavatory in the rear. There are three captain's chairs on one side of the aisle and two captain's chairs plus a custom-made dog bed on the other. I was sitting across the aisle from Hooker. He had a movie up on the screen but my mind was elsewhere. It was early evening, and we were flying into Concord, North Carolina. We dropped below the cloud cover, and familiar neighborhoods popped into view. Houses were sprinkled across the countryside and clustered around lakes. We flew over Kannapolis. That was Earnhardt country. Lots of open space and a rickety little town. A big strip mall toward one end. Lake Norman sprawled to the west. Mooresville attached to the northeast end of the lake and Huntersville attached to the southeast end. A lot of the drivers and crew chiefs lived in Huntersville and

134

Mooresville. There were condo complexes, high-end houses and golf-course communities, redneck bars, pretty shopping centers, and some fried-food restaurants.

The Citation touched down and skimmed over the asphalt runway. Five thousand five hundred feet long. It was a small airport used only by private planes. Hangars lined up on one side, with a terminal building in the middle. The NASCAR hangar sat at the far end. The sign on the terminal stated that this was NASCAR country. And it was accurate. NASCAR fans are all over the place, in every state, but you couldn't throw a stick without hitting one in greater Charlotte. NASCAR was on bumper stickers, personalized license plates, shirts, hats, flags, dog collars, jackets, lamps, clocks, boxer shorts, bobble-head dolls, and pajamas.

Hooker's black Blazer was parked by the Stiller Racing hangar. We loaded Beans into the back and watched Gobbles walk to a rusted-out Jeep.

"What happened to your 'vette?" Hooker asked him.

"Wife got it in the settlement. She painted it pink."

"Ow," Hooker said.

"I appreciate all you did for me," Gobbles said. "I'm sorry I got you into this shit. I didn't think it would turn into such a cluster fuck." He searched through the duffel hanging on his shoulder and came up with the remote. "I still have this. Maybe it'd be better if you keep it . . . in case something happens to me."

Hooker pocketed the remote; we got into the Blazer and followed Gobbles out of the lot.

"Do you think he'll be okay?" I asked Hooker.

"No. I have one of those Felicia feelings about Gobbles. I don't think his problems are over."

Corporate headquarters for many of the race teams are adjacent to the airfield. Hendrick, Penske, Roush, Huevo, and Stiller had campuses that housed engine shops and fabrication buildings, R & D centers, transporter bays, museums, corporate offices, and the main assembly buildings where the race cars are put together.

Stiller runs three full-time Cup cars and two Busch cars. At any one time, there are sixty race cars in the shop with two hundred new engines ready to race. The lighting is brighter than daylight, the floors are spotless, the inventory mind-boggling.

The season was over until mid-February, and the race-shop complex was a ghost town.

"Do you need anything at the shop?" Hooker asked.

"Nothing that can't wait," I said. "I'm looking forward to getting home."

Hooker took 85 north and got off at the Huntersville exit. If Disneyland had been built by the Gap, it would look like my Huntersville neighborhood. It's a contrived town with stores and restaurants at the ground level and apartments above. Surrounding the town are condo complexes. It's actually a wonderful place to live, especially when you're new to the area. The joke around the shops is that this is the place race-team members live when their wives throw them out of the house.

136

Hooker pulled into the lot behind my building, and his phone rang. The conversation was short, and he didn't look happy when he hung up.

"That was Ray Huevo," Hooker said. "Your purse got turned over to him, he found the gearshift knob in it, and as he puts it . . . something was missing."

"That answers a few questions."

"Yeah. Ray knew the chip was in the knob. And he wants the chip back. He said we could give it to him the easy way or the hard way."

"Did he elaborate on the hard way?"

"No. But I think it might involve a lot of bleeding."

"Maybe we should give him the chip."

"That's not going to prevent the bleeding. This has gone too far, and we know too much," Hooker said. "Not only do we know about the chip, we know about Oscar."

"I don't like the direction of this conversation."

"I think we're in a lot of trouble. I think we need to find out exactly what functions the chip performs and then go to NASCAR and the police with it. Better a live shoe salesman than a dead race-car driver."

"We've withheld information on a homicide," I told him.

"We'll deal."

"I know a guy at the university in Charlotte who might be able to help us. This guy is a total computer nut. He'd love the chance to check out a new toy. I haven't seen him in a while, but he's probably still at the same address. He was living with his parents, and I can't imagine him ever leaving. He's a great guy, but he'd starve to death if he didn't have a keeper. I have his phone number upstairs."

"I'll walk Beans and you make the phone call."

I live on the second floor of a three-story building. A florist is directly below me and Dan Cox is above. Cox is a motor sports journalist who covers NASCAR. He's a really nice guy. He's my age. And he looks like Gumby. Sometimes late at night I hear odd tapping sounds overhead, and I imagine it's Gumby's horse Pokey running around.

My apartment has two bedrooms and one and a half baths. My kitchen appliances are new, and the master bathroom has a marble countertop. The rooms are all freshly painted cream, and the carpet is stain free. My bedroom windows look down on a small patio and beyond that a parking lot. My living room windows look out at Main Street, USA.

Topper's is across the street. Decent food and ice-cold beer on tap. Its décor is a mix of hunt club and speed park. Big leather booths, a bunch of tall bar tables, and a nice long mahogany bar.

When I sit at my desk, I look out the window at Topper's. Most nights it's packed, but this was the day before Thanksgiving and there wasn't much going on. Teams were taking minivacations in the Florida Keys and visiting family.

Steven Sikulski had been easy to lure to the computer lab. I knew his only two weaknesses. A new computer problem to solve and cheesecake. Sikulski was a big, loose-jointed guy who looked like he should be setting out fruit in a supermarket. His face was unlined at fifty and perpetually looked like Sikulski didn't have a care in the world. And maybe he didn't.

I'd brought him the required offering of New York cheesecake, and now Hooker and I were pacing behind him, cracking our knuckles, waiting for Sikulski to solve the riddle of the chip.

"The small chip is obviously damaged," Sikulski said. "It's a microprocessor with wireless ability, and I'm guessing that the damaged portion contained leads to control some sort of mechanical process. The circuitry isn't complicated, but the miniaturization is impressive. That's all I can tell you on a quick look. The second chip is much more interesting. It can send and receive wirelessly. The fact that it was encased in a shell is fascinating. It would indicate that it doesn't attach to a wiring system. That it can perform its function entirely wirelessly. Perhaps this is a relay of some sort. The primary brain in a complicated routing system. The circuitry is much more sophisticated than the circuitry in the damaged chip. Again, it's microminiatur-ized. And here's the good part . . . it carries its own power source. It's riding on a veneer that seems to function as a battery. It's not my area of expertise, but I suspect the battery is the most exciting part of this little sweetheart. If I had more time, I could work my way through the circuitry and tell you more."

"Unfortunately, we haven't got more time. Is there anything else you can tell us?"

"Because I know the location of the chips, and because I know their suspected use, I can give you a hypothetical situation. A driver could adjust the mechanical function of a car, such as engine speed, with a remote. For that matter, anyone at the track could signal the circuit board. It's like one of those remote-control cars for kids, only this chip controls a real car. The puzzle is that there are two chips. It would seem to me the small chip could do the job."

"Anyone at the track could control this gizmo?" Hooker asked. "It wouldn't have to be the driver?"

"I'm speaking hypothetically," Sikulski said. "The remote would be a simple on/off switch. There's no reason why someone in the stands couldn't operate it."

"Would there be an advantage to a team member operating it? A spotter, for instance."

"I imagine a spotter would have a better sense of when to turn it on and when to turn it off." Sikulski closed the file on his computer. "You understand, this wireless technology could have other uses. It's total James Bond, Mission Impossible shit."

Hooker and I were in his Mooresville house, in front of his big-screen plasma, watching a ball game, eating Thanksgiving pizza. Beans was on the couch with us, waiting for scraps of crust, looking happy to be home.

I was happy to be home, too, but I couldn't get rid of the anxiety that periodically fluttered through my chest. Helping Gobbles had seemed like the decent thing to do. And if I had to do it all over again, I'd still try to help him. I just wish it had turned out better. If only we hadn't left Beans in the hauler . . .

"I was just so tired," I said. "I wasn't thinking right."

140

Hooker looked over at me. "I missed the first half of that."

"I'm worried."

Hooker slid an arm around my shoulders. "It'll work out okay. I've got a feeling."

"Another feeling? You've got a lot of feelings these days."

"You don't know the half of it. I'm a hotbed of feelings. If you'd just stop being mad at me, I'd explain some of them to you."

"I'm not mad at you. I'm disappointed. You broke my heart."

"I know. I'm sorry. Do you want the last piece of pizza? Would that make us even?"

"You slept with a salesclerk! You can't equate that with the last piece of pizza."

"You don't know much about men," Hooker said. "And this isn't any old pizza. This is extra cheese and pepperoni."

CHAPTER
EIGHT

"Not many people working the day after Thanksgiving," Hooker said, looking over my shoulder.

I was at my desk in my little cubicle at the Stiller R & D center, and I'd been the only person in the building until Hooker showed up.

"How did you know I was here?"

"Process of elimination. You weren't home, and it's too early in the morning for the mall to be open."

"I wanted to look at race tapes. And I had some models I wanted to run."

"Trying to gather evidence?"

"Yes."

"Having any luck?"

"I went over Shrin's car and found a chip on the engine. It's in worse shape than the one I got off the sixty-nine, but I'm hoping Steven can do something with it. I looked at it under a microscope, but I only know enough to see some remains of basic circuitry."

"What about the second chip? The sister chip to the one you found in the gearshift knob?"

"I didn't take Nick's car apart, but I looked in the obvious places and I didn't find a second chip."

"Maybe we should take it apart."

I'd tossed and turned all night with a long list of crimes replaying in my head. Multiple counts of grand-theft auto, destruction of personal property, withholding evidence, assault and battery, mutilation of a dead guy! I didn't want to add to the list.

"It would be good if we had permission," I said to Hooker.

"I'll call Bingo," Hooker said. "It shouldn't be a problem. The car is trash anyway."

Bingo is Nick's crew chief. He has three terrific kids, and a nice wife, and he was probably at the breakfast table eating leftover pumpkin pie.

I saved my computer program and swiveled in my seat, waiting for Hooker to get off the phone.

"Bingo wants to be here when you tear the car down," Hooker said.

"No he doesn't. He has a family, and he doesn't want to be part of this. Tell him if we find something, we'll tell him when it's safe for him to know."

By noon I was fairly certain there wasn't a second chip. Either it had been removed, or for some reason it wasn't part of the program.

Hooker was helping with the cleanup. "Most drivers know about cars," he said, wiping down a wrench. "I pretty much only know about driving. I can change the oil, I know the language, and I know some engineering, but I can't rebuild a carburetor. Didn't have an aversion to it, just never got around to it. I'd drive, and the guys I hung out with would drink beer. And then they'd fix my car, and *I'd* drink beer."

"You had a division of labor."

Hooker grinned. "Yeah. We were all specialists."

I wrestled the last tire back onto the car and tightened the lug nuts. "I love everything mechanical. I've been working with cars for as long as I can remember. I like the way they fit together. I like the way they sound, and the way they smell. I like the challenge of getting all the parts to work efficiently. I love my job in R and D, but sometimes I miss working in my dad's garage."

"Why do you suppose Shrin's car didn't have the second chip?"

I jacked the car down. "I don't know. I guess someone could have removed it, but that would mean there was a third Stiller employee involved, and I find that hard to believe. The car was immediately loaded into the truck by its crew, so I doubt Horse or Baldy had access. I'm guessing that for whatever reason, the second chip wasn't needed.

"I'm meeting Steven at four o'clock. I'm hoping he can tell me something interesting. And this time let's remember to bring the remote. I thought it might be helpful if we took it with us for Steven to see."

"This is *very* interesting," Sikulski said, studying the new chip. "This is diabolical. It looks to me like this little gem self-destructed."

He had all three chips under magnification and the guts of the remote exposed. He turned his attention to the chip I'd taken off the 69 engine.

"The two chips appear to be similar. Same size and same materials used in construction," he said. "They're

144

both too damaged to get a good read on the circuitry. Do you see this little bump right here on the original engine chip? I suspect this is the self-destruct charge. It wasn't activated. The remote you brought doesn't talk to this chip. I could probably blow the charge manually, but it will melt what remains, and probably you don't want to do that just yet."

We left Steven with more questions than answers and couldn't find much to say on the ride back to Huntersville.

"Would you feel safer at my house?" Hooker asked.

"Yes, but I don't think it's a good idea."

He dropped me at my door and rolled away. I trudged upstairs and went to my desk to catch up on e-mail. A little after seven I took a break and looked out the window at Topper's. Everyone was back from the holiday and the bar was filling up. I suspected Spanky would be there tonight to bask in his glory. It was the place Hooker would most like not to be, but I thought a Spanky spectacle held some potential. At the very least it was a diversion from my deadend thoughts.

I swiped on some mascara and lip gloss, gave my hair a shot of hair spray, sashayed across the street to Topper's, and claimed the bar stool next to my upstairs neighbor Dan.

"Has he come in yet?" I asked.

"Spanky? No. He's waiting to make an entrance. He'll be in around eight when he knows the place will be packed. Did you come to see the show?"

"I thought it might be fun."

"It's going to be painful. I had to get shit-faced before I could write the story for the last race. I can't believe this guy won. There's no justice in this world. I swear, halfway through the season it was like the sixty-nine car was driving itself."

"Huevo had a good setup on that car."

"Huevo had a *magic* setup on that car." Cox looked around. "Where's Hooker? He's usually half an inch behind you."

"He's staying in tonight."

"There were two guys looking for him earlier. Not from around here, but I think I saw them at Homestead. One guy looked like he'd had his head run over by a train."

Damn! I'd started to relax a tiny bit, thinking maybe we left our problems in Miami. And now I was back to having that horrible hollow feeling in my stomach and my heart was beating a little too fast.

"Was the second guy smaller and bald? And did the big guy have a snake tattooed on the back of his neck?"

"Yep. Friends of yours?"

"No. Not friends."

Hooker is the rock star of NASCAR. When he's at the track, cameras are constantly in his face, and the fans follow him everywhere. Hooker genuinely likes the press and the fans, but there are times when there's just a tad too much enthusiasm and Hooker ends up having half his clothes ripped off. And sometimes, in a state of ill-conceived adoration, the occasional fan will look a lot like a stalker. This year after a well-intentioned fan broke into Hooker's condo and accidentally set the kitchen on fire trying to make a romantic breakfast for two, Hooker moved out of Huntersville and bought a large house on a large tract of secluded land in Mooresville. And a couple months ago, after a tour bus drove up Hooker's driveway and dumped thirty people on his front lawn to take pictures, Hooker got security-gated, installed a large, steroid-angered gorilla in the little gatehouse, and had his property ringed with an electric fence. So I wasn't worried that Hooker would be caught offguard by the two Huevo henchmen.

Nevertheless, I called to warn him. "I'm at Topper's, and Dan says Horse and Baldy were looking for you earlier."

"I'll juice up the fence with a couple extra volts. I'm guessing you're barside, wanting to see the Spanky spectacle."

"Yep. Too bad you'll miss it. It's going to be awful."

"Darlin', you're hitting a new entertainment low."

I blew out a sigh because it was true. I disconnected and ordered a beer.

A half hour later, Spanky and Delores graced the room with their grandeur. As was expected, half the bar applauded and half booed. Dan and I did neither.

Dan threw back a handful of bar nuts. "I'm going to puke."

"You can't puke. You're an impartial journalist."

"No such thing. That crap went out with fedoras. To slightly change the subject, what do you make of Huevo's murder?"

I sipped my beer. "I haven't given it much thought. Do you have an angle?"

"No. But I think everything I've heard so far is wrong. Everyone is intrigued by the bite marks, but I don't think they have anything to do with the murder. The medical examiner said they happened later, after Huevo was already dead. I think they're accidental. I think someone killed Huevo and packaged him up to keep him on ice. Probably just used whatever was at hand. Which would lead me to think this wasn't planned."

"Someone just happened to have miles of shrink-wrap?"

Dan shrugged. "It's a common household item, and some people stockpile. If you shop at the big-box stores, you buy in quantity to save money. The teams do it all the time. Anyway, my theory is that someone killed Huevo and needed to keep things neat, so they wrapped him. They had him sitting in a corner, waiting for it to get dark so they could dispose of the body, and their dog decided Huevo looked tasty."

"So the killer had a big dog?"

"That's what I'm thinking. And it was an inside job, because Huevo was found in Spanky's truck. Someone was making a statement. And by the way, if I knew who the killer was, I'd send him a box of Godiva. Putting Huevo in Spanky's new Avalanche was genius. I hear Spanky threw up when he saw it. Plus, they impounded the truck as evidence."

"What kind of statement do you think the killer was making?"

"Don't know. Sometimes people commit crimes and actually want to get caught, so they leave clues.

Sometimes it's an ego trip and they want to leave a calling card. Or maybe this was a kind of revenge crime. Maybe someone was pissed off that Spanky won. If it had been me, I would have killed *Spanky* and left him in *Huevo's* car, but that's just me."

"Anything else?"

"According to the police, they scoured the parking lot and didn't come up with any evidence that said Huevo was killed there. Huevo and his entourage were staying in one of the big hotels on Brickell. He had a power breakfast scheduled but never showed."

"I can see you're fascinated by this," I said to Dan.

"There's a story here. I can feel it. We're just seeing the tip of the iceberg. And I don't think the dog is part of the murder, but I do think he's a place to start looking. If we go on the assumption that this was an inside job, then we just make a list of everyone who has a dog big enough to have swamp-monster teeth."

"Have you started the list?"

Dan's face flushed. "Yeah, but so far there's only one name on it."

"Probably you need to work harder on the list."

"My exact thoughts. There are probably tons of people out there with huge dogs with huge teeth. I just have to hunt them down."

Spanky and Delores were posing for pictures and signing autographs at the far end of the bar. Hooker'd had some run-ins with Spanky, but my relationship with Spanky was much more distant and cordial. Until finding the chip, I had no real reason for disliking either Spanky or Delores. And for that matter, I still had no reason. According to Steven Sikulski, the chip could be signaled from anywhere on the track. Realistically speaking, there are only two people who would be effective at controlling engine speed. One would be the driver and the other would be the spotter. My money was on the spotter. I didn't think Spanky was smart enough to pull off cheating at this level.

"An inside job for Oscar Huevo covers a lot of ground," I said to Dan. "From what I can see, he wasn't a popular guy. His wife hated him. His brother doesn't seem too broken up. And he stepped on a lot of toes in two countries. And I hate to rain on your parade, but I'm not so sure of the dog thing. If the Huevos were involved, it was probably a hired gun. The Huevos don't look like people who do their own killing."

Dan signaled the waiter for another beer. "Ray Huevo wouldn't hire out. He has people in his organization who would gladly do the job."

I took a handful of nuts. "Are you telling me Ray's a little dark?"

"Ray's very dark. I did an article on the family a year ago. It was next to impossible to get information on Ray. He doesn't talk to anyone, and he has offices in a separate building, a half mile from the bulk of Huevo Enterprises. I was eventually allowed entrance to the building but never got beyond the first floor. It's the R and D arm of Huevo, and God knows what they develop there. People who've actually gone through the building tell me it's filled with chemical labs and computer crap that looks like science fiction.

150

"I ended up writing nothing about him because I couldn't verify anything beyond his business address. What I suspect is that anytime something shady goes down, it gets funneled to Ray. Ray has development funds that could buy a third-world country and half the politicians in ours."

"Do you think Ray is dark enough to kill his brother?"

"I think Ray's dark enough to do anything, but I don't know what his motive would be for murder. It looks to me like Ray has his own little empire."

The dust was starting to settle around Spanky and Delores. The crowd had thinned to just a few hangers-on, and Delores was looking antsy, as if she couldn't wait to get home to her whips and chains and beat the bejeezus out of Dickie.

"I'm going to convey my congratulations," I said to Dan. "Are you coming?"

"I spoke to them at the track. Don't think I could get through it a second time."

I dropped a five on the bar and made my way over to Spanky. I stuck my hand out and smiled. "Congratulations, you drove a really good race."

"Thanks," he said. "Where's Hooker? I wanted to congratulate him on being second."

"I'll pass that along to him." Probably should take the bullets out of his gun first.

"I saw you guys sitting on the dock. What the heck were you doing?"

"We were just hanging out."

"It looked like you were watching us."

"Nope. Just hanging out."

Delores picked her nose up out of her cosmo. "Oh yeah? Well why did you start screaming when Ray's assistant invited you to breakfast? It was real rude of you to be there in the first place when Dickie and me were guests on the yacht. We knew what you were doing. You were trying to ruin our good time. You were jealous because you weren't on a yacht, because losers who come in second don't get invited on yachts."

And this is why everyone loves Delores. I wanted to talk to Spanky alone, but Delores was never more than three inches away. It was a wonder she let him drive the race car without her.

"Oh wow," I said to Delores. "You've got a big black seed right between your two front teeth. Were you eating those little crackers that are mixed in with the bar nuts?"

Delores swiped her tongue across her teeth. "Is it gone?"

"No," I told her. "You should go to the ladies' room and check it out. It's huge and black."

"Euuuw," she said. And she took off for the ladies' room.

"I didn't see any seed," Spanky said.

"I wanted to talk to you. Alone."

"I thought you were Hooker's girl."

"I'm his spotter. And I didn't like what I was seeing on Sunday."

"You mean me winning?"

"No. I mean you cheating. There was traction control on the sixty-nine."

"I drove the wheels off that car. And it was all legal."

"None of it was legal. The sixty-nine had a computer chip hidden in the gear shift knob, and the chip regulated engine speed."

"Yeah, right. And Batman is going to be my crew chief next year. Lady, you're looney tunes. You need to stop taking those drugs."

"You should ask Ray Huevo about it. And if you weren't the one controlling the engine speed, you should also talk to your spotter."

"What's Bernie got to do with it?"

"The chip is controlled by a remote, and you and Bernie are the only ones who could effectively work the remote."

"I'm not asking no one about it," Spanky said. "They'd think I was nuts. And how do you know all this?"

I was pretty sure I'd accomplished my task. No way to know for certain, but I was betting Spanky didn't know about the chip. I left the bar and crossed the street to my apartment. I put the key in the lock and the door swung open. The door hadn't been locked. If this had happened to me a year ago, I wouldn't have given it a second thought. Ten months ago, all that changed, and I got a firsthand education on breaking and entering. My brother had gotten himself into a lot of trouble, I'd gone to Florida looking for him and had stumbled onto his ransacked apartment. So finding my door unlocked when I was fairly confident I'd locked it was a little déjà vu.

I backed away and called Hooker on my cell. "This is probably stupid," I said to him, "but I just came back from the bar, and the door to my apartment is open, and I'm almost certain I locked it."

"Go back to the bar and wait for me."

A half hour later Hooker showed up at the bar. Only a handful of regulars remained. Most were watching hockey on the overhead television. Hooker wasn't big news to this group.

We went outside and looked up at my windows. No shadowy figures passing in front of the shades. We checked out the parking area. No gunner waiting with the motor running.

"Okay," Hooker said. "Let's do it. Let's go upstairs and see if anyone's home."

"Are you sure? It seems kind of dangerous. What if someone's actually there?"

"I'd hate that. I was counting on looking like a hero without any actual bad-guy contact."

Hooker pulled me into the shadows and made a gesture for me to be silent. My apartment door opened wide, and Horse and Baldy came out. They walked to the parking area and got into a car. The engine caught and the car pulled out of the lot and disappeared into the night.

"I have a cramp in a really uncomfortable place," Hooker said. "Gobbles's idea to move to Australia is starting to have some appeal for me."

I slipped out of the shadows, slunk to my door, and let myself in. Hooker grabbed my arm and jerked me back when I put my foot on the first step.

Hooker had his gun in his hand. "Let me go first."

Ten months ago, when Hooker and I got involved in my brother's disappearance we discovered some things about ourselves. One of the things we learned is that we can both be heroic if we have to . . . but we'd rather not. I was perfectly okay with letting Hooker go first. After all, he was big on driving the boat. And he had the gun.

I followed Hooker up the stairs, all the time holding my breath. He paused when he got to the top then looked around. He motioned for me to stay, and then he went room by room, making sure no one was there.

"Looks like it's just you and me," he said when he came back. "If they were searching for something, they were neat about it. Nothing seems out of place."

I filled my travel bag plus a couple brown grocery bags with clothes and other essentials. I hadn't had a chance to buy food, so there was very little in the refrigerator to worry about. I flipped the lights off and gave one of the bags to Hooker. "From what I could tell, they did a decent search. Things were disrupted in drawers. My bed had been taken apart."

"They were looking for the chip," Hooker said.

"Fortunately, I have the chip in my pocket," I said.

"I think it's time to get help. It was probably time to get help yesterday, but I was hoping it would all go away. I think we should go to my house tonight. We'll be safe there. First thing in the morning, we'll call Skippy and see if he'll send a NASCAR lawyer or at least a PR guy with us when we talk to the police."

155

Gus Skippy is vice president of a bunch of stuff. He was originally a newspaper guy, and now he was a NASCAR problem solver, shrink, babysitter, spin master, fashion icon, and the corporate communications guru who butt-kicked and bullshitted NASCAR through the millions of sticky situations that occurred during a season. He hung out with a big guy named Herbert who was known as the honorary mayor of NASCAR. They were both good old boys from Carolina, and when you put the two of them together, they were the Odd Couple of NASCAR.

We went down the stairs, locked the door behind us, and walked one block. Hooker'd taken the precaution of parking away from my building. He was driving the black Blazer, and Beans was waiting, nose pressed against the back window.

Hooker drove north to Mooresville and the collection of back roads that led to his property. He had close to fifty acres, and had placed his house squarely in the middle, behind a stand of pines. The house was only minimally visible to passing cars. He'd combined parcels of land, and three small ranch houses had gone along with the land purchase. Two of the houses were rented out to crew members. The third house sat at the edge of Hooker's driveway and served as a gatehouse. Butchy Miller lived in the gatehouse.

The story goes that Butchy was the local high school football hero who got lost in a bottle of steroids, bulked up to skin-popping proportions, shrank his wiener into uselessness, and developed anger-management issues. He consistently lost at poker, and he scared the hell out of anyone, living or dead. Hooker considered him to be the perfect security guard, and had installed him in his gatehouse, not because he actually needed a security guard but more because he frequently needed an extra hand for poker.

Hooker stopped at the side of the road and looked at his gatehouse. "The lights are off."

"It's late. Butchy's probably asleep."

"Butchy's afraid of the dark. He sleeps with the lights on. When he goes out, he leaves the lights on so it's not dark when he comes home."

Hooker unbuckled his seat belt. "Stay here. I'm going to take a look."

He quietly jogged to the house and disappeared in deep shadow. He reappeared on the far side, and I could see he was peeking in windows, inching his way around. He got to the front door, opened it, and stepped inside. Minutes later he emerged, closed the door, ran to the truck and got in.

"Butchy's dead," Hooker said, putting the truck in gear, pulling onto the road. "Shot in the head. Like Huevo."

"Omigod, I'm so sorry. He was your friend."

"We weren't exactly friends. It was hard for anyone to be friends with Butchy. It was more like having a three-hundred-pound paranoid rottweiler on the property. Still, I feel bad that he's dead. Especially since I'm probably to blame."

"Was he shrink-wrapped?"

"No. He was sprawled on the living room floor. He had an arsenal in that house, so he must have been

157

taken by surprise. Or maybe this was done by someone he knew."

"Someone like Bernie Miller?"

"I don't think he knew Bernie. The Huevo people tend to keep to themselves. And Bernie is new to the area. Bernie came on the scene as Spanky's spotter at the start of the season, just like you. He used to race modifieds, had a bad crash last year and screwed up his knee. Couldn't drive anymore. Got a job spotting for Huevo and the sixty-nine car."

We were barreling down a dark country road. "Where are we going?" I asked Hooker.

"I don't know. I wanted to put some space between us and the crime scene. I deliberately tripped the silent alarm when I left. If there's anyone at the main house, the police will walk in on them when they come to investigate."

"And they'll find Butchy?"

"Yeah, the police will find Butchy and take care of him. He's a local boy. Everyone knows Butchy."

"You don't think we should go back and wait for the police?"

"Darlin', right now I'm more afraid of the man with the gun than of the police. One thing's going to lead to another with the police, and they're going to want us to stay in the area. I'm not sure that's a good idea. I'm afraid we'd be like shooting fish in a barrel."

Hooker drove to a budget chain motel in Concord. I registered us under a phony name, paid in cash, and hoped no one saw Hooker and Beans sneak in. It was a generic motel room with dark industrial-grade carpet and a dark floral bedspread designed to hide cheap wine stains. No Childress Vineyard wine consumed here. This was a wine-by-the-gallon-box-type room. It felt like I'd stayed in a gazillion of these rooms since I'd started the race season. We found a plastic ice bucket, which we filled with water and set on the floor for Beans.

Hooker and I crawled into bed and then thrashed around, unable to sleep all night. We gave up at daybreak and tuned the television to the local news.

The camera crew was set up in front of Hooker's gatehouse. The gatehouse was ringed in yellow crime scene tape. The tape cut across Hooker's driveway entrance, limiting traffic. The on-scene reporter was talking about Butchy. Shot in the head. Found in his living room. No one at home in the main house. Police are looking for Sam Hooker. Wanted for questioning.

Hooker had his head in his hands. "I feel really bad about Butchy."

I leaned against him. "You were nice to Butchy. You gave him a place to live when he had no money. You gave him a job when no one else would hire him. You invited him into your poker games."

"I got him killed."

"You didn't get him killed."

"I set the wheels in motion."

I wanted to comfort Hooker, but I didn't have a good answer for him. At the moment, I was low on intelligent thought. I was tired. I was confused. I was scared.

I pulled a knit hat out of one of the clothes bags and tugged it onto my head. "I'm going to take Beans for a walk and then I'll get us some breakfast." I zipped a winter jacket over my long-sleeved T-shirt and pocketed the room card and the keys to the SUV. I clipped the leash on Beans and led him out of the room, down the hall, and out into the crisp morning air.

The sky was flawlessly pale blue. The sun not yet visible. It was cold enough for my breath to make frost clouds, and I could feel the cold air clearing my head, jump-starting my brain. Beans and I were the only ones in the parking lot. We crossed the lot to a hardscrabble grassy field and walked around until Beans was empty. I loaded him into the SUV and set off in search of coffee.

CHAPTER
NINE

Hooker was showered and shaved when I got back to the hotel room. "I hope you don't mind," he said. "I borrowed your razor. I made up for its pinkness by swearing a lot while I shaved."

"The razor is fine. When you start borrowing my underwear, we need to talk."

I unpacked two cups of coffee and two plastic cups of orange juice from one bag, and I had a second bag filled with breakfast sandwiches. I handed a sandwich to Hooker, kept one for myself, and gave the rest of the bag to Beans. "Everything you could possibly want for breakfast with the exception of pancakes," I said to Hooker. "An egg, a sausage patty, cheese, and a biscuit."

"Yum," Hooker said. And he meant it. Gourmet food was lost on Hooker.

I finished my sandwich, juice, and coffee and took a shower. Hooker was back to watching television when I came out of the bathroom.

"This isn't good," he said. "They're saying the murder weapon that was used on Butchy was also used on Oscar Huevo. I'm now wanted for questioning by

161

the local police and the Miami police. And I hate to tell you this, but they're looking for you, too."

"Me?"

And as if on cue, my cell phone rang. It was my mother. "I just got home from the cruise, and I heard your name on television," she said. "They said you were wanted for murdering two men."

"No. I'm only wanted for questioning. And it's all a mistake. Don't worry about it. I'm fine."

"Don't let them take you to jail. I saw a show on it once. They watch you on television when you go to the bathroom."

More information than I needed right now.

"My mother," I said to Hooker when I disconnected. "She suggested I don't go to jail. She thought I wouldn't like it."

"If you don't want to go to jail, we need to check out of this motel," Hooker said. "It's too easy to spot my SUV sitting out there in the lot. There's an empty factory that's up for sale on the road to Kannapolis. It's been vacant for over a year. I took a tour of it a couple months ago, thinking I might want to buy it for a shop. Maybe build my own cars someday. It wasn't right for a shop, but it might be okay to use as a hiding place while we think this through. There's no alarm on it, so it'll be easy entry. And it's on a secluded stretch of road."

I added breaking and entering to my mental crime tally.

The building had originally been a tool-and-die factory. When the factory went belly-up, the place had been

162

gutted and used to store motor oil and assorted car-care products. Those products had since moved on, and we now sat in a dark, damp, cavernous cinder-block bunker of a building. It hadn't been locked, and one of the garage-bay doors had been left open, so we were only guilty of entering. Hooker drove the SUV into the interior and parked close to the wall where we were in shadow and not visible from the outside.

"For a short time it felt like things might get normal," I said to Hooker. "But now they're worse than ever."

"One step forward, two steps backward. Let's test-drive a couple things. We know Ray was using illegal technology to cheat. We're not sure why because Ray never seemed to be interested in racing. We also know Ray employs two goons who kill people. And we're not absolutely sure, but it feels like Ray knew his brother was in the locker. In fact, chances are probably good that Ray killed Oscar."

"There's something very high stakes here. Something we don't understand," I said to Hooker. "There has to be more going on than cheating at a race."

"I agree. I think we need to find out why Ray killed his brother."

"You were thinking Madam Zarra and her crystal ball would tell us?"

"I was thinking Ray would tell us. All we have to do is kidnap Ray and beat the crap out of him until he talks to us."

I felt my mouth drop open, and I guess I must have looked as horrified as I felt.

"What?" Hooker said.

"Do you have an alternative plan?"

"Not at the moment."

"What makes you think he'll talk if we beat him?"

"I've been beat on a lot, and I *always* talk."

"Let's go on the assumption that the chip has something to do with the murders. Ray really wants that chip back."

"If we gave the chip to NASCAR, he could lose the championship," Hooker said.

"Yeah, but he's never cared about the car side of the business before. Why does he care so much about the championship now? And his dead brother would take the hit. Ray would say he knew nothing about it. Ray would come out clean. And anyway, NASCAR would impose a fine and some sanctions, but they wouldn't take the championship away. They'd have to undo too many things that are already in motion. Photo ops and satellite radio tours and television appearances. Not to mention party favors for the banquet next week."

"So?"

"I think there's something else going on with the chip."

"Like it has some secret James Bond code on it that can be used to destroy the world?"

"Nothing that glamorous. I was thinking more about the things Steven told us . . . a breakthrough in computer technology. Or a new and better battery."

Hooker looked doubtful. "Do you think someone would kill for a better battery?"

"A better battery could be worth a lot of money."

Hooker kissed the nape of my neck.

"What are you doing?" I asked him.

"I'm getting friendly."

"There's no getting friendly. We don't get friendly anymore."

Hooker was a good lover for the same reason he was a good race-car driver. He never gave up. It didn't matter whether he was closing in on the leader, or if he was twenty laps down, he put out the same effort. And if he was in cruising mode, it was only because he was pacing himself and reorganizing. Hooker wasn't a quitter . . . not in a car and not in bed. And apparently that characteristic carried over to not giving up on failed relationships. Or hell, what do I know? Maybe he just didn't spend enough quality time in the bathroom this morning.

"Suppose we go to jail? Suppose the bad guys find us and kill us? Don't you want to get one last orgasm in?" Hooker asked.

"No!"

Hooker kissed me, and somehow, when I wasn't paying attention, his hand had wandered to my breast. Turns out race-car drivers also aren't good with *no*. *No* isn't a word they entirely comprehend.

"Not in front of the dog," I said to Hooker, pushing his hand away.

"The dog isn't looking."

"The dog *is* looking."

Beans had climbed out of the cargo area and was sitting with his butt on the backseat. I could feel his breath on the back of my neck.

"Would you get friendly if the dog wasn't looking?" Hooker asked.

"No. Could you please put your libido on hold? I have some ideas. We could talk to Spanky's spotter."

"You mean we could beat the crap out of him."

"Yeah, okay, we could beat the crap out of him. Anyway, it seems like there's some potential for information there. Or we could break into Huevo R and D . . ."

"Huevo R and D is in Mexico," Hooker said. "Not that Mexico is impossible, but the police probably have my plane grounded. We'd have to fly commercial. And that would be chancy."

"How about residences. Does Ray Huevo have a house in the Concord area?"

"Oscar had a house on Lake Norman. I'm not sure how much he used it. I know Mrs. Oscar wasn't in love with North Carolina. Sometimes I'd hear that Oscar was in town, but I never saw him out and around. I think it was . . . take care of business and get out of Hicksville. I don't think Ray has anything here. There might be a corporate condo somewhere."

"Am I missing anything?"

"The goons. Horse and Baldy. Huevo's henchmen. We could try to get something out of them."

"You mean like get them to confess to murdering two people?"

166

"Yeah," Hooker said. "Of course we'd have to beat the crap out of them."

"I'm seeing a pattern here."

"My talents are limited. Basically, I'm only good at three things. I can drive a car. I can beat the crap out of people. And you know the third thing. It involves a lot of moaning on your part."

"I don't moan!"

"Darlin', you *moan*."

"This is embarrassing. Let's get back to beating the crap out of people. Who would you like to take on first?"

"The spotter, Bernie Miller." Hooker dialed a number on his cell phone. "I need some help," he said. "No. Not that kind of help, but thanks, I might need it later. Right now I just need some information. I need an address for Bernie Miller, Spanky's spotter."

Hooker cradled the phone between shoulder and ear, listening while he rummaged around in the console and the door pocket. He came up with a pen and a crumpled Dunkin' Donuts napkin, handed them over to me, and repeated the address. He disconnected and put the SUV in gear.

"Miller is recently divorced, so with a little luck, he's alone in his house."

"Who did you call?"

"Nutsy. He offered the use of his plane if I needed to get out of the country fast."

Nutsy drives the Krank's Beer car. He's one of the older drivers and is a real good guy. He knows everyone and has probably forgotten more about racing than I could possibly learn.

"That address you gave me is on the lake," I said to Hooker. "That's a pricey neighborhood for a spotter."

"Maybe he can give you some financial advice while we're beating on him," Hooker said, cranking the engine over and putting the SUV in gear.

It wasn't a long ride to Bernie Miller's house in terms of miles, but I was having an anxiety attack and the trip seemed endless. It was midday when we cruised into his cul-de-sac. The house looked new. Probably not more than two years old. The yard was neatly trimmed, with sculpted flower beds and bushes that hadn't yet reached lush status. A gray Taurus was parked in the driveway.

"So, how do we go about this beating thing?" I asked Hooker. "Do we just go up and ring the doorbell and then sucker-punch him when he answers?"

Hooker grinned at me. "Getting into this whole brutality mind-set?"

"Just wondering. Maybe that approach would be too aggressive for a guy with a gray Taurus parked in his driveway. Maybe that's the approach we'd use if we were talking to a guy in a double-wide."

"I used to live in a double-wide."

"And?"

"Just throwing that into the mix," Hooker said.

"Did you get sucker-punched a lot?"

"No. I used to answer the door with my gun in my hand."

I looked over at the house. "That could slow down our interview progress. Might be hard to beat the crap out of a man who answers the door with his gun in his hand."

We'd been idling in the middle of the road, not in front of Miller's house but one house down. Hooker slowly rolled past Miller's house and continued down the block to the corner. He hung a U-turn at the corner and came back down the street. He pulled to the curb and parked. We were now on the opposite side of the street from Miller. And again, we were one house down.

"You don't seem too anxious to do this," I said to Hooker.

"Scoping out the scene," Hooker said.

"I thought maybe it was cold feet."

"I don't get cold feet. Creepy-crawly scrotum and tight sphincter, a lot. Diarrhea, sometimes. Never cold feet."

Beans got up, turned around twice, and flopped back down with a big dog sigh.

"Are we waiting for your sphincter to relax?" I asked Hooker.

"I don't feel comfortable with this. I don't like the car sitting out in the driveway. I know lots of people never use their garage, but this feels off somehow. And I can't see Bernie driving a gray Taurus."

Miller's garage door slid open, and we both scrunched down in our seats. A car engine cranked over in Bernie's garage. Horse jogged out of the garage and got into the Taurus. The Taurus engine caught, and the car backed out of the driveway and idled in front of Miller's house. A blue Lexus sedan backed out of the garage, the garage door slid closed, and the Lexus pulled into the street and rolled past the Taurus. Bernie wasn't driving the Lexus. Baldy was driving the Lexus.

"This isn't doing anything for my sphincter," Hooker said. "In fact, my nuts just went north."

We followed the Taurus and the Lexus out of the subdivision, south on Odell School Road. After a couple miles the two cars pulled off Odell, onto a rutted dirt road that disappeared into a patch of woods. It was the sort of road used by kids for drinking beer, and smoking weed, and getting unexpectedly pregnant. Hooker cruised past the road and parked in a driveway that belonged to a small yellow-and-white ranch-style house. There was a bike and a plastic wading pool in the front yard. It was November and the pool was empty. We were maybe an eighth of a mile beyond the dirt road.

"Now what?" I asked.

Hooker swiveled in his seat and looked back at Odell. "We sit and wait. I don't think that dirt road goes anywhere."

Ten minutes later the two cars reappeared, turned back onto Odell, and continued south, driving past us without so much as a sideways glance. Hooker put the SUV in gear, and followed them.

The air was still cool, but the sky was no longer blue. Clouds had pushed in overhead and threatened rain. The Lexus took Derita Road, and the Taurus followed. We drove past the entrance to the airport. The

NASCAR corporate building was to our right. The two cars continued on and finally turned onto Concord Mills Boulevard and minutes later drove into the mall parking lot.

Concord Mills is a monstrous mall. Over two hundred stores, a twenty-four-screen theater, race-car simulators, an indoor and outdoor go-cart track. It was a Saturday, early afternoon, and the lot was packed. The Lexus driver didn't mess with trying to find a good spot. He went straight to the end of a line of cars where there was room to park. The Taurus parked next to him, both men got out, and they took off for the mall.

We were a row over.

"This is strange," Hooker said. "Huevo's henchmen driving two cars, one of which I'm guessing belongs to Bernie, and they go shopping."

"Maybe it's not Bernie's car. Maybe these guys are staying with Bernie, and they're driving their own cars. Maybe Bernie's deeper in this mess than we originally thought."

A drizzling rain had started misting onto the windshield. Hooker had his phone in one hand and the Dunkin' Donuts napkin with Miller's address and phone number on it in the other hand. He punched Miller's number in and waited.

"No answer," Hooker finally said.

We cut our eyes to the Lexus.

"Maybe Miller's subleasing his house to the thugs," I said.

Hooker nodded. "I guess that's possible."

We unbuckled our seat belts, got out of the SUV, walked over to the Lexus, and looked inside. Nothing out of the ordinary. Clean. No Dunkin' Donuts napkins.

"Nice car," I said, looking it over. "Except it's got a drip in the rear." I bent to take a closer look. "Uh-oh."

"What *uh-oh*?"

"The drip is red, and I think it's coming from inside the trunk."

Hooker came over and squatted next to me. "Uh-oh." He stood and knocked on the trunk. "Hello?"

No one answered.

Hooker ran his fingers around the trunk. "We need to get this open."

I tried the driver's-side door. Open. The morons hadn't locked the car. I reached inside and popped the trunk.

"Double uh-oh," Hooker said when the trunk lid popped up.

The red drips were coming from Bernie Miller. He was curled up in the trunk, and he'd been shot . . . everywhere.

"I wish I wasn't looking at this," I said to Hooker.

"You aren't going to hurl or faint or get hysterical, are you?"

I chewed on my bottom lip. "I might."

"Look on the positive side. One less guy to beat the crap out of."

"Yeah, but it's a crime against nature to do this to a Lexus. The trunk upholstery is going to be ruined."

172

This was my best shot at bravado. The alternative was uncontrollable weeping.

Hooker closed the lid. "These guys are stepping up the house cleaning. Since they loaded Bernie into his car and shot him off his property, I'm guessing they were going to make him disappear. The question of the day is . . . why have they parked him here?"

I glanced back at the mall entrance just as Horse and Baldy came out. They were each holding coffee-to-go cups.

"Looks like they parked him here so they could get their triple-shot cappuccinos," I said to Hooker.

"Man, that's harsh. Shoot a guy and then park him so you can get a cup of coffee. That's so *Sopranos*."

The rain had changed from misting to definitely raining, and the men were hustling toward us, heads down, getting wet. We ducked down and scuttled behind a van.

"You should make a citizen's arrest," I whispered to Hooker. "This is our big chance. We can catch them red-handed. Where's your gun?"

"In the SUV."

Huevo's men were between us and the SUV.

"Do we have a plan that doesn't involve a gun?" Hooker asked.

"You could call the police."

Hooker looked over at the SUV, and his mouth tightened a little at the corners. "Do we have a plan that doesn't involve a phone?"

The two Huevo men got into their cars, backed out of their parking slots, and drove away. Hooker and I ran for the SUV, and in seconds we were out in the drive lane, moving in the same direction as the Lexus. The rain was slanting in, the windshield wipers beating it away. I was forward in my seat, trying to see.

"I've lost them," I said to Hooker. "I can't see through the rain."

Hooker was stuck in traffic. "I can't see them either, and I can't move. It starts raining and people get nuts."

I had the phone in my hand, debating a police call. I had no license numbers to give them. And I had no credibility. The rain was washing the blood off the pavement.

Beans was on his feet and panting. Hooker cracked the windows for him, but Beans kept huffing.

"He probably needs to tinkle," I said to Hooker. "Or worse."

Hooker inched his way out of the lot, got back onto Concord Mills Boulevard, and pulled off when he saw an island of grass. Five minutes later, Beans and Hooker were back in the car, and they were both soaking wet.

"This sucks," Hooker said. "We need to do something to turn this around, because it just keeps getting worse, and I'm losing my good mood."

"Maybe you need lunch." Food solved all problems in my family.

Concord Mills Boulevard crosses Route 85 and becomes Speedway Boulevard. Every possible fast-food chain has a spot on that stretch of road. Hooker took us to a drive-thru window, and we ordered bags of food. Then we cleverly concealed ourselves behind fogged windows and sheets of rain in the Cracker Barrel parking lot.

I filled our stolen motel ice bucket with water for Beans and gave him a bunch of burgers. Hooker and I had shakes and fries and burgers.

Hooker ate the last of the fries and slurped up the last of his shake. "It's amazing how consuming large quantities of salt and artery-clogging fat always makes me feel happy," Hooker said.

"Don't get too happy. We have lots of problems."

"We need to find those two guys."

"How are we going to do that? We don't even know their names."

Hooker called Nutsy again. "I need some more information. There are two guys looking for me. They're on the Huevo payroll. Probably working for Ray. Muscle in suits. One guy is big and has a snake tattooed onto the back of his neck. Dark hair cut short. Just recently got his head bashed in. The other guy is bald. I want to know who they are, and it would help if I knew where to find them."

We moved the SUV back to the mall lot where we felt less conspicuous and waited. Hooker and Beans fell asleep, but I stayed awake. My mind wouldn't shut down. It was making lists. Pick up the cleaning. Buy baby-shower gift for Nancy Sprague. Try to cut back on the swearing. Call mother more often. Forgive Hooker. Get car serviced. Have lock fixed on apartment front door. Adopt a cat. Clean out hall closet. Get manicure.

After two hours, I woke Hooker up so he could change locations in the lot. "Do you think we'll get out of this?" I asked him.

"Sure," Hooker said. And he went back to sleep.

It was a little after four when Nutsy called. Hooker put his cell phone on speaker mode so I could hear.

"The guys' names are Joseph Rodriguez and Phillip Lucca," Nutsy said. "The big guy with the tattoo is Lucca. The little bald guy is Rodriguez. They're part of Ray Huevo's entourage. Security detail. Usually travel with Ray, but Ray's in Miami, and these guys are here. So I don't know what that means. I imagine it isn't good since you're in shit up to your eyeballs and you need this information."

"Just want to send them a candygram," Hooker said. "They've been nice to me."

"Yeah, I bet. I don't know where they're staying. They're operating independently of everything here. I'd guess they're at one of the chains in Concord."

Hooker disconnected and started calling hotels, asking for Joseph Rodriguez. He hit gold on the fifth try. The desk rang the room, but no one answered.

"Probably out looking for us," I said to Hooker. "Got a couple bullets left with our names on them."

"We need a different car," Hooker said. "The police are looking for us, and the bad guys are looking for us, and everyone probably knows my plate by now."

I hated to part with the car. It was reliable and comfy. I looked around the lot. "What we need is a different *plate*. Just swap ours for someone else's. Most people would never notice if their plate was changed."

176

Hooker scrounged around in the console compartment and came up with a small screwdriver. Fifteen minutes later, we had new plates, and Hooker was back in the car, drenched to the skin. He tossed the screwdriver back into the console and turned the heat up full blast.

"If I don't get dry pretty soon, I'm going to start to mold."

He put the SUV in gear and drove across the highway to the motel lot. He backed the SUV into a slot at the far end where we had a good view of the lot and the hotel back door. As good a hiding place as we were going to get.

We'd just settled in when the Taurus pulled into the lot. No Lexus. Hooker had his gun out. Rodriguez and Lucca got out of the Taurus and hunched against the rain. Hooker reached for the door handle, and another car pulled into the lot and parked. Hooker took his hand off the door handle.

"This is like when you're taking a test in school, and you don't know half the answers, and the fire alarm goes off," Hooker said. "You're sort of saved, but you know eventually you're going to have to go back to the test and you'll totally screw up."

Rodriguez and Lucca crossed the lot and disappeared into the building. They were soaking wet, and their shoes and the bottoms of their trousers were muddy.

"It looks like they've been digging," I said to Hooker.

"Yep, the boys have been busy."

"You think they buried the car, too?"

"The car's probably at the bottom of Lake Norman."

Hooker's phone rang. It was Nutsy.

"You know that property you bought for a future shop?" Nutsy said on speaker mode.

"On Gooding Road?"

"Yeah. I had to go by it a while ago, dropping my kid off at a friend's house. Anyway, I think those guys you were asking about were on your property. I can't be sure it was them, with the rain and all, but they seemed to fit your description. The big guy had a bashed-in head. They were just standing by their cars. Guess they were looking for you."

"What kind of cars?"

"A Taurus and a blue Lexus."

Hooker disconnected and thunked his head on the steering wheel.

"What?" I asked. And then it hit me. "Omigod, you don't think they buried Bernie on your property? How would they know it was yours?"

"Everyone knows it's mine. I didn't buy the tool-and-die building, but I bought this warehouse. I haven't started construction, but the warehouse has a big sign on it advertising it as the future home of Hooker Motor Sports." Hooker rolled the engine over. "We're going to have to check it out. It would be a smart move for them to bury Bernie on my land. It would tie everything up nice and neat. There are three murdered men. One has tooth marks that perfectly match my dog's teeth. The other two are found on my property. All undoubtedly shot with the same gun. And

I'm sure they're counting on me being too dead to defend myself."

We drove a half mile and Hooker cut off into a strip mall that was anchored by a Wal-Mart.

He parked and gave me a wad of cash. "Buy a shovel . . . just in case. I'd go in but I'm afraid I'll be recognized."

Twenty minutes later I wheeled a shopping cart out of the store and into the rain. I had two shovels, a flashlight, and a box of giant-sized garbage bags. All just in case. I also had a bag of dog food and three gallons of water for Beans, plus dry clothes for Hooker. And I'd run next door to the supermarket and gotten a rotisserie chicken, some cookies, and a six-pack of beer. I loaded everything onto the backseat and jumped in.

I opened a bag of cookies and fed one to Hooker. "I hope we don't have to use the shovel. Digging up a water-logged corpse isn't high on my list of favorite things to do."

CHAPTER
TEN

The rain had slowed to a steady drizzle, the sky was heavily overcast, the light was somewhere between gloom and the twilight zone. Hooker's property was on a country road that was dotted with small race shops and supporting businesses. The structure was classic cinder-block warehouse, smaller than the warehouse we'd gone to earlier. It was surrounded by a cement apron that led to three bays in the back and a door in the front. Beyond the apron was hard-packed dirt and scrubby grass. Beyond the dirt was woods.

Hooker drove to the rear and parked. We got out and walked the property. We stopped when we reached a piece of ground at the far back corner that was newly disturbed. It was slightly mounded and the smell of freshly dug earth hung heavy in the air. There were footprints and tire tracks in the surrounding mud. Details had already been obscured by rain.

"Fuck," Hooker said. More a sigh than a swear.

I was in total agreement. "How did this happen?" I asked him. "This is a nightmare. I didn't sign up for this."

Hooker turned and trudged through the muck, back to the SUV. I followed him, no longer caring where I stepped. I was in mud to my ankles. My hair had succumbed to the relentless drizzle and was plastered to my face. My jeans were soaked through to my underwear. And I was cold clear to the bone.

Beans popped up when Hooker opened the side door. Beans was wearing his excited *now what* expression, looking like he wanted to be part of the adventure.

"Sorry, big guy," Hooker said. "Too much mud. You're going to have to stay in the car."

Here's the irony of it. The dog would have loved to roll in the mud, and he had to stay in the car. I wanted to stay in the car, and I had to wallow in the mud.

I grabbed a shovel and the flashlight, and I followed Hooker back to the gravesite. I took a stance, rammed the shovel into the dirt and flung the dirt about ten feet to my side. I just kept ramming the shovel in and throwing the friggin' dirt away. I looked up and found Hooker watching me.

"You keep digging like that and you're going to rupture something," Hooker said. "And you have that look on your face like your underwear's riding up."

"I'm wearing a thong. It's always up."

"Oh, man," Hooker said. "I wish you hadn't told me that. It's all I'm going to be able to think about."

"Then I'm happy to be able to supply a diversion, because the other things we have to think about aren't pleasant."

Actually, I was digging like a demon because I was furious. There was no justice in the world. This had all started out as a good deed, and good deeds weren't supposed to end like this. Where's the reward for being a good person? Where's the satisfaction?

I plunged my shovel into the dirt and hit something solid. Not a rock. A rock would go *chink*. This hit with a muffled *thud* that caused my breath to catch in my chest. I pulled my shovel back and a ragged scrap of material clung to the shovel tip. My mind went numb, and I froze with the shovel a foot off the ground. Cold horror slid through my stomach, my pulse pounded in my ears, and it was lights out. I heard someone call to Hooker. I guess it was me.

When I regained consciousness, I was in the back of the SUV and Beans was standing over me panting. Hooker's face hovered beside Beans's big dog head. They both looked worried.

"I think I found Bernie," I said to Hooker.

"I know. You turned white and went face-first into the mud. Scared the crap out of me. Are you okay?"

"I don't know. Do I look okay?"

"Yeah. A little muddy, but we'll get you cleaned up and you'll be good as new. You can breathe through your nose, right?"

"Yeah. Now that we've found him, what should we do with him?"

"We have to move him," Hooker said.

"No way! It's so horrible. The rain, and the mud, and the body's probably all wormy."

"I'm pretty sure it's too soon for maggots, but there are some real good night crawlers back there. Big suckers."

The bells started clanging in my head again.

"I feel like a grave robber," I whispered.

"Darlin', we're doing him a favor. He doesn't want to be buried behind my shop. He didn't like me. We'll put him in a nice clean garbage bag and take him to a better place. We could even buy him flowers."

"Flowers would be nice."

I thought I saw Hooker roll his eyes, but I could be wrong. I was still sort of cobwebby.

"Stay here with Beans," Hooker said. "I can finish up."

I lay perfectly still, willing my head to clear. Beans flopped down next to me, warm and reassuring. When the feeling returned to my lips and my fingertips, I crawled out of the SUV. It was dark and still drizzling. No moon. No stars. No streetlights. Only degrees of blackness to differentiate between sky and building.

I heard Hooker before I saw him. He was dragging Bernie. And it looked like he had Bernie by the foot, although it was hard to tell since Bernie was bagged and wrapped with bungee cords.

"It's sort of an odd shape for a body," I said to Hooker.

"Yeah, I don't know how he got like this. He had to have been folded up in the trunk when he went rigor-mortis central. Only thing I can figure is his arms popped out when he started to bloat."

I clapped a hand over my mouth and told myself this wasn't a good time to get hysterical. I could get hysterical later when I found a bathroom and I could drown out my screaming by flushing the toilet.

Beans was dancing around in the back of the SUV, barking, eyes focused on Bernie.

"We can't put him in the back," I said to Hooker. "Beans will want to play with him."

We looked up at the roof rack, and then we looked over at Bernie. He was all odd angles inside the shiny black plastic bags.

"He's heavy," Hooker said. "You're going to have to help me get him up there."

I gingerly felt the bag.

"I think that's his head," Hooker said. "Maybe it would be better if you came over here and took his foot."

I clenched my teeth and grabbed what I hoped was a foot, and after a lot of maneuvering we got Bernie onto the roof rack. Not sure we could have done it if he wasn't so stiff. Hooker secured the body with the bungee cords, and we both stepped back.

"That's not so bad," Hooker said. "You wouldn't know it was a body. It looks like we wrapped up a bicycle or something. See, doesn't it look like he's got handlebars?"

I clapped my hand over my mouth again.

Hooker tossed the shovels into the back of the SUV and closed the door. "Let's roll."

Ten minutes later we were still rolling without incident. The garbage bags were rattling in the wind as we drove, but the bungee cords were holding. We were taking the scenic route, avoiding the highway, Hooker reasoning that it would be easier to retrieve Bernie if he blew off the roof on a country road.

184

"Where are we going?" I asked Hooker.

"Back to Concord. My original plan was to leave him someplace where he was sure to be found. On the doorstep to Huevo corporate, or maybe take him back to his house. But now I'm thinking I don't want him found right away. With the kind of luck I'm having, Rodriguez and Lucca will be the ones to find him. And they'd probably rebury him in the same shallow grave. I don't want to have to dig him up a second time.

"I'd still like to leave him on Huevo property, but someplace where he'd be on ice for a while. I was thinking we could leave him in a motor coach. We keep our coaches parked on shop property, hooked up to electric. The air runs all the time so the coach doesn't get funky and the veneers stay nice. Huevo probably works the same way. We could put him in Spanky's coach. Spanky won't be using it until February. All we have to do is turn the temperature down."

I stared at Hooker in openmouthed stupefaction.

"What?" Hooker said. "Do you have a better idea?"

The Huevo campus is huge. Acres of landscaped lawn and clusters of perfectly maintained, brilliant white, two-story blocky buildings that house the Huevo offices, cars, transporters, and shops that build the cars. We wound our way between the buildings to the transporter garage, and just as Hooker had predicted, six motor coaches were parked in stalls, hooked to electric. The coaches were dark, no lights burning, not even running lights. There were security floods on the buildings, but not a lot of the light reached to the bus lot.

Hooker parked, and we both got out and looked up at Bernie. He looked none the worse for the trip. His garbage bags were still intact.

"You take the bungee cords off, and I'll get a towel," I told Hooker. "I don't want Bernie getting Spanky's coach all wet."

Motor coaches have keypad locks, but everyone in the drivers' lot uses the same universal code. I was hoping that held true when the coaches were stored. I punched in the standard number of O's and blew out a sigh of relief when the door unlocked. I switched my flashlight on, went inside, and found my way to the rear bathroom. I grabbed a couple large towels, leaving one on the bed, taking the other with me.

"Okay, let's do it," Hooker said.

We tugged at Bernie, and he tumbled off. A lot easier to get him down than it had been to get him up. Hooker took what he thought was Bernie's head, and I grabbed Bernie's foot again, and we tried to wrestle him into the coach.

"The coach door is too narrow," I said to Hooker after several attempts. "Try turning him again."

"Darlin', we've turned him every possible way."

"It's this thing sticking straight out. It must be his arm. It just doesn't fit through the door."

"Go inside and see if you can find something to grease him up with. Maybe if we get him slippery."

I took the flashlight and went through the cabinets, but they'd all been emptied. I was checking the refrigerator when I heard a sound like a baseball bat hitting a tree trunk.

I went to the coach door and looked out at Hooker. "What was that?"

"I don't know, but I think he'll fit now."

"What are you holding behind your back?"

"A shovel."

"That's disgusting. That's desecration of the dead."

"I'm a desperate man," Hooker said.

We wrangled Bernie through the door, I dried the garbage bag off as best I could in the stairway, and we carted Bernie back to the bedroom and set him on the towel on the bed.

"Maybe we should take the bag off," I said. "I'd hate to have someone discover him and think he was garbage."

"No!" Hooker said. "Trust me. You don't want to do that. He's a lot better in the bag. A *lot* better."

Hooker adjusted the temperature, and we closed the door on Bernie. We walked Beans around so he could tinkle and stretch his legs, and then we all piled into the SUV and headed for the abandoned factory that Hooker hadn't bought.

The factory was just as we'd left it. No SWAT teams. No flashing police strobes or crime scene tape. Our hidey-hole was still our secret. Inside the building it was pitch black and cold. At least it was dry. It had a bathroom that worked. I took my grocery bag filled with clothes into the bathroom and changed. When I came out Hooker was already dressed and feeding Beans.

187

We sat in the SUV and ate the rotisserie chicken and drank the beer, then polished off the bags of cookies.

"Do we have a plan for tomorrow?" I asked Hooker.

"Yeah. We abduct Rodriguez and Lucca and beat the crap out of them."

"And we're doing this why?"

"To get information. And after we get the information, we'll get them to confess to everything. I have it all figured out. I can put my cell phone on movie mode and send the confession to the police."

"Is that legal?"

"Probably not. The police will have to beat their own confession out of Rodriguez and Lucca to make it entirely legal. Our video would be more of a *How to Solve the Crime Without Unjustly Arresting Hooker and Barney* guide."

I woke up tucked in between Beans and Hooker. Light was dim in the building interior where Hooker had parked the SUV, but the sun was bright beyond the open garage-bay door. Beans was still asleep, his warm broad back pressed against me, his breathing deep and even. Hooker had me in a stranglehold. His leg was thrown over mine, his arms tightly wrapped around me, his hands inside my shirt, one hand cupping a breast.

"Hey," I said. "Are you awake?"

"No."

"You've got your hands inside my shirt . . . again."

"My hands were cold," Hooker said. "And your boobs are nice and warm."

"For a minute there I thought you were getting friendly."

"Who me?" And he lightly brushed his thumb across my nipple.

"Stop that!" I struggled to slide out from under him and drag myself up to a sitting position. "I'm starving."

I crawled out of the SUV and cleaned up as best I could in the sink. I washed my hair and finger-combed it dry. Hooker used my toothbrush, but he didn't tempt fate a second time with the pink razor, so he was looking a little mountain man.

We hit the McDonald's drive-thru in Concord, and when Hooker reached for the bags of food, he was recognized.

"Omigod," the girl at the window said. "You're Sam Hooker. The police are looking for you."

Hooker handed the bags and coffees over to me. "Sorry," he said to the girl. "He's my cousin. Family resemblance. Happens all the time. Sometimes I even sign autographs for him."

"I hear he's a real asshole," the girl said.

Hooker rolled his window up and drove away.

"That went well," I said to Hooker.

He cut across Speedway Boulevard and looked for a place to hide. It was Sunday morning and the shopping-center lot was empty. Not good for losing ourselves. We finally settled on one of the chain-restaurant lots and dug in.

"So, how much do you know about this interrogation stuff?" I asked Hooker.

"I watch CNN."

"That's it? Everything you know about abduction and interrogation you learned from CNN?"

"Darlin', I drive cars for a living. I don't have a lot of opportunity for interrogation."

"What about beating the crap out of people?"

"I have some experience at that," Hooker said.

"We might need some equipment if we're going to kidnap Rodriguez and Lucca," I said. "Maybe we should get some rope to tie them up with. And rubber hoses so you can beat them."

"I don't need a rubber hose. But the rope might come in handy. And some doughnuts wouldn't hurt either."

Hooker found a Dunkin' Donuts drive-thru and ordered a dozen assorted doughnuts. When he reached for the bag, he was recognized again.

"Hey, you're Sam Hooker," the girl said. "Can I have your autograph?"

"Sure," Hooker said. And he signed a napkin and pulled away, back onto Speedway.

"Not going with the cousin routine?" I asked him.

"It seemed like a good line at the time."

We finished eating and Hooker dropped me off at a Wal-Mart where I bought rope, some chains and locks, pillowcases (because CNN had shown terrorists wearing pillowcases), and a second flashlight. Minutes later, we were back in the motel lot with one eye on the back door and the other eye on the Taurus. And nothing was happening.

"Why aren't they out looking for us?" Hooker asked.

"Maybe they're taking Sunday off."

"There's no Sunday off if you're a hit man. Everybody knows that. I could do a lot of damage on a Sunday. I could decide to go to the police. I could talk to the press."

"All because you were ignored on a Sunday?"

"It could happen," Hooker said.

"You should call them. Tell them to get their slacker butts out here."

Hooker grinned. "I like that. That's not a bad idea." He called the hotel and asked for Rodriguez. "Hey," Hooker said when Rodriguez answered. "How's it going? I was just wondering what you guys were doing? I would have thought you'd be looking for me. Ray's not going to be happy to find out you're sitting around in your underwear taking the day off."

"Who is this?" Rodriguez said.

"Jeez," Hooker said, "how many guys are you looking for?"

"Where are you?"

"I'm at the mall. Thought I'd go to a movie. Get a slice of pizza."

"Real cocky, aren't you?"

"So far I haven't seen anything to get worried about."

"Asshole."

Hooker hung up.

"Two out of three people can't be wrong," I said to Hooker.

We slouched in our seats and waited to see if Rodriguez and Lucca would go to work. Hard to believe that Hooker was watching a movie or eating pizza, but if it was me, morbid curiosity would dictate that I checked it out.

Sure enough, five minutes later Rodriguez and Lucca emerged from the back door, got into the Taurus, and drove off.

"They came out of the hotel and walked straight to their car," Hooker said. "Didn't even look for us."

"Probably didn't think we'd be dumb enough to be sitting here."

"Happens to me all the time," Hooker said. "People are always underestimating my dumbness."

The movie theater is twenty-four screens big and attached to the mall. Hooker watched the Taurus turn onto the service road and stop at the light. The light changed and the Taurus crossed Speedway Boulevard.

"One more time to the mall," Hooker said, putting the SUV in gear.

Probably Hooker could drive the route blindfolded by now.

Rodriguez and Lucca were already out of their car and walking toward the theater entrance when we swung into the lot.

"Now what?" I asked. "Are you going to run over them? Or are you going to snatch them at gunpoint?"

"Race-car drivers aren't supposed to run over people. You don't lose points, but you could get a big fine and community service."

"But it's okay to kidnap them at gunpoint?"

"The rule book doesn't actually cover kidnapping."

Hooker cruised down the lane and stopped behind the Taurus. "Can you do something to their car so it won't start?"

"Sure."

I got out and tried the door on the Taurus. Not locked. I popped the hood and disconnected a hose and some wires. I got back in the SUV, and Hooker drove one lane over and parked.

"This is part of your plan, right? Disable their car so they can't get away?" I asked him.

"Darlin', I don't have a plan. I just wanted to mess with them."

Thirty minutes later, Rodriguez and Lucca sauntered back down the car lane. They were talking, and they each had a soft-drink cup. Lucca was carrying a pizza box. They got in the car and a couple minutes passed. Hooker smiling the whole time.

"I can't believe you're getting off on this," I said. "We're wanted by the police. We're about to abduct a couple killers. And you're having fun with them."

"You have to take fun where you find it," Hooker said. "Anyway, this throws them off their game a little. Gives them something to think about besides us."

The car doors opened and Rodriguez and Lucca got out. They popped the hood and took a look.

"Probably don't know a gasket from a water pump," Hooker said.

They slammed the hood down and looked around, hands on hips, pissed off.

Now I was starting to enjoy it. "We have them wondering."

Rodriguez took out his cell phone and made a call. There was a lot of head nodding. He looked at his watch and wasn't happy. I'm not proficient at reading lips, but it was obvious what he said into the phone.

"Bad move," Hooker said. "Not only is that physically impossible, it's also not going to get the road-service crew out here anytime soon."

Rodriguez flipped his phone closed and looked around some more. He stared directly at us, and my heart skipped a couple beats before his gaze moved on.

"He didn't spot us," I said.

"Might not be at the top of the charts as far as hit men go."

"Yeah, and they've killed two men. Probably three. Imagine how many people they could have killed if they were really good."

"At least three more," Hooker said.

Rodriguez ran his hand over his bald head and looked at his watch again. There was a discussion, and Rodriguez got behind the wheel and horse-wanger Lucca returned to the mall.

"Divide and conquer," Hooker said. "It'll be easier to snag just one of them. Let's move."

We got out and walked over to the Taurus. Hooker had his gun in one hand and his other hand on the Taurus door handle. He yanked the door open and pointed the gun at Rodriguez.

"Get out," Hooker said.

Rodriguez looked at Hooker, and then he looked at the gun.

"No," Rodriguez said.

"What do you mean, no?"

"I'm not getting out."

"If you don't get out, I'll shoot you."

Rodriguez stared Hooker down. "I don't think so. You're not a shooter. I bet you never shot anything."

"I hunt," Hooker said.

"Oh yeah? What do you hunt, bunnies?"

"Sometimes."

I tried not to grimace. "That's disgusting."

"Women don't understand about hunting," Rodriguez said to Hooker. "You gotta have cojones to hunt."

I did an eye roll. "Now that you two big-game hunters have bonded, how about getting out of the car."

"Forget it," Rodriguez said.

"Okay," I said to Hooker. "Shoot him."

Hooker's eyes opened wide. "Now? Here?"

"Now! Just friggin' shoot him."

Hooker looked around the lot. "There are people . . ."

"For crying out loud," I said. "Give me the gun."

"No!" Rodriguez said. "Don't give her the gun. I'll get out. Christ, she almost killed Lucca with that six-pack."

Hooker and I took a step back and Rodriguez got out.

"Hands on the car," Hooker said.

Rodriguez turned and put his hands on the car, and I did a pat down. I took a gun from a side holster and a gun from an ankle holster and his cell phone.

Hooker's phone rang. "Yeah?" Hooker said. "Uh-huh, uh-huh, uh-huh." He shifted from side to side.

"Uh-huh. Uh-huh. No problem. I'll be there. I'm ready to get on the plane."

"Who was that?" I asked Hooker when he disconnected.

"Skippy. He wanted to make sure I remembered about the banquet. He said murder charges wouldn't exempt me."

It was Sunday, and Skippy was probably already in New York preparing for an entire week of NASCAR promotion with the top-ten winning drivers. And he was justifiably worried that he'd have only nine guys safely tucked away in their rooms at the Waldorf. Probably at this very moment his thumbs were flying over his BlackBerry, composing a damage-control article on Hooker and me that could be shipped out to the media at a moment's notice.

Hooker reached into the car and popped the trunk. "Get in," he said to Rodriguez.

Rodriguez paled. "You're kidding."

Rodriguez was thinking about Bernie Miller. Thinking about how easy it was to shoot a guy in a trunk. And I was thinking I liked seeing Rodriguez coming to terms with it. This wasn't the movies. This was real life. And shooting people in real life wasn't nice. Especially when you were the guy getting shot.

"I could shoot you now," I said. "Be easy to get you in the trunk with a couple bullets in your head."

I couldn't believe I was saying this. I had to get somebody else to kill a spider. And I hated spiders. Not only was I saying all these dumb tough-cookie things . . . I was almost believing them.

196

Rodriguez looked into the trunk. "I've never climbed into a trunk before. I'm gonna feel like an idiot."

Guess this was one of those situations where having cojones doesn't do you a lot of good, eh?

Hooker made an impatient sound and raised his gun, and Rodriguez went into the trunk headfirst. He had his ass up in the air, looking like Pooh Bear going into the rabbit hole, and I almost burst out laughing. Not because it was all that funny, but because I was borderline hysterical.

A bunch of high school kids walked by on their way to the mall.

"Hey, it's Sam Hooker," one of them said. "Dude!"

"Hey, man, can I have your autograph?"

"Sure," Hooker said, handing me the gun. "You got a pen?" he asked the kid.

"What's with the guy in the trunk?" one of the kids wanted to know.

"We're kidnapping him," Hooker said.

"Way to go," the kid said.

The kids left, and we closed the lid on Rodriguez.

"You drive the SUV, and I'll take the Taurus," Hooker said. "We'll take him to the factory."

I reattached the hose and wires on the Taurus, jogged to the SUV, Hooker backed the Taurus out, and we took off.

CHAPTER
ELEVEN

It was late afternoon. We'd stopped at a grocery store, and I'd done some shopping while Hooker walked Beans. After the grocery store, we drove to the deserted factory and parked the two cars deep in the cavernous interior. Now we were standing behind the Taurus, wondering what the heck we were supposed to do next.

"How about this," Hooker said. "We haul him out of the trunk, and we chain him to that pipe over there. We can wrap the chain around his ankle and lock it. He'll be able to move around a little, but he won't be able to get away."

It sounded like an okay plan to me, so I held the flashlight and Hooker felt around for the trunk latch. He got the lid up, looked in at Rodriguez, and Rodriguez kicked out with both feet, catching Hooker square in the chest, knocking him on his ass. Rodriguez rocketed out of the trunk and hit the ground running. He tried to push past me. I whacked him hard in the knee with the flashlight and he went down like a sack of sand.

Hooker was on all fours with the chain in his hand, trying to wrap it around Rodriguez's ankle, but Rodriguez was a moving target, rolling on the cement floor, holding his leg, swearing and moaning. I threw myself on top of Rodriguez, Rodriguez let out an *oouf* of air, and I pinned him long enough for Hooker to secure the loop of chain with a padlock.

I rolled off Rodriguez and looked at Hooker, still on hands and knees. "Are you okay?"

Hooker dragged himself up to standing. "Yeah, aside from having size-ten footprints on my chest, I'm peachy. Next time I open a trunk with a killer in it, I'll step back."

We waited for Rodriguez to quit swearing and writhing in pain, and then we dragged him across the room and chained him to the pipe.

Rodriguez propped himself up against the wall, his knee outstretched. "You broke my fucking knee," he said.

"It's just a bruise," I told him. "If I'd broken it, you'd see swelling."

"It feels swollen."

"I'm sure it's not swollen."

"I'm telling you it's fucking swollen. You goddamn broke my knee."

"Hey!" Hooker said. "Could we forget the knee for a minute? We're in an unfortunate situation, and we need you to answer some questions."

"I'm not answering nothing. You could cut off my nuts and I'm not answering nothing."

"There's an idea," I said to Hooker. "I've never cut off anybody's nuts before. It might be fun."

"Messy," Hooker said. "Lots of blood."

"How about this, we could hang him upside down until all the blood rushes to his head, and then we could cut off his nuts."

Hooker smiled at me. "That might work."

Rodriguez groaned and put his head between his legs.

"I think he's feeling sick," I said to Hooker.

"Maybe we should give him a break," Hooker said. "He's probably not such a bad guy. Only doing his job."

"You're such a softy," I said to Hooker.

"Trying to be fair."

I was still holding the flashlight and I gave it a little waggle. "Can we at least beat the crap out of him?"

"I know that was our original plan," Hooker said, "but I think we should give him a chance to save his ass. I bet he could tell us some interesting stuff."

We both looked down at Rodriguez.

"Shit," Rodriguez said. "You're playing me."

"True," I said. "But that doesn't mean we won't cause you a lot of pain if you don't cooperate."

"And if I *do* cooperate?"

"No pain," Hooker said.

"What do you want to know?"

"I want to know about Oscar Huevo."

"He wasn't such a nice guy. And now he's dead," Rodriguez said.

"I want to know how he got dead."

"It was an accident."

I had the flashlight trained on Rodriguez, making him squint past the glare.

"He had a big hole in the middle of his forehead," I said to Rodriguez. "It didn't look like an accident."

"Okay, it wasn't an accident. It was more like good fortune. Oscar and Ray got into a big fight. I don't know what it was about, but Ray came out of it mad and decided he needed to get rid of Oscar. So Lucca and me got the job. Problem is, Oscar has his own muscle, and there aren't a lot of opportunities to gracefully make Oscar disappear, if you know what I mean. We watched Oscar for a couple days, and we were worrying it wasn't gonna happen, and then it got dropped in our lap.

"Oscar had a girlfriend stashed in South Beach. He'd sneak out of his hotel on Brickell and spend the night with his girl, and then his guy, Manny, would pick him up and bring him home real early in the morning. Manny'd drop Oscar off a couple blocks from the hotel, and it'd look like Oscar was out getting exercise. Oscar was laying low on account of the divorce. Figured why stir up any more trouble than he already had. So Manny's supposed to pick Oscar up, only Manny's eaten some bad clams or something and he can't get himself out of the bathroom long enough to get his shoes on. That's how Lucca and me got the call to go get Oscar.

"We drive over there and it gets even better. The girlfriend opens the door and tells us Oscar's in the bathroom, and he's in trouble. Turns out he took some of that stuff to, you know, help him out in the sack, and his dick won't go down. He's buck naked in the

201

bathroom, and he's trying everything he knows, and his dick won't go down. So we shot him."

"That explains a lot," Hooker said.

"Yeah, I honestly thought it would help his situation, but even after we shot him, his dick wouldn't go down," Rodriguez said. "I'm telling you, I'm *never* taking that stuff."

"What about the girlfriend?"

"We shot her, too. One of those unfortunate necessities."

"Had to be messy," I said.

"Hey, Lucca and me are professionals. We're not stupid about this. We shot them both in the bathroom. Wall-to-wall marble. Easy cleanup. Had to use a brush on the grout, but overall it wasn't bad."

We were discussing a grisly double murder and Rodriguez was telling us all this in the same sort of conversational tone a person might use to pass on a favorite lasagna recipe. And I was responding with the same enthusiasm a new cook might show. I was simultaneously horrified and impressed with myself.

"Tell me about the plastic wrap," I said to Rodriguez. "What was that?"

"Ray figured he had a way to get rid of Oscar *and* Suzanne. He figured he'd take Oscar back to Mexico and bury him someplace where the widow Huevo would look guilty . . . like in her flowerbed in the hacienda backyard. Ray wanted to make it look like Oscar had gone back to Mexico and had it out with the missus. And the perfect way to get him to Mexico was in the hauler since it was already supposed to take the

202

car back to the R and D center. Only thing was, Ray said we had to make sure we didn't get anything dirty. He didn't want blood smears all over the hauler. And he didn't want Oscar stinking things up.

"We would have put him in a big garbage bag, but there was only one left in the kitchen at the girlfriend's condo, and we used it on the girlfriend. So we were left with the plastic wrap. Good thing there was a lot of it. A couple giant rolls. I don't know what they were doing with all that wrap. Probably something kinky. Oscar had some odd tastes. Anyways, we found a couple boxes by the Dumpster outside the condo, and we put Oscar and the girlfriend in the cardboard boxes and carried them out like they were going into storage. We tossed the box with the girlfriend into the Dumpster. And we brought Oscar onboard the hauler. We thought he was hidden better in the locker, so we threw the box away and stuffed him in.

"Originally we were gonna put Oscar onboard when the hauler made a rest stop, but it had an engine problem and it turned out we were able to transfer him at the track. We drove up just as everybody was leaving. The two drivers went to take a leak, and we got the box out of the SUV we were driving and into the hauler. It was real sweet . . . until you stole the truck."

"Guess we ruined the plan," Hooker said.

"Big-time. And you got the gizmo. Ray don't like that you got the gizmo. He needs it bad. He's on a rant."

"What's so special about the gizmo?"

"I don't know exactly. I guess it's one of a kind."

Hooker had his phone in his hand. "Now all you have to do is tell all this to the police."

"Yeah, right," Rodriguez said. "How many murders you want me to confess to? Maybe I'll get off easy and they'll only fry me twice."

Hooker looked over at me. "He's got a point."

"You could change the story," I told Rodriguez. "You could say Ray killed Oscar. We don't care if you tweak the facts a little."

"Right," Hooker said. "We just want to look squeaky clean, so we can get on with our lives."

"Ray was always with people," Rodriguez said. "He'll be able to account for his time."

"Okay, how about you say Lucca killed Oscar? You could plea-bargain," Hooker said. "They do that all the time on television."

Rodriguez had his arms folded across his chest and his mouth set in a tight line. He'd said all he was going to say.

Hooker and I walked away and huddled.

"We have a problem," Hooker said. "Rodriguez isn't going to confess to murder to the police."

"Gee, huge surprise there."

Here's the thing. I'm not Nancy Drew. I grew up wanting to build and race stock cars. Solving crimes was never on my list of top-ten desired vocations. Don't have any aptitude for it. And from what I knew of Hooker, ditto. So when you talked about being up the creek without a paddle, you were talking about us.

"How about this," I said to Hooker. "We make an anonymous phone call to the police to come get him.

204

And when they get here he's got the murder weapon on him."

Hooker looked over at me. "Would that be the gun that's stuck in your pocket? The one with your prints all over it?"

I gingerly removed the gun from my pocket. "Yep, that's the gun."

"It might work," Hooker said. "And I have the perfect spot for him."

Forty minutes later, we had Rodriguez locked inside Spanky's bus. We'd shoved him in, chained him to the stairwell hold bar, and handed him his empty, freshly wiped clean, fingerprint-free gun.

Hooker'd closed the motor coach door. We'd jumped into the SUV, driven off Huevo property, and parked in the little airport lot where we hoped we looked unworthy of notice. We had a clear view of the road leading to Huevo Motor Sports. All we had to do now was call the police, and then we could sit and wait for the fun to begin.

I was about to cross the lot and go into the building to use the pay phone when Spanky's motor coach came roaring down the road and barreled past us.

Hooker and I went slack jawed.

"Guess I gave him too much chain," Hooker said.

"We really need to stick to racing," I said to Hooker. "We're total police-academy dropouts."

Hooker rammed the SUV into drive and took off after the coach. "I prefer to think we're on a learning curve."

Rodriguez fishtailed to a stop at the end of the airport road. He made a wide left turn and headed for Speedway Boulevard.

An average motor coach is about 12 feet high, 9 feet wide, and 45 feet long. It weighs 54,500 pounds, travels on diesel, and has a turning radius of 41 feet. It's not as complicated to drive as an eighteen-wheeler, but it's big and unwieldy and requires some care when maneuvering.

Rodriguez wasn't taking care. Rodriguez was overdriving the coach. It was rocking from side to side, sliding back and forth over the centerline of the two-lane road. The coach veered onto the shoulder, took out a residential mailbox, and swerved back onto the road.

"Good thing he can kill people," Hooker said, dropping back, "because he sure as hell can't drive."

We followed the coach onto Speedway and held our breath as Rodriguez merged into traffic. Speedway is multiple lanes and heavily traveled. It was dusk, and cars were leaving the shopping center and seeking out fast-food restaurants for Sunday dinner. Ordinarily traffic on Speedway was orderly. Tonight, Rodriguez was causing havoc. He was straddling lines and oozing into adjoining lanes, scaring the heck out of everyone around him. He sideswiped a panel van and sent it careening across the road. A blue sedan hit the van and probably a few more cars were caught in the mess, but it was all behind us.

"Do you think he knows he hit that van?" I asked Hooker.

"Doubtful. He's slowed down, but he still can't control the sway on the coach."

We were coming up to a major intersection with traffic stopped at a light. The coach was cruising at 40 miles per hour, and I wasn't seeing his brake lights.

"Uh-oh," I said. "This isn't good. We should have put a seat belt on Bernie."

Hooker eased off the gas and increased the space between us.

"Brake!" I yelled at Rodriguez. Not that I expected him to hear me. I just couldn't *not* yell it. *"Brake!"*

When his lights finally flashed, it was too late. He fishtailed and swung sideways, the right side of the coach scraping a truck hauling scrap metal. The right-front coach skin peeled away as if it had been cut with a can opener, four cars slammed into the left side, and the entire mess moved forward like an advancing glacier or lava flow or whatever bizarre disaster you could conjure up. There was one last crunch and the behemoth bus came to rest on top of a Hummer.

A headline flashed into my head: Bonnano Motor Coach Humps Hummer on Speedway Boulevard.

We had fifteen to twenty cars between the motor coach and us, not counting the cars directly involved in the crash, and cars were in gridlock behind us.

"I really want to run up there and take a look," Hooker said, "but I'm afraid to get out of the car."

"Yeah," I said to him. "You'd probably have to sign autographs. And then the police would come and take you away and do a body-cavity search."

I climbed out of the window and stood on the ledge to see better.

Caught in the glare of headlights and smoky road haze, a lone figure ran between wrecked cars. He had a chain and part of a handrail tethered to his ankle. Hard to tell from my vantage point if he was injured. He approached a car stopped at the intersection, yanked the driver's door open, and wrenched the driver out of the car. He angled himself into the car and drove off with the chain caught in the door and the handrail clattering on the pavement. So far as I could see, no one stopped him or followed him. The driver of the stolen car stood in frozen shock. Sirens screamed in the distance.

I slipped back inside and took the seat next to Hooker. "Rodriguez carjacked a silver sedan and drove off into the sunset."

"He did not."

"Yep. He did. Still had the chain and handrail attached."

Hooker burst out laughing. "I don't know who's more pathetic . . . him or us."

I slouched in my seat. "I think we'd win that contest."

Beans sat up and looked around. He gave a big Saint Bernard sigh, turned twice, and flopped down.

"This could take a while," I said to Hooker. "They're not going to sort this out in fifteen minutes."

Hooker reached over and ran a fingertip along the nape of my neck. "Want to make out?"

"No!" Yes. But not here and not now. I wasn't going to give in on a freeway. If we were going to have make-up sex, it was going to be good. It for sure wasn't going to be in the backseat of an SUV.

"Just some kissing," Hooker said. He put his hand over his heart. "I swear."

"You're not planning on doing any touching?"

"Okay, maybe some touching."

"No."

Hooker blew out a sigh. "Darlin', you're a hard woman. You're doggone frustrating."

"And it's not going to do you any good to drag out your Texas drawl," I told him.

Hooker grinned. "It got me where I wanted to go when I first met you."

"Yeah, well, it's not going to get you there now."

"We'll see," Hooker said.

I narrowed my eyes at him.

"Come on, admit it," Hooker said. "You want me bad."

I smiled at him, and he smiled back, and we both knew what that meant. He held my hand, and we sat there, holding hands, staring out the windshield, watching the cleanup spectacle like it was a television show.

There were fire trucks and medical-emergency trucks from three counties and enough flashing strobes to give a healthy man a seizure. The medevac helicopter didn't drop out of the sky, and no one seemed to be rushing around, frantically trying to save a life. So I was hoping that meant no one was critically injured. All but one of the fire trucks left the scene. And one by one the EMT trucks left, some with flashing lights. None of the EMT trucks sped away with sirens blaring. Another good sign.

Tow trucks and police were working on the outer perimeter of the crash, moving cars. The road was still blocked, but the problem was shrinking. A tow truck inched into the heart of the wreck.

"They're going to try to get the coach off the Hummer," I said to Hooker. "I'm going out for a better view."

I was afraid to climb onto the car again. Too many lights now. Too many people looking around. So I stood beside the SUV with my sweatshirt hood up and my hands in my pockets, hunched against the cold.

After a lot of discussion, the tow-truck driver attached a chain to the coach and slowly winched it back. The rear on the Hummer had been squashed down to about three feet of compressed fiberglass and steel, so the coach didn't actually have all that far to drop. It came off with a decent amount of grinding noise and a loud *wump* when it hit the ground. It bounced and jiggled a little, and then it went stoic, silently enduring its disgraced condition.

Now that the motor coach was off the Hummer, it was easy to see how Rodriguez had escaped. The right front had taken the biggest hit, and the shell of the coach had completely peeled back, leaving a gaping hole where the door used to be. Rodriguez had probably gotten yanked out of his seat and then found that the handrail had broken free of its moorings.

210

Hooker had his head out. "What's going on?"

"They pulled the coach off the Hummer. And now I think they're going in to investigate. Probably want to make sure no one's inside."

Hooker pulled his head back into the SUV and slunk down. They were about to discover poor Bernie Miller in the motor coach bedroom. And he wasn't exactly Sleeping Beauty.

I watched two cops enter with flashlights. Long moments passed while I held my breath. The cops came out and stood beside the bus. One was on his talkie. More cops came over. Some suits pushed through the crowd. A uniform unrolled yellow crime scene tape, securing the area around the bus.

I leaned into the SUV. "They found him," I whispered to Hooker.

Hooker looked at me. "Why are you whispering?"

"It's too horrible to say out loud."

An unmarked cop car with its Kojak light flashing cut through traffic and eased up to the outer perimeter of the smashed cars. Two suits got out, followed by Spanky and Delores. They all power-walked to the bus, and even from my distance, I could see Spanky's eyes go wide. He stopped and stared, mouth agape, arms dangling at his sides. If I'd been closer, I'm sure I could have seen the blood drain from his face and his breathing get shallow. He swayed slightly, and one of the cops moved him forward, toward the coach. They got to the door and stood talking. One of the cops was gesturing at the coach, and Spanky was appearing to listen, but I suspected nothing was registering in his brain.

I popped back into the SUV and grabbed a bag from the back. "I have my binoculars in here somewhere," I said to Hooker. "I need to see this. I think they're going to take Spanky into the coach. I bet they want him to ID the body!"

Hooker put his hood up and pulled the drawstring. "No way I'm going to miss this."

I found the binoculars, and we both got out and stood beside the SUV. Spanky was obviously inside the coach with the police. Delores was at a slight distance, flanked by two uniforms. A news helicopter hovered overhead, and a mobile satellite truck from one of the Charlotte stations crept up to the tangle of cars.

I had the binoculars trained on the hole where the door used to be, waiting for Spanky to appear. A cop came into view first, then Spanky. A normal person would be horrified by finding his spotter dead on his bed. And Bernie was especially horrifying since we'd dug him up. On the heels of the horror, you'd expect sadness or at least a solemn respect for the dead. Spanky, true to form, was pissed off. And it would seem he wasn't pissed off because someone had killed Bernie. Spanky was pissed because his coach was ruined. I'm not a professional at reading lips, but this was easy. Spanky was in a rage, stomping around, hands on hips, screaming the f word, his face brick red, the cords standing out in his neck.

"Fuck, fuck, fuck!" He threw his hands into the air and pointed at his trashed motor coach. "How the fuck

212

did this happen? Who fucking did this? Do you know how much this fucking coach cost?" he asked a cop.

He was pacing and gesturing and somehow our eyes caught. I saw recognition register. For a long moment he seemed in suspended animation. Not sure what to think. Not sure what to do. Finally, he snapped his mouth shut, turned on his heel, and stalked back to the unmarked cop car. He pulled the door open and rammed himself into the backseat. Delores minced over in her high-heeled boots. The two plainclothes cops followed, looking like maybe they should check their bullets at the door so they wouldn't be tempted to shoot Spanky.

"This might be a good time to try to leave," I said to Hooker. "I think Spanky spotted us."

The traffic wasn't moving forward yet, but some cars had crossed the median and some SUVs had done the all-terrain thing and rumbled over curbs and climbed embankments to reach intersecting parking lots and ultimately other roads. The traffic jam wasn't nearly as dense as it had originally been, and Hooker was able to work his way through the pack and go off-road.

The SUV lumbered over hill and dale, and as luck would have it, ended up at a fast-food joint. We bought a bag of food, stopped at a neighboring gas station and filled up, bought more food at the gas station convenience store, and skulked away.

Hooker drove north out of habit. We couldn't go back to the warehouse. We were afraid to check into a motel. We didn't want to involve friends. So we parked in a supermarket lot and fed Beans and started eating our way through a bag of doughnuts. I was on my second doughnut when Hooker's phone rang. It was Spanky, and Hooker didn't need to use the speakerphone function for me to hear. Spanky was yelling into the phone.

"You sonovabitch," Spanky yelled. "I know you're responsible for all of this. I saw you sitting there watching. You think this is funny, don't you? You did this just to ruin my week. You knew I had a new motor coach that was better than yours. So you had it wrecked. And it wasn't enough to waste Oscar and your poor retard rent-a-cop, you had to leave Bernie in my bed. You are such a dumb sick fuck."

"Okay, let me get this straight," Hooker said. "You think I killed three men and arranged to have your motor coach trashed because why?"

"Because you're jealous of me. You can't stand that I won the championship. And I know you put Oscar in my new truck, too. I'm gonna get you for this. You better watch your ass."

Hooker disconnected. "Spanky's an idiot."

Hooker's phone rang again.

"Uh-huh," Hooker said. "Uh-huh, uh-huh, uh-huh."

"Now what?" I asked when he was done.

"Skippy calling back. He wanted to remind me that the banquet was black tie."

"It's Sunday, and the banquet is Friday. There's no way."

"Obviously you've never been called into the NASCAR hauler after a race you just screwed up and had to face Skippy. Remember the time I flipped Junior

214

the bird on national television? And the time I got pissed off and punted Shrub into the wall and caused a seven-car wreck? Trust me, we'll make the banquet."

"Where are we going?" I asked Hooker. "Where are we going to sleep tonight?"

"I thought I'd go to Kannapolis. I figure they won't look for us there. No one intentionally goes to Kannapolis."

"This is it?" I asked Hooker. "This is where we're going to spend the night?"

"You don't like it?"

"We're parked in front of a house."

"Yeah, we're tucked between a bunch of cars that belong here. We're invisible. And my buddy Ralph lives two houses down. He lives alone in one of these ramshackle little houses, and he'll leave for work tomorrow at six in the morning. And he never locks his house. Got nothing worth taking, if you don't count a fridge full of Bud. So we can go in and use his bathroom and not get busted."

"That's great, but I need a bathroom *now*."

"There's a patch of woods two blocks from here. I was planning on walking Beans and hiding behind a tree. You're welcome to join me."

"You've got to be kidding. Women don't hide behind trees. We aren't built for it. Our socks get wet."

Hooker looked down the block at Ralph's house. "We could probably trust Ralph to let us stay with him tonight. Ralph's the one person who wouldn't get accused of aiding and abetting. Nobody would ever think Ralph knew what he was doing. He's a good guy, but his primary skill is his ability to open a beer can."

Hooker searched for Ralph's name and dialed it. "Hey, man," Hooker said. "How's it going? Are you alone? I need a place to crash tonight."

Five minutes later, we were standing at Ralph's back door. Hooker, Beans, and me. I had a bag of clothes. Hooker had a bag of junk food. Beans had himself.

Ralph opened the door and looked out at us. "Whoa, dude, you got a family." He stepped to one side. "Me casa is your casa."

Ralph was raw-boned skinny. His snarled brown hair was shoulder length. Baggy jeans hung frighteningly low on plaid boxers. His shirt was rumpled and unbuttoned. He had a beer can in his hand.

Hooker made the introductions, and then he and Ralph did one of those complicated bonding handshake things that men do when they don't want to hug.

"We're sort of hiding out," Hooker said to Ralph. "I don't want anyone to know we're here."

"Gotcha," Ralph said. "Her old man's looking for her, right?"

"Yeah," Hooker said. "Something like that."

Ralph draped an arm across my shoulders. "Honey, you can do better than him. He shops at Wal-Mart, if you know what I mean. Hangs out there on a Friday night with his bag of candy."

I cut my eyes to Hooker.

"I haven't done that for a couple weeks now," Hooker said. "I'm changing my ways."

216

Ralph scratched Beans on the top of the head, and Beans affectionately leaned against Ralph and pushed him into the refrigerator.

"Ralph and I have been friends since grade school," Hooker said. "We grew up in the same town in Texas."

"We both used to race cars," Ralph said. "Only Hooker was always good, and I never had the killer instinct."

Hooker got a couple beers out of the fridge and handed one over to me. "Yeah, but Ralph's famous," Hooker said. "He won the sixth-grade spelling bee."

"Yep, I was pretty smart back then," Ralph said. "I could spell anything. Pissed it all away. Can't hardly spell my name anymore. Living the *vida loca* though."

"Ralph hooked up with DKT Racing early on, and they brought him here to the stock-car capital of the world. And he's still with DKT."

"Probably could have a brilliant future there," Ralph said, "but I prefer to keep my head up my ass."

The kitchen appliances were avocado green and at least thirty years old. A blackened pot appeared to be stuck to a stove burner. The sink was filled with crumpled beer cans. Hard to tell the exact color of the walls and linoleum floor. No room in the kitchen for a table.

We moved to the dining room. Pool table in the dining room. Ralph had pulled a chair up to the pool table, and a pizza take-out box was open on the tabletop. There was one piece of pizza left in the box. It looked like it had been there for a long time.

"Don't shoot a lot of pool?" I asked.

"Comes and goes," Ralph said. "I like to use this for a dining room table because the bumpers stop the food from falling off."

Beans walked up to the table and sniffed the pizza. He turned his head to look at Hooker, and then he looked at me, and then he put his two front paws on the table edge and ate the pizza.

The living room furniture consisted of a lumpy couch with a large burn hole in one of the seat cushions, a coffee table that was completely covered with beer cans, take-out coffee cups, crumpled burger wrappers, empty grease-stained French fry containers and fried chicken buckets, and a large-screen television occupying an entire wall.

"Bathroom?" I asked.

"Down the hall. First door on the left."

I poked my head in and took a fast look around. Not terrifically clean, but there weren't any dead men in it, so I thought I should be grateful. There was a stack of dog-eared publications on the floor. Mostly automotive with a few girlie magazines in the mix. A bottle of Johnson's Baby Shampoo on the edge of the tub. Plastic shower curtain decorated with gobs of soap and streaks of mold. A single towel hung on a hook on the wall. Good chance that this was Ralph's only towel.

Hooker, Beans, and Ralph were watching a game on television when I returned to the living room. They scooted over to make room for me, and we all sat there until close to midnight, drinking beer, pretending we were normal.

218

"I gotta go to bed," Ralph finally said. "I gotta go to work tomorrow. Where are you guys staying?"

"Here?" Hooker said.

"Oh yeah," Ralph said. "Now I remember." And he shuffled off, down the hall, past the bathroom. A door opened and closed and then there was quiet.

"How many bedrooms does Ralph have?" I asked Hooker.

"Two. But he keeps his Harley in the second bedroom. He's rebuilding the bike, and he doesn't have a garage."

"So we're sleeping on this couch?"

"Yep." Hooker stretched out on his back. "Hop onboard. We'll sleep double-decker. I'll even be a good guy and let you take the top."

I rolled onto him, and he grunted.

"What was that grunt?" I asked him.

"Nothing."

"It was *something*."

"I just don't remember you as being this heavy. Maybe we should cut back on the doughnuts."

"Good grief."

Beans came over to investigate. He looked at us with his droopy brown eyes and then he climbed on top of us and settled in with a sigh, his huge dog head on mine.

"Help!" Hooker gasped. "I can't breathe. I'm squashed. And there's a spring poking me in my back. Get him off."

"He's lonely."

"If he doesn't get off, he's going to be an orphan."

Five minutes later, we were all stretched out on the pool table.

CHAPTER
TWELVE

Hooker, Beans, and I were awake but still on the pool table when Ralph staggered past us on his way to the kitchen.

"Morning," Ralph said.

I looked at my watch. Six thirty. I had no good reason to get up, but I was uncomfortable enough not to want to stay where I was. I crawled over Hooker and wriggled myself clear of the bumper. I expected Ralph to make coffee and pause for breakfast, but he ambled through the kitchen and out the back door. He got into a truck parked in his small backyard and drove off without a backward glance.

Hooker came up behind me. "Ralph's not a morning person. He sleeps in his clothes so he doesn't have to decide what to wear when he rolls out of bed."

"No shock there. Do you think he's got coffee?"

"Ralph's only got beer and takeout."

I felt my shoulders slump. I really wanted coffee.

Hooker hugged me to him and kissed the top of my head. "I can see you're crushed by that news. Never fear. You take a shower, and Beans and I will go out and get coffee."

"Do you think it's safe to take a shower in there?"

"Sure. Just leave your socks on."

When I came out of the bathroom, Hooker had hazelnut coffee waiting for me. My favorite. Plus a fruit cup and a bagel with lite cream cheese. Not subtle, but thoughtful. He'd also bought newspapers.

"'Body found inside championship race driver's million-dollar motor coach,'" I read. "'Police are withholding information until relatives can be notified, but sources close to the driver say the deceased was part of the Huevo race team. The body was discovered as the result of a bizarre seventeen-car crash in which the motor coach driver fled on foot and then stole a car from an innocent bystander. The motor coach was heavily damaged in the crash.'"

Hooker sipped his coffee. "Does it say anything about the driver? Has he been identified?"

I read through the article. "He hasn't been identified, but they give a reasonably good description of him. It says he was limping and thought to be injured. The car he stole hasn't been found. At the end, there's a quote from Spanky where he accuses you of masterminding the entire disaster."

"Nice. I wish I could mastermind us *out* of the disaster."

"I was counting on you to have a clever plan."

"I'm out of plans. I'm at a dead end."

"What about beating the crap out of people?"

"Turns out, it doesn't entirely work. And it's embarrassing because you're better at it than I am."

"Here's part of the problem. It would be better if Ray had done the actual killing. Eventually, Rodriguez

221

would have ratted Ray out. Unfortunately, there's no reason for Ray to feel sufficiently threatened to talk to the police about Rodriguez."

Hooker's phone rang, and I looked at my watch. It was early in the morning to be getting a phone call.

"'Lo," Hooker said. "Uh-huh, uh-huh, uh-huh. Thanks, but I'll take care of that myself." He disconnected and grinned at me. "The Lord works in mysterious ways, darlin'."

"Now what?"

"That was Ray Huevo. And he sounded . . . nervous. He wants the chip from the gearshift knob. Said maybe we could work something out. He wanted to fly us down to Miami so we could negotiate in person, but I declined. I didn't think it was healthy to get on Ray's private plane." Hooker tapped a number into his phone. "I need a favor," he said. "I need a ride to Miami."

I mentally cracked my knuckles until he disconnected. "Nutsy?"

"Yeah. He said the police are watching the airport in Concord. He suggested we drive to Florence and catch his plane there. No one will think to watch Florence. It's a three-hour drive, so we should get moving."

I called Felicia from the road. "We're coming back to Miami," I said. "I was wondering if we could stay with you again? And it's a secret. We don't want anyone to know we're there. We're trying to keep a low profile."

"Of course you can stay," Felicia said. "My neighbor's boy will be so excited to see Hooker again.

222

And my cousin Edward was out of town last time. I have to go buy hats to get signed. I have a list."

Hooker glanced over at me when I disconnected. "She's not going to tell anyone, right?"

"Right."

Two hours out of Concord, Hooker's phone rang and he did a small grimace when he looked at the readout. It was Skippy. Hooker still had speakerphone mode up.

"Where are you?" Skippy yelled. "Do you know what day this is?"

"Monday?" Hooker answered.

"That's right. And you need to be driving your car around Manhattan on Wednesday. And by the way, I'm not saying you were responsible, but the body in the motor coach was a nice touch. I understand Dickie messed his pants when he saw it. When they arrest you and you get your one phone call, make sure it's to me." And Skippy hung up.

Florence is a nice little town with a nice little airport that has a few commercial hops in the morning. The National Guard uses the airport, and it serves as home base for a few private planes. And once a year, when the races are at Darlington, the airport bustles.

It was close to eleven when Hooker swung into the lot and parked. We unloaded Beans, grabbed our bags of clothes, and walked from the car directly to Nutsy's Citation. It was the only plane on the runway. It was the same model Hooker owned. I'd called ahead, and they were ready to roll the second we were onboard.

A private plane seems like an outrageous luxury, but the schedule for the top Cup drivers is so insane it's virtually impossible to manage any other way. There are corporate meet-and-greet sessions, commercial tapings, charity functions, and, of course, the races. Forty races a year at twenty-two different tracks spread across the country. Plus all of those drivers have wives and girlfriends and kids and dogs and proud, insane parents who need visitation time.

Just like Hooker's plane, Nutsy's plane carried seven passengers and two pilots. Hooker and I took seats opposite each other. Beans tried to fit in a seat, but couldn't get comfortable and finally settled himself in the aisle.

A Citation goes up fast. One minute you're on the runway, and then ZOOOM you're above the clouds and leveling off. The Citation seat was infinitely more comfortable than Ralph's pool table. I instantly fell asleep and didn't wake until we were descending for the approach into Miami. I heard the wheels go down, and I looked out at the red tile roofs and shimmering waterways of south Florida. Odd how the mind works. I was wanted by the police and two hit men and all I could think about was the New York banquet looming in front of me. I needed a manicure. I needed a haircut. I needed a gown. If I couldn't get back to my apartment, I didn't even have the right makeup.

We disembarked, and we were a ragtag little family standing in the Signature Aviation lobby, our dog on a leash, and all our worldly possessions in grocery bags plus my one travel bag. Hooker had a decent beard going, and I felt like a street urchin beside him.

I looked across the room to the car-rental counter. "What are the chances they'll rent us a car?" I asked Hooker.

"Chances are good," Hooker said. "Nutsy left his credit card in the plane. I just have to bullshit my way around giving them my license."

Ten minutes later we were on the road in an SUV.

"Are we going to see Ray now?" I asked Hooker.

"No. We're going to Little Havana so we can hide the chip from the gearshift knob in Felicia's house. It seems to be the only chip Ray cares about. Then we're going to see Ray."

No one was home when we got to Felicia's house, but the key was in the flowerpot next to the back door, just like always. We let ourselves in and Beans rushed ahead, jumping around, all excited, skidding on the kitchen linoleum. Probably remembering Felicia's pancakes and pork barbecue. We trooped upstairs to the little bedroom, and Hooker taped the chip to the back of the picture of Jesus.

"Doesn't get any safer than that," Hooker said.

After sleeping in the car and on top of a pool table, I was thinking the little bedroom looked like paradise. The comfy bed with the clean sheets, the immaculate bathroom just down the hall . . .

"Maybe we should test the bed out," Hooker said. "See if it's still too small."

"Good grief."

"Well, you had *that look*."

"I was thinking about the bathroom."

"Works for me," Hooker said. "Warm water, slippery soap . . ."

"Good grief."

"You keep saying that. That sounds so hopeless. I'm dying here. I need something to hang on to. Throw me a crumb, for pity's sake."

I did a big fake sigh. "Maybe we can get together sometime later."

Hooker looked like the joy fairy had just unlocked the door to the bakery. "Really? How much later?"

"After we get cleared of murder and grand-theft auto."

"Do you think we could shorten that to . . . *in fifteen minutes?*"

"I thought it would give you an incentive."

"You think I need more incentive than not going to jail for the rest of my life?"

"Okay. Fine. Great. Just forget it then. I didn't mean it anyway." And I turned and flounced out of the room and down the stairs. I wasn't all that annoyed, but it seemed like a good exit line.

Hooker was close behind me. "Too late to take it back. You promised."

"I didn't promise. I said maybe."

We were in the dining room and Hooker pushed me against the wall and leaned into me and kissed me. There was a lot of tongue involved in the kiss, and Hooker pressed against me until there wasn't any space left between us, and it was obvious there was more of Hooker than there had been five minutes ago.

226

"Tell me about the maybe," Hooker said. "Was it a *probably* or was it a *probably not.*"

"I don't know. I'm working on it."

"You're killing me," Hooker said. "You're more of a threat than Ray Huevo. And by the way, I like that you've got your hand on my ass."

Crap! He was right. I had my hand on his ass.

"Sorry," I said. "It was an accident."

Hooker was grinning. "It was no accident, darlin'. You're hot for me."

I smiled back at him and shoved him away. "You're right, but it's still a maybe."

When we got to the kitchen, Hooker filled a bowl with water for Beans. Beans put his face into it and did a lot of loud slurping. The water slopped over the sides when he drank, and when he picked his head up, the water leaked out of his mouth and dripped off his lips.

I mopped up the water with paper towels while Hooker called Ray Huevo.

"I'm in town," Hooker said. "Do you want to talk?"

There was some negotiation and Hooker hung up.

"I'm meeting him on the beach in a half hour," Hooker said. "At Lincoln Road. I declined on a boat meeting. I didn't want to get thrown off his boat again. And this meeting is between Ray and me. I want you and Beans to stay here."

"And why is that?"

"I don't trust Ray. I don't want to put you in jeopardy."

"I appreciate the thought, but there's no way you're going without me. We're in this together. And suppose someone gets the crap beat out of them? You think I want to miss that?"

"My fear is that it might be me," Hooker said.

The compromise was that we left Beans in Felicia's house and I went with Hooker. Hooker had stripped down to a T-shirt and jeans when we arrived in Miami. I'd been left with jeans and a long-sleeved turtleneck, making me a tad conspicuous on South Beach. You could be naked on South Beach and not cause a ripple of excitement. A turtleneck shouted tourist, fresh off the plane. Hooker parked the rental on the street, and I popped into a shop and swapped my turtleneck for a tank top.

The Ritz-Carlton sits at the end of Lincoln Road, and a pretty bricked footpath gently undulates alongside the hotel, giving beach access to all. We took the footpath and walked out onto the hard-packed sand. It was a breathtaking blue-sky day in Miami. Eighty degrees with a gentle breeze. The beach is white sand and wide here. The Ritz had its royal blue beach chairs out in orderly rows. Plus a row of cabanas. There were some bronzed and oiled-up bodies on the lounges. Attendants moved from body to body, serving drinks, handing out towels. The ocean rolled in on foamy waves. No one was swimming.

I looked over Hooker's shoulder and saw three men step off the footpath onto the sand. Ray Huevo, Rodriguez, and Lucca. Rodriguez was on crutches. He had a Band-Aid across his nose and two black eyes. Lucca's six-pack bruise was turning green. Ray Huevo looked like a billion dollars.

228

Huevo moved toward us. Rodriguez and Lucca stayed behind.

"How's his knee?" I asked Huevo.

"He'll live." He glanced back at Rodriguez. "For a while."

Hooker and I exchanged a look that said *yikes*.

"For security purposes, I would prefer this conversation was one-on-one," Huevo said.

I nodded agreement, and Hooker and Huevo walked away from me. They stood at the water's edge, their conversation lost in the surf. After a couple minutes, they turned and walked back.

Huevo inclined his head when he passed me. "I'll have positions open in security if you're interested in career advancement."

I looked at Hooker. "What did he mean by that?"

"He's not happy with Rodriguez and Lucca. They keep killing people. And even worse, they keep getting beat up by a girl."

"That would be me."

"Yeah. So he wants to sacrifice them for the chip we found in the gearshift knob. He says Lucca and Rodriguez are a liability. If we give Ray the chip, he'll turn Lucca and Rodriguez over to the police, and he'll pretend the hauler was never stolen."

"Hard to believe the chip is that valuable. Especially now that Oscar is out of the picture. Ray can pretty much do whatever he wants."

Hooker shrugged. "That's what he said. And as an act of trust, he's going to turn Rodriguez and Lucca in before we give him the chip."

"That's sweet."

"Not entirely. He has Gobbles." Hooker handed me a photo of Gobbles standing with his hands tied behind his back, not looking happy, Rodriguez on one side, Lucca on the other. "We get Gobbles back when Ray gets the chip and verifies its authenticity."

"We should never have let Gobbles go off on his own."

"Hindsight," Hooker said. "Anyway, we get him back when we give Ray the chip." Hooker nuzzled my neck and kissed me behind the ear. "I think we should celebrate."

"I think a celebration is premature."

"Darlin', I *really* need to celebrate. I haven't celebrated in a long time. In fact, it's been so long, it's probably appropriate if it's a premature celebration because it's going to be a premature —"

"Stop!" I had my hand up. "Let's celebrate with onion rings at the bar."

Hooker just stared at me.

"Earth to Hooker."

"Onion rings at the bar," he repeated. "Sure, that would be good. That was my second choice."

The Ritz has a fabulous bar set right on the beach. It's just behind the footpath, nestled into a cement cave and garnished with palm trees. It's shaded and South Beach glitzy. Not exactly rocking at three in the afternoon, so we had no problem claiming bar stools. We were halfway through our onion rings and Buds when a familiar figure strolled by on the footpath. It was Suzanne walking Itsy Poo.

230

"It walks," Hooker said. "Who would have thought?"

Suzanne looked over the top of her sunglasses at me. "Barney? Hey, girlfriend, I thought you'd moved on."

"I came back. Missed the heat."

Suzanne put Itsy Poo in her bag and joined us at the bar. "You've been making headlines."

"It's all a misunderstanding."

"Our mutual friend Dickie Bonnano seems to feel Hooker is responsible for everything evil in the world."

"I do the best I can," Hooker said, "but I can't claim responsibility for *everything*."

"I figured you didn't do Oscar," Suzanne said, "but I was kind of hoping you set Dickie up with the stiff and the coach crash."

Suzanne was total Dolce & Gabbana in a gauzy leopard-print shirt, wide jeweled belt, tight white slacks, and strappy gold sandals. I was Wal-Mart and Gap. Hooker still hadn't shaved. Hooker was Detroit wino raised by wolves.

"I thought you would have left South Beach by now," I said to Suzanne.

"I like it here. Thought I'd stay for a while." She lit a cigarette and took a deep drag, letting the smoke curl out of her nose, dragon-style.

"Are you still at Loews?" I asked her.

"I moved into a condo building. Majestic Arms." She took another drag on her cigarette. "Corporate rental, so it's sterile, but the location is prime, and it's full service. And most important, Itsy Poo adores it." Suzanne put her face into the dog bag. "Don't you wuv it, Itsy Poo? You do! I know you do. You wuv the new condo."

Hooker ate the last onion ring and sent me a look that said he'd throw up if I ever asked Beans if he *wuvved* something.

I returned my attention to Suzanne. "How's the boat battle going?"

"It's been ugly, but it's about to improve. Men like Oscar and Ray always underestimate women." Suzanne's mouth curved into a joyless smile. "Not a smart thing to do with a bitch like me."

Hooker instinctively crossed his legs.

"Sounds like you have a plan," I said to Suzanne.

She took a drag, tipped her head back, and blew out a perfect smoke ring. "I have a plan and a half." She slid her ass off the bar stool. "Gotta go. Got a cake in the oven. Remember, I'm at the Majestic if you want a giggle."

"Do you think she really has a cake in the oven?" I asked Hooker when Suzanne was back on the footpath.

"If she does, you're not going to catch me eating it."

"What happens next?"

"Ray had an appointment that he didn't expect to last long, and then he was going to take care of Rodriguez and Lucca. Apparently there's a buyer for the chip coming in on a flight tonight, and Ray doesn't want to disappoint him. So we should have this nightmare wrapped up before the day is over."

I rested my forehead on the bar and took a deep breath. I was so relieved, I was close to tears. "Do we need to go back and get the chip?"

"No. I don't want it on either of us until I'm sure we're off the hook. Ray said he'd call me when he had everything in place. He expected he'd be back in touch by eight at the latest."

Hooker's phone rang. "Sure," Hooker said. "Barbecued chicken would be good. Just us, though, right? We don't want anyone to know we're here."

"Felicia?" I asked.

"Yeah," Hooker said, returning his phone to his pocket. "She wanted to know if we'd be back for dinner."

We sat at the bar for a while longer, and then we took off for Little Havana. Every light was lit in Felicia's house when we arrived. Cars were double-parked on the street and people were milling around on the sidewalk in front of her small front porch. Hooker slowed the SUV in front of the house and a cheer went up.

"Good thing we told Felicia to keep this a secret," Hooker said. "Otherwise she'd have to rent out the Orange Bowl for dinner."

We drove around back and parked in a spot that had been held empty for us with a sign on a garbage can. The sign read RESERVED FOR SAM HOOKER.

"Thoughtful," Hooker said on a resigned sigh.

Felicia was at the back door. "We've been waiting for you! I just took the chicken off the grill. And I have hot fry bread."

I could see Beans bouncing around behind Felicia. He saw Hooker get out of the car, and he pushed past Felicia and bounded down the stairs. He gave a *woof*

233

and hurled himself into Hooker, taking Hooker to the ground.

"Guess he missed you," I said to Hooker.

"Look, doggie!" Felicia said, waving a piece of bread. "I have a nice big treat for you."

Beans's ears perked up and he swiveled his head in Felicia's direction. His nose twitched, he shoved off Hooker and galloped at Felicia. Felicia threw the bread into the kitchen, and Beans bounded in after it.

Hooker picked himself up, ambled to the kitchen door and looked in. "You've got a lot of people packed in there," Hooker said to Felicia.

"Just family. And no one will tell anyone you're here. It's a secret."

"I'm relieved," Hooker said.

"Hooker's here!" Felicia shouted into the house.

Another cheer went up.

"We're serving buffet style," Felicia said. "Help yourself."

Every flat surface held food. I fixed myself a plate and looked over at Hooker. He had a piece of chicken in one hand and a Sharpie in the other. He was signing hats and foreheads and eating barbecue. Who says a man can't multitask?

"Look at him," Felicia said to me. "He's such a sweetie. He's even nice to Uncle Mickey. Everybody loves him. He thinks they love him because he's a good driver, but everybody loves him because he's a good person."

Rosa was next to Felicia. "I love him because he got a cute tushie."

234

They turned and looked at me.

"What?" I said.

"Why do *you* love him?" Rosa wanted to know.

"Who says I love him?"

Rosa forked up some pulled pork. "You have to be nuts not to love him."

I remember when I was in high school and I had a terrible crush on this guy who worked in my dad's garage. I'd go in after school, and he'd flirt with me and say he'd call. So I'd go home and wait, and he wouldn't call. I'd wait and wait and wait. And he never called. And then one day I heard he got married. All the time he'd been telling me he'd call, he'd been engaged. That's how tonight was feeling. I was waiting for the phone call. Ten percent of my mind was listening to Rosa, but the other ninety percent was dedicated to the rising panic that the call might not happen. Deep inside, I was a cat on a mouse. Tail twitching, eyes unblinking, whole body vibrating while I stalked the phone call that would make my life right.

Eight o'clock and no phone call. Hooker looked at me from across the room. Hooker was better at this than I was. He could compartmentalize. He knew how to focus on one thing and set everything else aside. If Hooker was on a racetrack, his mind was working to win. Hooker had only one sequence of thought. How do I get to the front and stay there. When I was racing, other thoughts would creep in. I had no control over which thoughts would stay and which would get set aside for another time. Why wouldn't the cute guy in the garage call me? What if I was in a wreck and broke

235

my nose? And there were always lists. Algebra homework, laundry, clean my room, find my house key, call Maureen, study French . . . So now Hooker had chosen to be in the moment enjoying Felicia's friends and food, and my mind had chosen to obsess about the phone call.

Eight o'clock I pantomimed to Hooker. Hooker glanced down at his watch and excused himself from the people around him. He started toward me and stopped to answer his phone.

My breath stuck in my chest. This was it.

Hooker had his head down and he was nodding at the caller . . . yes, yes, yes. His head came up, our eyes caught, and I didn't like what I saw. Hooker was concentrating to hear over the room noise, talking into the phone. He disconnected and signaled me to head for the kitchen. I pushed through the crush and met Hooker on the small back stoop. There were a couple people huddled in the yard, laughing and talking. Smokers evicted from Felicia's house. They smiled but didn't come forward for an autograph. Smoking took precedence.

Hooker steered me past them, to the SUV. He slid behind the wheel, and I sat next to him and asked the question. "The phone call?"

"It was Rodriguez. Ray Huevo is missing. He told Rodriguez and Lucca to wait for him in the car after he talked to us. Said he would be a half hour tops. He never showed. They don't know who he was meeting or where the meeting took place. They were calling because they decided we snatched Ray. I guess they've

236

been out beating the bushes looking for us and finally gave up and made the call. They're in a panic because the buyer is due to arrive at nine. I don't know who the buyer is, but Rodriguez and Lucca are scared."

I was stunned. Of all the things I expected to hear, this wasn't even close. "I'm a little flummoxed," I said to Hooker.

"Then I've got you beat because I'm a *lot* flummoxed."

"Maybe Ray got cold feet and took off. Maybe he's in Rio."

"It's possible, but he seemed like he had other plans when he talked to us."

"Something must have gone wrong at his meeting," I said. "Maybe he's swimming with the fishes."

"God, I hope not. We need him to get us out of this disaster."

"What about Gobbles?"

"I spoke to Gobbles," Hooker said. "He was there with Rodriguez and Lucca. He sounded rattled."

"At least he's not dead."

"Not yet, but I'm worried. Rodriguez and Lucca have a history of solving their problems by shooting people."

"It's odd no one knew who Ray was going to see. He has staff. They keep his calendar, they make his phone calls, they read his e-mails. Even bad guys with secrets have people around them who are entrusted with sensitive information. So I'm thinking the meeting had to either be not important enough to mention to staff, or else something spontaneous, arranged at the last minute.

"Did Rodriguez say anything about the chip buyer? Who it is? Why the chip is so important?"

"No," Hooker said. "Just that the buyer was arriving at nine. For all I know, he could be selling his fancy-ass battery to the battery bunny. Or how about this, maybe the chip is a homing device for an alien probe."

"You got that from *Star Trek*."

"Yeah, that was a great movie. It had whales and everything." Hooker plugged the key into the ignition and cranked the motor over. "Let's drive out to the airport. I want to see who's arriving tonight."

CHAPTER
THIRTEEN

Hooker was stretched back in his seat, hands locked behind his head, eyes closed against the ambient light from the terminal.

"Surveillance doesn't actually work if you keep your eyes closed," I told Hooker.

"Are *your* eyes open?"

"Yes."

"Good enough."

We were parked to the side of the Signature terminal, and there wasn't a lot of activity.

"The plane's late," I said to Hooker.

"If they're coming from out of the country, they have to go through customs and immigration, and it's in a different part of the airport. After they clear customs, they'll get back into the plane, and the plane will taxi them over here. I've been through the process at this airport, and it usually goes pretty fast, but the plane still has to get from point A to point B."

At nine thirty-five, three men in suits and two men in uniform exited the terminal. The men in uniform and two of the suits carried luggage. Three small rolling suitcases and a computer case. They were traveling light. The third man was luggage free. They were all

Caucasian. The uniformed men were young, in their twenties. Flight attendants. The three men in suits were forties to fifties. I didn't recognize any of them. That didn't say a lot because I *never* recognized anyone. Okay, maybe if Brad Pitt walked by. The Russian premier, the queen of England, our own vice president (what's-his-name), the ambassador to Bulgaria, were all safe with me.

"Do you think this is our man?" I asked Hooker.

"Seems to be the only plane with a nine o'clock landing."

"Do you recognize any of these guys?"

"No. They look like average middle-management businessmen."

A six-seat limo pulled up, the luggage was loaded, the three suits got into the limo, and the limo pulled away with us a couple car lengths behind. We followed the limo south on Route 95 and then east on 395, across the MacArthur Causeway. The lights of South Beach were directly in front of us. Four behemoth cruise ships parked at the Biscayne Bay cruise ship docks were to my right. I'd expected the limo to take Collins and head for Loews or the Delano or the Ritz. Instead, the limo right turned onto Alton.

"He's going to the boat," I said to Hooker. "What does that mean?"

"I'm guessing no one's told him about the missing Ray."

The limo pulled into the marina lot and stopped at idle in front of the walkway leading to the piers. Lights still on. Motor running. Hooker cut his lights and slid into a shadowed slot at the back of the lot.

Two uniformed crew members came running from dockside. They were followed by someone who was also in uniform but clearly was higher on the food chain. Maybe the captain or purser. The limo driver got out and popped the trunk. The three suits got out, and after a brief conversation, the luggage was turned over to the crew members, and everyone headed for the boat. The limo driver got into his car and drove away.

"Looks like these guys were invited to stay on the boat and the invitation stands," Hooker said.

Hooker and I got out, quietly closed the car doors, skirted the lot, and found a dark bench on the marina boardwalk where we could watch the action. Problem was, there didn't seem to be any action to watch. The three men had disappeared into the bowels of the ship and all was quiet.

"This is sort of boring," Hooker said. "We should do something."

"What did you have in mind?"

He inched closer to me.

"No," I said.

"Do you have any better ideas?"

"I want to see what's going on inside the boat. Let's walk down the pier and look in the windows."

We passed through the gate that said OWNERS AND GUESTS ONLY and walked the length of the wood dock. The Huevo boat was still tied up at the very end of the pier. Both decks were lit, but the salon and cabin windows were tinted and not much could be seen. A uniformed crew member stood watch.

Hooker took his cell phone out of his pocket and called the boat number. We could very faintly hear Huevo's phone ringing inside the salon. A male voice answered and said that Ray Huevo was not available. Hooker didn't leave a message.

"He could be in there," I said. Wishful thinking.

"It's unlikely."

"But not impossible. Maybe we could see more from the other side."

"Darlin', there's water on the other side."

"Yeah, we need a boat."

Hooker looked down at me. "And you would get one how?"

"We could borrow one. There are lots of little boats here. I bet no one would mind if we borrowed one for a couple minutes."

"You want to steal a boat?"

"*Borrow*," I said.

"Okay," Hooker said, taking my hand. "Let's go for a stroll and look around."

We got to the last pier and Hooker stopped in front of a medium-size cabin cruiser. Dark inside. Nobody home.

"I know the guy who owns this boat," Hooker said. "He's only here weekends. And he keeps a dingy tied to the back. It should be easy to *borrow*."

We climbed onto the boat and made our way to the back where the dingy was tied, just as Hooker had predicted. We scrambled into the boat, Hooker released the rope and turned the key. The motor hummed to life and Hooker pushed off.

"Keep your eyes open," Hooker said. "I don't want to run into anything."

There was just a sliver of moon in the sky. The piers were lit and some of the boats had their running lights on. A few boats had interior lights on, as well, but not much light reflected onto the black water. The air was still. No wind. Not a lot of tide running.

Boats occasionally came and went at night here, but none was currently under way. Only us. We came abreast of the Huevo boat and sat at a distance, watching. Not much was happening. Windows and doors were closed and sound wasn't carrying.

"Huh," I said. "Disappointing."

Hooker was fidgeting around in the dingy. He'd turned to the back and was poking through a watertight chest. "I might be able to produce some action. At least get everyone on deck so we can take a head count."

I looked over his shoulder, into the chest. "What did you have in mind?"

Hooker pulled a snub-nosed, fat-barreled gun out of the chest. "Flare gun. I could lob a flare over the boat and maybe draw them out." He two-handed the gun, holding it at arm's length, raised the barrel so the flare would arc high, and pulled the trigger. A flare went off with a loud *phunnf* and sailed into the night sky. The flare gracefully curved up and away from us, reached its zenith, fell on a sloping downward trajectory toward the Huevo yacht . . . and crashed through a window on the first deck.

"Oops," Hooker said.

The flare exploded with a burst of light that danced around the main salon like fireworks on the Fourth of July. Sound carried out through the gaping hole in the tinted window, and we could hear the hiss of the flare and the panicked voices of the people inside.

Hooker and I sat in stupefied, bug-eyed silence. There was a small explosion, and then the crackle of fire, and a yellow flame licked up the side of the salon.

"Oh shit," Hooker whispered. "If I didn't have bad luck, I wouldn't have any luck at all."

"You have some good luck. You have *me*."

"I don't have you. You won't even sleep with me."

"That's true, but I'm here with you now."

Hooker got that look in his eyes.

"No," I said.

"How about you tie the anchor to my ankle and throw it overboard."

"I have a better idea. How about we sneak away before someone sees us sitting out here."

Five minutes later, we eased up behind the cabin cruiser, secured the line, and scrambled out of the dingy. Emergency vehicles were on the scene four piers down. Fire and rescue. Police. Lots of people. Strobes flashing. The unintelligible chatter of police band. No one paying attention to Hooker or me. And thank goodness, no smoke or flames shooting out of the Huevo boat.

Hooker stayed back in the shadows, but I edged closer to the pier. One of the three men who'd flown in earlier stood off to the side on the cement walkway, watching the activity. I moved next to him and gestured to the boat.

"What happened?"

He shrugged. "Something came through the window and started a fire. It didn't burn much. Everything on the boat is fire resistant."

I was thrown for a moment. I'd expected a foreign accent. Russian maybe. His accent was New Jersey. "Wow," I said. "Was it a firebomb?"

"I don't know. They're investigating. I was below in a stateroom when it happened. I didn't actually see anything."

I was scanning the crowd as I was talking, looking for Ray Huevo. "I can't help noticing, you're not wearing Miami clothes. Did you just arrive in Florida?"

He looked down at his wool suit slacks. "I flew in earlier. It's been a long day."

"Let me guess. Jersey?"

"Not for a lot of years."

"But originally, right?"

"Yeah, I guess you never really get rid of the Jersey in you."

I stuck my hand out. "Alex."

"Simon."

"Where are you living now?"

"The world."

"That narrows it down," I said.

"My employer travels, and I travel with him."

"Is your employer originally from New Jersey, too?"

"Yeah. Originally."

He was looking down at me, and there was a quality to his eyes and the set of his mouth that I'd seen before. It was the same look Hooker got . . . a lot. "And now?" I asked.

"The world."

"Oh yeah. I forgot."

I could see him weighing his desire to stay anonymous against his desire to get a playmate for Mr. Frisky. He shifted slightly, leaned a little closer to me, and I knew Mr. Frisky was at the wheel.

"For the last couple years, we've been based in Zurich," he said.

"That would explain the suit."

"We ran into some problems when we arrived, and I haven't had a chance to change. What about you? Do you live here?"

"Sometimes. Mostly I live in the world."

"Trying to make fun of me?" he asked.

"Trying to flirt with you," I said. Might as well use the few weapons I had in my arsenal, right? I just hoped Hooker was armed and keeping close watch.

That got a smile from him. "Nice," he said.

And just for the record, I was fully aware that he would have smiled and said *nice* if I had scabs over two-thirds of my body and had an ass like Francis the Talking Horse.

"So, what is it that you do in Zurich?" I asked him.

"I'm an expediter."

In my neighborhood in Baltimore, an expediter is someone who makes sure things move along smoothly. For instance, if the owner of a bar isn't making his

246

protection-money payments on time, an expediter might go talk to him and break his kneecaps as a performance incentive.

"An expediter," I said. "What kinds of things do you expedite?"

"You ask a lot of questions."

"Making conversation. I read somewhere that men like it when you seem interested in their work."

More smiling. "The guy I work for is in the import-and-export business. I facilitate movement."

"What does he export? Carburetors?"

"Maybe we should take this conversation somewhere else," he said. "Like over to the bar."

The night's game plan. Get the dumb chick liquored up. "Sure," I said.

We walked a short distance and went up the stairs that led to the outdoor bar attached to Monty's. We wrangled a couple stools and ordered drinks. I looked over Simon's shoulder and saw Hooker watching from an alley, making signs like he was going to hang himself.

"Excuse me," I said. "I'll be right back."

I followed Hooker down the alley and around the corner.

"What was that all about?" I asked him.

"Did you order a drink?"

"Yeah."

"Oh man, you're gonna get drunk, and then I'll have to rescue you from King Kong there. He's got about thirty pounds on me. It's going to be ugly."

"I'm not going to get drunk."

247

"Darlin', you're just about the worst drinker I've ever seen. You get drunk on fumes when you open a bottle of merlot. What did you order? I bet you got one of those froufrou drinks with the fruit and the umbrellas."

"I got a beer."

"Lite beer?"

I narrowed my eyes. "Do you want me to try to get information out of this guy, or what?"

Hooker stood hands on hips. Unhappy. "The only reason I'm agreeing to this is because I know how good you are at saying no."

I returned to the bar. "So, talk to me," I said to Simon. "Tell me about this importing and exporting. I imagine you import and export race cars."

"Race cars?"

"You're visiting on the Huevo boat, so I assumed you were involved in racing."

"Not even a little. Huevo Industries has their finger in a lot of pies."

He was drinking Jack Daniel's on the rocks. He slugged his down and glanced at me. I was sipping my beer like a lady. He looked like he wanted to tell me to hurry up, but he got himself under control and ordered another Jack.

"What do you do?" he asked.

"I sell ladies' undies."

I have no idea where that came from. It just popped out. And from the expression on his face, it was a good choice. A lot better than telling him I was a mechanic, for instance.

"Like at Victoria's Secret?" he asked.

248

"Yep, that's me. I'm a Victoria's Secret lady."

He belted back the second Jack. "I always wanted to meet a Victoria's Secret lady."

"Well, this is your lucky day."

He nudged my knee with his. "I like the sound of that. How lucky do you think I'm going to get today?"

"You might get pretty darn lucky." Not.

I swiveled on my bar stool and watched the fire truck pull out. The ambulance had already departed. The only emergency vehicle left was a lone police car. Most of the crowd had dispersed, and crew members moved around on the first deck. "It looks like everyone's back on the boat," I said. "Hopefully there wasn't too much damage."

A third Jack magically appeared on the bar.

"Wouldn't bother me if the whole friggin' boat went down," Simon said. "This operation is turning into a lost cause. If it was me, I'd write it off and go home."

"Your employer doesn't feel that way?"

"My employer's on a mission."

"I bet Ray Huevo isn't happy about this fire. I'm surprised he didn't get off the boat with everyone else."

"Ray isn't here. Ray's out of town. Him and his two clowns."

The bartender was standing in front of us, polishing glasses. "If you're talking about Rodriguez and Lucca, I just saw them in the parking lot. I took a bag of garbage to the Dumpster and walked past them."

Simon turned his attention to the bartender. "Are you sure?"

"Yeah, they were sitting in their car. Black BMW."

Yes! Excellent. Hooker and I could sneak up on them and rescue Gobbles.

"I need to talk to them," Simon said.

No! Not good. Talk could mean *make them mysteriously disappear if they don't come up with the right answers.* That would hinder my ability to rescue Gobbles. And I needed the police to find Rodriguez and Lucca with the murder weapon.

"Probably just a look-alike," I said.

"I saw the tattoo on his neck," the bartender said.

"Lots of thugs have tattoos," I told him. "Look at this guy next to me. I bet he's got a tattoo."

"Not on my neck," Simon said. He stood and dropped a couple twenties onto the bar. "Sweetheart, I'm going to have to cut out on you."

"Boy, that's too bad," I told him. "I had plans. I was going to make you *real* happy. I was going to do things to you that don't even have names."

He slid a bar napkin my way. "Give me your number, and I'll call you when I get off work."

"Yeah, but the moment will be gone then. I'll be all cooled off. I don't stay hot forever, you know."

"This won't take long."

"Okay, I don't do this for everyone, but I'll let you look down my shirt if you forget about the guys in the lot. Take it or leave it."

"That's it? Look down your shirt?"

"Hey, I've got good stuff hidden away under this shirt."

"I'll look down your shirt," the bartender said. "I'll even throw in a beer."

250

"Why are you so interested in those guys in the lot, anyway?" I asked Simon.

"I want to talk to them."

"That's it?"

"Yeah, more or less."

"Can't you talk to them some other time?"

He grinned at me. "Boy, you want me bad. Guess you don't get around much, huh? When was the last time someone slipped you the old salami?"

Now there was a pretty mental picture. What woman doesn't have romantic fantasies about a man who refers to a penis as a salami?

"It's been awhile," I admitted. And that was true. "Guess that's why I'm so hungry for your . . . uh, salami."

"I'd like to accommodate you," Simon said, sliding off his stool, "but I have to do this first."

I jumped off the bar stool and crossed the patio to Hooker.

"We have a problem," I said to Hooker. "The bartender just told the chip buyer's expediter that Rodriguez and Lucca were in the parking lot."

"Expediter?"

"The gorilla at the bar. They're Americans, but they're living in Zurich. And Ray has definitely disappeared."

We crept into a thicket of shrubbery at the edge of the lot and watched as Simon rapped on the BMW's driver's-side window with his gun barrel and persuaded Lucca and Rodriguez to get out of the car. They stood talking for a couple minutes. Looked amicable. Simon

251

gestured that they should go to the boat, and Rodriguez shook his head no. Rodriguez didn't think that was a good idea.

Bang. Simon shot Rodriguez in the foot.

"Fuck," Rodriguez said. And he sat down hard on the pavement.

I jumped back when the shot went off, and I felt myself go light-headed. Hard to watch someone get shot with such cold calculation. Of course, I'd just whacked the poor guy in the knee with a flashlight, but it had seemed different at the time. I put my head down and did some deep breathing.

Even at this distance, in the dark, I could see Lucca was dumbstruck, eyes glazed.

"Do something," I whispered to Hooker. "We can't afford to have Rodriguez and Lucca disappear. We need them."

"Darlin', the gorilla has a gun."

"So do you."

"Yes, but the gorilla likes to use his. Mine's just for show."

"Call the police!"

Hooker punched in the emergency code.

"There's a mugging going on in the South Beach Marina parking lot," Hooker whispered into the phone. "Who is this? You want my name? My name is Dickie Bonnano. And you should hurry or someone might get dead or kidnapped." Hooker snapped his phone closed and pocketed it.

"You didn't tell the dispatcher about the shooting," I said.

"I thought that was included in the mugging."

"Not all muggings involve shootings. A shooting is much more serious than a plain old mugging."

"Not necessarily. You could get beat to death in a mugging. And you might just get your toe nicked in a shooting."

"Are the police on their way?" I asked.

"I guess so."

"What do you mean, you guess so? What did the dispatcher say?"

"She said I should stay calm."

Simon had also made a phone call, and three minutes later his traveling companion arrived on the scene. They did a pat down on Lucca and Rodriguez and loaded them into the BMW's backseat.

"Where are the police?" I said, feeling a little panicky. "I don't hear any sirens. I don't see any flashing lights. You should have told the dispatcher about the shooting. You should have been more assertive."

"I was assertive. I just wasn't *freaked.*"

"Well, maybe you needed to be freaked because I don't see any cops on the scene."

"Well, maybe next time *you* need to make the stupid call."

"Count on it."

"Okay then."

"Okay."

We were glaring at each other, standing nose to nose, hands on hips.

Hooker's mouth curved at the corners with the beginning of a smile. "Did we just have a fight?"

"Discussion."

"I think it was a fight."

"It was *not* a fight."

"Felt like a fight to me."

"Forget it. We aren't having make-up sex."

"It was worth a try," Hooker said.

Simon and the other guy got into the BMW and the BMW cruised out of the lot. Hooker and I scrambled for our rental, and we all drove north.

"I learned something interesting from Simon."

"The guy at the bar?"

"Yeah. He said they weren't associated with racing. He said Ray had his finger in a lot of other pies."

"Did he mention any of the other pies by name? Apple, blueberry, poontang?"

"Nope. No mention of poontang pie."

The BMW worked its way through traffic and, true to form, we lost them after a couple blocks and a couple traffic lights.

"Okay," Hooker said, "here's my assessment of the situation. If Gobbles is in the trunk, they'll find him and probably his status won't change much. At least not for a while. And as far as we're concerned, we're screwed."

"Anything else?"

"We need to find Ray. And we need to identify the chip buyer. And before we do any of those things we need to go back to Felicia's because I'm out on my feet."

CHAPTER
FOURTEEN

I woke up with Hooker on top of me, and Beans breathing Saint Bernard breath in my face. The disturbing thing is that I didn't mind either. I slithered out from under Hooker, went to the Ibarras' bathroom and took a fast shower, got dressed, grabbed some gallon-size plastic bags from the kitchen, and took Beans for a walk.

It was a little after seven and Felicia's neighborhood was on the move. Pickup trucks and secondhand sedans motored down the side streets, people stood in line at the bus stop, dogs barked from postage-stamp backyards, and cats sat on stoops, soaking up the first sun of the day. The language spoken was Spanish, the kitchen smells were Cuban, and the skin tones were darker than mine. The rhythm of life felt normal and comforting, the setting seemed exotic.

Felicia's niece was manning the Ibarra stove when I returned. Hooker was at the table with a pack of kids and an older man I didn't know. Beans slid under the table, waiting for food to drop to the floor.

"Finish your breakfast," Lily said to her youngest. "The bus will be here and you won't be ready again."

Hooker had coffee, juice, and a breakfast burrito in front of him. He had his hand wrapped around his burrito and his phone to his ear.

"Sure," Hooker said into the phone. "You bet."

I poured myself a mug of coffee and took a chair at the table.

"That was Skippy," Hooker said to me when he disconnected. "He wanted to remind me that it was Tuesday."

I was surprised Skippy was up this early. Skippy was known to come to track meetings in his pajamas if the meeting was called before nine o'clock.

"Skippy's starting to sound nervous," Hooker said. "There's a ton of media scheduled for tomorrow, including the parade of cars that starts at Times Square."

It wouldn't be good for Hooker to miss the parade of cars. This is where the top-ten drivers get into their race cars and drive them through midtown Manhattan. It's televised and photographed and thousands of fans line the parade route. "Maybe we should go to New York."

"I'll get arrested and charged with multiple counts of —" Hooker looked at the kids at the table — "misbehaving."

"You don't know that for sure," I said to Hooker.

"Even if I'm just called in for questioning, it'll create a ton of bad press. And if they decide to hold me, you'll be left on your own to get us out of this disaster."

Lily put a massive breakfast burrito in front of me and refilled my coffee. I ate half of the burrito and gave the other half to Beans.

Forty-five minutes later, Hooker and I were in the marina parking lot. The black BMW had returned and was neatly wedged between two other cars. We parked the SUV at the edge of the lot, far away from the BMW, and got out to take a look, bringing a tire iron with us.

"No blood dripping from the trunk," Hooker said, standing to the rear of the car. "That could be a good sign."

Hooker rapped on the trunk and called *hello*, but no one answered. I tried the door and found it locked, so Hooker rammed the tire iron into the crevice by the trunk lock and popped the trunk open. Empty. No blood. Hooker mashed the trunk down to make it catch.

I peeked through the driver-side window. "No blood on the seats or splattered on the windshield. The floor mat is missing from the back. Probably Rodriguez bled on it big-time. There are a few smears on the carpet but nothing major. Maybe they just drove Rodriguez to a doctor. Maybe they didn't whack them or anything."

"I can't decide if I'm relieved or disappointed."

We crossed the lot to the cement walk that ran the length of the marina. Two piers down, the Huevo yacht was a hub of activity as crew members worked to clean up the damage caused by the fire. Five men in slacks and short-sleeved dress shirts stood talking on the dock, not far from the boat. From time to time, one of the men would gesture at the boat and everyone would look that way. Two of the men held clipboards.

"Insurance agents," I said to Hooker.

After a couple minutes, the three men from Zurich emerged from the main salon and left the boat without a backward glance, two crew members trailing behind them carrying luggage.

"Dollars to doughnuts they're going to be coming our way," Hooker said. "I'm guessing they're heading for the parking lot. We need to make ourselves disappear."

We stepped off the walkway and were immediately swallowed up by the birds-of-paradise bushes and dwarf date palms that provided a greenbelt between the walkway and the parking lot. We snaked around the palms, skirted the lot, and hid behind the SUV.

The men from Zurich and the luggage toters weren't far behind us. They crossed the lot to the black BMW, went to the trunk, and stared at the gouges we'd just made. They looked around. They did some disgusted head shaking. They tried to open the trunk. It was jammed. They loaded the suitcases into the backseat and got into the car.

"They're leaving," Hooker whispered. "They're going home. What does that mean?"

"They aren't going home. Home is Zurich, and it's cold in Zurich now. They'd have their suits back on if they were going home. These guys are all in short-sleeved shirts. I think they're just getting off the boat. Probably everything smells like smoke."

We waited until the BMW left the lot, and then we hopped into the SUV and tailed them to Collins. Easier this time. No lights. Less traffic. They drove up to a small boutique hotel where they valet-parked the car, gave their luggage over to the bell captain, and followed him into the lobby.

"I'd really like to know who these guys are," Hooker said. "Maybe one of us could go talk to the guy at the desk and be incredibly charming and get some information out of him."

I did an eye roll. "I can't just walk up to the desk and start asking questions."

"You could if you hiked your T-shirt up so the desk clerk could see some skin."

"You're pimping me out," I said.

"And?"

I reached for the door handle. "If I'm not out in ten minutes, come in guns blazing and rescue me."

I pulled my T-shirt out of my jeans and tied the hem into a knot so it sat just below my boobs, leaving a lot of skin exposed. I sashayed across the street and swung my ass Suzanne style into the lobby.

It was a pretty little lobby with black and white marble floor tiles and potted palms and an elaborate gold-trimmed art deco reception desk. An immaculately tailored and turned-out man stood behind the desk. His nails were buffed, his hair was perfectly cut, his skin was flawless. He wore a tiny rainbow pin in his lapel. I untied my shirt and tucked it back into my jeans. It was going to take more than a bare stomach to entice this guy. The bare stomach was going to have to be attached to equipment I didn't possess.

"Oh, sweetie," he said to me. "You're too perfect to cover up. This is South Beach. You work out, right?"

"Sometimes."

"What can I do for you? If you're looking to make rent money, I might have something for you."

Okay, so I came in half naked and swinging my hips . . . it was still sort of upsetting that I was instantly sized up as a hooker. "I'm not cheap," I said to him.

"Of course not! Although, a manicure might not be a bad idea. And you are showing some roots."

I shoved my hands into my pockets. "Three men just checked in. Would one of them be looking for a . . . lady? The one with the blue shirt and touch of gray at the temples?"

"He didn't request one. Although, Mr. Miranda has stayed here before, and in the past has used our services to obtain female companionship."

"I thought I recognized him. I did him last year. He was here for the Orange Bowl, right? I remember him because he has a crooked . . . you know."

"Don't you hate that?" the desk clerk said. "Did you charge extra?"

"What's his first name again?"

"Anthony."

"Anthony Miranda. Yep, that's the guy." I borrowed the pen on the counter and wrote a fake number on the back of a hotel brochure. "Here's my cell number," I said to the desk clerk. "Tell Anthony Miranda that Dolly says hello." I swung my ass out of the lobby, across the street, and into the SUV. "Anthony Miranda," I said to Hooker.

"Anything else?"

"That's it. Just a name. I probably could have learned more, but I would have needed a manicure."

260

Hooker returned to the marina lot, parked, and got Skippy up on the speakerphone.

"I need some help," Hooker said to Skippy.

"No shit."

"I need information on a guy. Anthony Miranda. Know anything about him?"

"No."

"Well, Google him or something and call me back."

"Whatever happened to the good old days when all NASCAR had to worry about were pregnant pit lizards and trashed hotel rooms? Earnhardt Senior wouldn't have called up and asked me to Google for him. He was a *driver*."

"Can't argue with that," Hooker said, disconnecting.

"You're a good driver," I said to Hooker. "You just suck as a detective."

A limo pulled into the lot and idled at the path leading to the marina. The limo door opened, and Suzanne Huevo got out. She was wearing a pale yellow suit, her hair was pulled tight, her doggie bag was on her shoulder, and her earlobes were weighed down with diamonds.

"Damage inspection," Hooker said.

Suzanne disappeared down the path, and the limo waited at idle. Five minutes later, Suzanne reappeared, got into the limo, and the limo took off.

Hooker put the SUV in gear. "Might as well follow her," he said. "We follow everyone else. And we haven't got anything else to do."

The limo rolled down Collins and pulled into the porte cochere on a condo building a couple doors down from the Ritz. Suzanne got out and strutted into the building. The limo left.

"Huh," Hooker said. "That didn't amount to much. This is where she's living now."

"Do you have any other ideas?"

"There's a Starbucks around the corner. We could get coffee and one of those cranberry cakes with the icing on top."

"I meant do you have any ideas about how we can get ourselves off the Most Wanted list."

"Nope," Hooker said, putting the car in gear, heading for Starbucks. "I don't have any of those ideas."

Ten minutes later I was leaving Starbucks with two large cups of coffee and two cranberry cakes. I pushed through the large glass door, took the steps to the sidewalk, and looked across the street just in time to see the SUV pull away, followed by the black BMW.

My first reaction was disbelief. For a moment the earth stopped spinning on its axis and nothing moved. Time stood still. And then a horrible ache grew in my chest, and I couldn't breathe. And my vision blurred behind tears. And I knew it was real. Hooker was gone. The bad guys had him. And these bad guys were a cut above Lucca and Rodriguez. Lucca and Rodriguez were thugs. I suspected Simon and his partner were polished professionals.

I sat down hard on the cement steps behind me and put my head between my legs, sucking in air. Get a grip, I thought. This is no time to fall apart. I blew my nose in a Starbucks napkin. I sipped some coffee, trying to calm myself, trying to think. "Here's what has to be done," I said to myself. "You have to find Hooker before they hurt him. You need help. Call Rosa and Felicia."

I was still on the steps in front of Starbucks when Rosa pulled to the curb. I was wired on two cups of coffee and a piece of cranberry cake. I'd managed to stop the flood of tears, but I was feeling horrible that Hooker had been snatched by the bad guys. And I was determined to get him back in useable condition.

Rosa was driving a magenta Toyota Camry that had been customized with a rear spoiler and a fluorescent red-orange-and-green-flame paint job. Felicia was in the seat next to her. And Beans was in the backseat, his nose pressed against the window, staring out at me.

I slid onto the seat next to Beans and my attention was caught by the arsenal tucked into the pockets on the seat backs. Three semiautomatics, two revolvers, a stun gun, and a bear-size can of pepper spray. Plus what looked like a sawed-off shotgun on the floor.

Felicia saw me looking at the guns. "You never know," she said. "Better to be prepared, right?"

Prepared for what? World War III?

"What do we do now?" Rosa wanted to know. "We're ready to go get those sonsabitches. Do you know where they took Hooker?"

"No. But I know where they're staying. It's the little white hotel on Collins that has the big front porch with the rocking chairs. I thought we could start looking there."

"I know the hotel," Rosa said, edging into traffic. "The Pearl."

I sat back and called Skippy.

"I'm calling for Hooker," I said. "Did you get anything on Anthony Miranda?"

"Turns out there are a lot of Anthony Mirandas. There's a drummer, a New York cop, a politician, a guy who has a Zurich-based export company —"

"That's the one. The exporter."

"I knew it would be the exporter. From what I read, he mostly exports guns and illegal military technology."

"Not good news. I was hoping for chocolate."

"Where's Hooker?" Skippy asked.

"You know how there are all those movie-star impersonators? You might want to try to find a Hooker double . . . just in case."

"I'm getting too old for this shit," Skippy said. And he hung up.

Rosa parked on the street, half a block from the Pearl Hotel. We left Beans in the car, guarding the guns, and Rosa, Felicia, and I took the lobby like here-come-the-hookers.

The same immaculately turned-out guy was at the desk, and his eyes got wide when we all barreled in.

"Oh dear," he said. "Maybe too much of a good thing."

"Anthony is expecting us," I told him.

"He didn't say anything . . ."

Rosa was wearing a V-neck red sweater that showed a lot of boob squished so tight together a man would suffocate if he got his nose caught in her cleavage. "We've been invited for brunch," Rosa said.

"He didn't order any brunch," the desk clerk said.

"Honey pie," Rosa said, "we *are* brunch."

"But they aren't here. They all went out about a half hour ago. Something about out coffee not being up to their standards, and they were looking for a Starbucks."

So maybe Rodriguez and Lucca told them about Hooker, and the Zurich chip buyers ran into him by accident. How crappy is that?

"Anthony said we should go upstairs and get ready," I told the clerk. "He said you'd let us in his room."

"Oh, no. I can't do that. I couldn't possibly."

"Okay, then we'll get ready here," Rosa said. And she stripped off her sweater.

"Eek!" the desk clerk said. "No, no, no. You can't do that in the lobby."

"Here goes me, too," Felicia said, unbuttoning her lavender-flowered shirt.

The desk clerk clapped his hands over his eyes. "I can't look. I'm not looking."

"Unless you want to see Felicia's granny panties hit the floor, you'd better give me the key," I said.

He shoved a card at me. "Take it. *Take it and go!* Get out of my lobby. Room 315."

Felicia, Rosa, and I flounced off to the elevator and rode to the third floor. I let us into the room, and we went through everything.

"This guy has no imagination," Felicia said. "Look at his boxers. They're all the same color. No pictures or anything."

I turned on his laptop. Nothing on its desktop. Nothing interesting in his hard drive. I went into his mail program. Wiped clean. Nothing on his calendar.

"There isn't anything here," I said. "He must export everything onto a memory stick." I looked around for a memory stick but came up empty.

"There's a little safe in the closet," Rosa said. "Probably he got the good stuff in there because it's locked. Nothing in his jacket pockets."

Felicia's cell phone rang. "It's my niece," Felicia said, handing the phone to me. "Hooker is there with three men, and he wants to talk to you."

"Hey," I said to Hooker. "How's it going?"

"It could be better. I'm here with three gentlemen who are interested in the computer chip. Turns out it's not behind the picture of Jesus anymore."

"I had Felicia take it. I thought I might need it to ransom you."

"Oh man, that's a relief. So you have the chip with you?"

I looked over at Felicia. "You have that little chip from the back of the Jesus picture, right?"

"Yes and no," Felicia said. "I got it, and then when I was looking for the guns, I put the chip on the table, and Beans ate it."

"*What?*"

"How was I to know? I left the room for three seconds and when I come back, Mr. Sneaky Dog had his tongue on the table and the chip was gone."

I was speechless.

"It could be worse," Felicia said. "At least we know where it is. You just have to wait for him to poopie."

"Hello," Hooker said. "Are you still there?"

"The chip is temporarily unavailable," I told him. "Let me talk to Miranda."

There was some fumbling and Miranda came on the phone.

"Listen," I said, "there's a small problem here, and the chip is temporarily unavailable, but we know exactly where it is, and we're going to get it to you as soon as possible. Now here's the thing, if one hair is out of place on Sam Hooker's head you'll *never* see the chip."

"Now here's *my* thing. Get me the chip or you're going to have a dead boyfriend."

"Technically, he isn't my boyfriend."

"You've got twenty-four hours," Miranda said. He gave me his cell phone number and disconnected.

"We have twenty-four hours to swap the chip for Hooker," I said to Rosa and Felicia.

"Maybe we feed doggie some prunes and it make things go faster," Felicia said. "Works for me."

"Maybe we wait for the bad guys to return and we kick their ass," Rosa said.

I thought they both sounded like okay ideas. "Let's get out of here," I said. "One of you can do surveillance on the hotel, and the other can come with me to buy prunes."

"I don't want to do surveillance," Rosa said. "It's just sitting and waiting."

"I don't want to do it either," Felicia said. "I want to be where the action is. I'll call my nephew Carl. He can do surveillance. He's between jobs. He'd be happy to have something to do."

"Carl," Rosa said. "I know him. Wasn't he busted for possession?"

"Yeah, but he's clean now. He lives in a group home a couple blocks from here, and he's probably sitting around watching television. He used to bag at a supermarket, but they switched to plastic bags, and he couldn't get the hang of it."

Ten minutes later, we were out of the hotel and across the street with Carl. He was a chunky five seven, with dark skin, shoulder-length black hair, too big jeans, and a shiny gold tooth in the front of his mouth. We sat him on a curbside bench and gave him descriptions of the men and cars, including Hooker. He had a cell phone, a quart bottle of soda, mirrored sunglasses, and a ball cap . . . everything he needed for a day of Miami surveillance.

"Carl don't look too bright," Rosa said when we got back to the Camry.

"He's fried his brain a little with the drugs, but he'll be fine," Felicia said. "He's very conscientious. He found Jesus."

"He looks like he found Him in a pool hall," Rosa said.

"There's a convenience store attached to the marina," I told Rosa. "We might be able to buy prunes there, and we can check the parking lot for the black BMW."

Beans was sitting beside me on the backseat, breathing hot dog breath down Felicia's neck.

"Someone give doggie a mint," Felicia said. "He needs a mint real bad. Next time no breakfast burritos for him."

"We'll get mints when we get the prunes," I told her.

"I brought him with because we have to watch him all the time so we don't miss the *big event*," Felicia said.

I didn't want to think about the *big event*. I couldn't imagine how I was going to find the teeny-tiny chip in the midst of the *big event*. I was going to need a contamination suit and gas mask.

Rosa went all the way on Collins, rolled past Joe's Stone Crabs, and cut into the parking lot next to Monty's. She crept up and down the aisles, so we could check out the cars, but we didn't see the BMW.

"I still want to take a look at the boat," I said. "And I'd like to let Beans stretch his legs."

Felicia turned and looked Beans in the face. "Do you have to poopie?" she asked him.

"It's too soon," Rosa said, nosing the Camry into a slot and cutting the engine. "He hasn't had any prunes yet. And anyway, it doesn't just go in and out *bing, bang, boom*. It's not like it's sex!"

"It does if you eat *enough* prunes," Felicia said. "And you should stop having sex with bing, bang, boom men. That's married sex. If I was divorced like you, I'd set the egg timer on *me first*. No bing and bang without a boom."

269

"It's a crap shoot out there," Rosa said. "You roll the dice and sometimes you get a bing and a bang and sometimes you get a boom. That's why God gave women shower massage."

We all got out of the car and walked toward the marina.

"You better watch what you say about God," Felicia said. "He listens, you know. If I was you, I'd say some Hail Marys tonight just in case."

Rosa looked sideways at Felicia. "I suppose you never used the shower massage?"

"Well, sure, but I don't bring God into it. I think shower massage might have been invented by the devil. God invented the missionary position."

We were on the dock, looking out at the piers. Everything was business as usual, except the Huevo yacht was missing. I walked Beans down to the pier where the yacht used to be tied and approached a guy who was getting ready to shove off on a Hatteras.

"Where's the Huevo boat?" I asked.

"It just left. It's going to Fort Lauderdale for repairs. They had a fire in the main salon."

One less place to look for Hooker.

We went up the steps, past the outdoor bar, and walked around the building to the deli on the street side. I stayed outside with Beans and ten minutes later Felicia and Rosa emerged with two bags of food.

"Wow," I said. "Is that all for Beans?"

"No," Rosa said. "The prunes and the gallon-size plastic bags are for Beans. The rubber gloves are for you. The macaroni salad, chocolate cake, meatball subs, and soda are for all of us."

We sat on a bench outside the store and Felicia opened the box of prunes. "Anybody want a prune?" she asked. "Prunes are good for you. Full of iron."

We all declined prunes. Saving ourselves for the chocolate cake.

"How about doggie?" Felicia said to Beans. "Does doggy want a prune?"

Beans was sitting straight, eyes bright, ears perked. He sniffed the prune Felicia held in her hand and then very delicately took it from her. He held it in his mouth for a while, drooling, not sure what one actually did with a prune. He opened his mouth, and the prune fell out.

"We got him a meatball sub," Felicia said. "Just in case." She unwrapped one of the subs, stuffed prunes into the meatballs, and gave the sub to Beans.

Beans wolfed the sub down.

"Now we just have to wait for the poop to come," Felicia said, handing us our subs, passing plastic forks around for the macaroni.

We ate our lunch, drank our sodas, and Felicia called her nephew for a progress report.

"He reports no progress," she said. She stuffed the crumpled wrappers and used forks into the bag we'd designated as trash, and she looked around. "Where's the box of prunes? I had it on the bench next to me."

All eyes focused on Beans. He was sitting on the grass not far from us. He was drooling, his eyes looked droopy, and there was a piece of the cardboard prune box stuck to his lower lip.

"Oh boy," Rosa said. "He ate a *lot* of prunes."

Beans stood and lifted his tail and there was a sound like air escaping a balloon. We all jumped off the bench and moved away.

"He could peel paint off a building," Rosa said.

Felicia was fanning the fumes away with the garbage bag. "It smells like burrito. And look at him. I think he's smiling."

I felt like I should be doing more to find Hooker, but I didn't know where to start. Maybe a property search. I hauled my phone out and called Skippy.

"I was wondering if you could get some more information for me," I said. "I want to know if Anthony Miranda has property in the Miami area. A house or an office building. Anything."

"I want to talk to Hooker."

"He isn't here."

"Where *is* he?" Skippy asked.

"He's sort of . . . kidnapped."

There was silence on the other end, and I was worried Skippy had fainted or had a heart attack.

"Are you okay?" I asked.

"I'm dandy. My scrotum is so tight my balls are choking."

"It's not as bad as it sounds," I said to Skippy. "I'll be able to get Hooker back as soon as the dog poops."

"I'm not even going to ask," Skippy said. "Do you have a phone number I can call when I get information on Miranda?"

272

I gave him my number and disconnected.

"Maybe we should go back to the hotel and see if Carl needs a potty break or wants to get lunch," Felicia said.

We went back to the lot, piled into the car, and Rosa headed for Collins. After three blocks, Beans made the balloon noise again, Rosa pulled the car to the curb, and we all got out and waited for the air to clear.

We were standing not far from the take-out part of Joe's Stone Crabs. A black limo glided to a stop in front of us and Suzanne got out.

"Omigosh," she said when she saw me. "Barney. How've you been? Where's Hooker?"

"He's been kidnapped."

"Jeez," Suzanne said, "that's too bad. There's so much of that going around these days. Excuse me a minute. I have to get my stone crabs."

"Who's that?" Rosa wanted to know. "She looks like a big bitch. I like her already."

Suzanne was carrying a large bag when she came out. "So what are you up to?" she asked me, handing the bag over to the chauffeur.

"I'm trying to find Hooker. These are my friends Rosa and Felicia."

"Have you gone to the police?" Suzanne asked.

"No. Hooker and I are sort of wanted for multiple counts of murder. Oscar, Spanky's spotter, Hooker's security guy . . . and they've probably added Ray by now."

"That's ridiculous. Ray isn't dead," Suzanne said.

"Are you sure?"

"Yeah, Ray's with me. You want to see him?"

CHAPTER
FIFTEEN

Felicia, Rosa, and I got back into the Camry, rolled the windows down, and followed the black limo to Suzanne's condo. We valet-parked the car and rode the elevator to the twelfth floor. All the time, I was dying to jump up and down and yell and be embarrassingly excited because I'd found Ray. Since I hadn't a clue as to what was going on, and I didn't want to screw anything up, I just kept my lips pressed tight together and my hands balled into fists at my side and tried to look calm.

"It's just a temporary rental until I get everything straightened out," Suzanne said, plugging her key into the lock. "Still, it's not bad, and it's got a great view."

The condo stretched across the back of the building with floor-to-ceiling windows that looked out on the ocean. The décor was modern, mostly white with touches of pastel. The kitchen was high tech and looked totally unused.

"Where's Itsy Poo?" I asked Suzanne.

"She goes to play group on Tuesdays. And then she gets a whirlpool bath and a pedicure."

Beans was pressed into my leg as if he understood pedicure and didn't think a lot of it.

Suzanne set the stone crabs on the kitchen counter. "Follow me, ladies, and I'll show you what pissed-off mothers do for fun."

We all marched into the bedroom, which was about half the size of a football field. Her bed was one of those four-poster things, draped in white gauze. The carpet was white. The woods were pale. The upholstered pieces were white. The curtains were drawn, and I thought this was probably to keep the sun out so she didn't go snow blind.

"This unit has his and hers bathrooms," Suzanne said. "My bathroom is through the door to the right. And *his* bathroom is in here."

Suzanne took a key off the dresser, unlocked the door to *his* bathroom, and stepped back. Ray was prisoner in the little room, still dressed in the clothes he'd worn to the beach meeting. He was tethered with an elaborate system of clunky chains that wrapped around the toilet and the pipes under the sink. His hands were free to do whatever he needed to do, but he didn't have enough chain to do what he really *wanted* to do . . . which was to choke Suzanne. He had a pillow and a quilt, a stack of magazines, and a tray with leftovers from takeout.

"Now you're all accomplices to kidnapping," Ray said. "If you don't get me out of here, you're all going to jail for the rest of your lives."

"What did he do?" Felicia asked. "He cheat on you?"

"No. He's my brother-in-law," Suzanne said. "He rudely killed my husband before I had the chance to do it myself. And now he's planning to swindle my kids out of their inheritance."

"You have no proof," Ray said.

"It's always a mistake to mess with a mother," Suzanne said.

"So this is where Ray went after he talked to Hooker and me," I said.

"It was easy," Suzanne said. "I told him I wanted to talk to him in private about transferring the boat over to him. He came up here. I hit him with a blast from a stun gun, trussed him up, and I was in business. I guess the moron never told anyone he was coming here."

"Ask her about the chip," Ray said to Suzanne.

"Shut up."

"*Ask her!*"

"What about the chip?" I said to Suzanne.

"Ray and Oscar have a product in R and D that's worth a *lot* of money. They didn't realize I knew about it, but I keep my ears open.

"I knew it was ready for sale, and I knew Oscar was using it on the cars. It got him a championship, but more than that, it was a flashy way to demonstrate the technology to prospective buyers. I was willing to be the good corporate wife and keep my mouth shut. I was even willing to be the good ex-corporate wife and keep my mouth shut. I'm *not* willing to be the widow who sits by and watches the slimebag brother rape the company." Suzanne's frozen eyebrows narrowed ever so slightly. "So I had to bring Ray in for questioning, right, Ray?"

Ray gave her the death glare. And Suzanne ignored it.

"And now the prototype has disappeared, and Ray doesn't want to tell me where it's wandered off to," Suzanne said.

"I told you where the chip is," Ray said. "Jesus, why don't you just ask her?"

Suzanne kept her eyes on Ray. "Ray has this insultingly ridiculous story he's constructed about the product disappearance. His contention is that you and Hooker have it. And it gets even better. He claims you got this particular product by stealing a car hauler. The same hauler that was supposed to carry Oscar back to Mexico."

"Are you talking about the gizmo in the gearshift knob?" I asked her.

Suzanne turned to me, mouth dropped open, eyes as wide as they'd go on Botox. "I thought he was lying. The story was insane. I mean, who would believe something like that? Don't tell me it's true!"

"It's true," I said.

Suzanne tipped her head back and gave a whoop of laughter. She looked over at Beans. "I guess the tooth marks in Oscar make sense to me now. You should give him an extra dog biscuit for that one."

"He thought Mr. Dead Guy was a big chew toy," Felicia said. "He's just a puppy inside."

"So where's the circuit board?" Suzanne asked. "Do you have it?"

"Not exactly. But I know where it is."

"And it's safe? You can get it for me?"

"Yes."

Suzanne gave a sigh of relief. "You can't imagine how much time and money went into the making of that thing. It's my sons' future."

"So it wasn't about the boat?"

"Not entirely. The boat was just part of it. By the time Ray's executorship ran out, there wouldn't have been anything left of the company. Ray would have stripped every asset from it."

Ray didn't say anything. They'd obviously had this conversation before and it didn't end well for Ray.

"There are a couple things I don't understand," I said to Suzanne. "I know the value of traction control in a race car, but I get the feeling this is bigger than just rigging a contest. Why is this one little circuit board so important?"

"The technology has the potential for wide use," Suzanne said. "Everything on that tiny circuit card is exclusive to Huevo. The concept, the programming, the wireless technology, and the battery composite are all straight out of development and have never before been seen . . . anywhere. If the circuit board fell into the wrong hands, it could eventually be unraveled and the technology could be stolen. The battery alone is worth hundreds of millions. The wireless technology will revolutionize the aircraft industry."

"So you wanted to get it back just so it wouldn't get duplicated?"

"It's more complicated than that," Suzanne said. "Idiot Oscar amused himself by producing a microprocessor that could easily be embedded in an

278

engine and regulate engine speed. It was illegal and made use of the new battery and wireless technology, but it was a simple program, and it self-destructed each week when given the signal. At the same time, Oscar had established a partnership with a technology broker."

"Anthony Miranda?"

"Yes. Miranda has an overseas client who is willing to pay top dollar. Unfortunately, some of that technology could have been used in very bad ways by Miranda's client. I would have stepped in sooner, but I didn't know that part of it until I got to Florida.

"Anyway, a prototype circuit board had been produced for Miranda. It was programmed to demonstrate the wireless technology that could be used in aircraft. So genius Oscar brought two different circuit boards to Florida and somehow managed to put the wrong circuit board in the sixty-nine car."

"It was Rodriguez," Ray said. "He picked up the wrong package. I had both packages labeled and locked away in the hotel's safety-deposit box. Miranda's man was flying in the day after the race to pick up the prototype for demonstration. I didn't even know about the mix-up until the day after the race when I went to get Miranda's package."

"Wait a minute," I said. "Let me get this straight. Rodriguez put the wrong circuit board in the number sixty-nine?"

"The chip that actually controls engine function is embedded directly onto the engine, but since the signal was traveling some distance to the car, we found it to be a more reliable system if we added a second chip that picked up the start signal and relayed that signal to the primary. Because we powered the relay chip with the new battery material, we kept the chip close to us until the last moment. And as a final precaution, it was programmed to self-destruct. Plus, we only used the second chip on Huevo cars. The morning of the race Rodriguez was in a hurry and grabbed the wrong package out of the safe. And Rodriguez placed the chip in the knob without examining it."

"Could that prototype circuit board control the car?"

"No," Ray said. "And it wasn't programmed to self-destruct, either."

"So you're telling me Dickie actually won the race?"

This was the first time Ray smiled. "Yes," he said. "Isn't that a kicker? Who would have thought he could actually drive that car?"

"Why didn't you hurry up and make another circuit board for Miranda?"

"There's no way to hurry. The prototype circuit board and battery could have been reproduced . . . but not quickly. Certainly not in the two week window we were tied to. The demonstration schedule was in place."

"Why didn't you just reschedule?"

"Imagine that Miranda is Darth Vader," Ray said. "And you had to tell Lord Vader that he needed to reschedule his demonstration. Miranda is ruthless. Miranda has no tolerance for mistakes. And when the chip didn't get dropped into Miranda's hand as promised, his twisted paranoid mind screamed *double* cross. Miranda's assumption was that I was selling the chip elsewhere. And things turned very ugly."

"Anybody mind if I have some stone crabs?" Felicia wanted to know.

"Omigod," Suzanne said. "I forgot about the stone crabs. Let's all go into the kitchen, and I'll have a pitcher of booze sent up."

"Hey!" Ray said. "Pay attention here! What about me?"

"What about you?" Suzanne asked.

"I'm chained!"

"Don't whine, Ray," Suzanne said. "It's unattractive."

"I told you everything you wanted to know," Ray said. "You're just keeping me here because you're a sicko. Not my fault that you turned into a dried-up old hag and Oscar dumped you, sweetie pie."

Suzanne lunged at Ray, and we all jumped on her and dragged her back from the bathroom.

"Not a good idea to wrestle with him," I told her. "I need him to be alive and coherent so he can set Rodriguez and Lucca up as murder suspects." I looked at Ray. "You're still going to do that, right?"

"Sure," Ray said. Sullen but hopeful.

"Unfortunately, Rodriguez and Lucca have disappeared and might be dead, so you'll have to work that into your plan," I told him.

I looked over at Suzanne. "Do you mind keeping him here awhile longer? He's probably safer here than out on the street where Darth Vader might run into him."

"Sure. We're having a good time together. And I know it seems crass to bring this up, but I want the circuit board. It belongs to Huevo Enterprises."

Rosa, Felicia, and I cut our eyes to Beans.

"He ate it," I said.

"I put it down for only one minute," Felicia said. "And he did a big lick on the table, and the little thingy was gone. And now we're waiting for him to make poopie."

Suzanne went dead still. "Are you serious?"

"Yes," we all said.

She stood with her hands slack at her sides and her face expressionless. "Let me get this straight. We're waiting for that dog to shit out my billion-dollar circuit board."

"Yes," we all said.

"This is priceless," Suzanne said. "I've been keeping Ray here for two days because the true story he was telling me was too insane to be believable, and now it turns out a Saint Bernard ate the circuit board. Is there anything else I should know?"

"Miranda is holding Hooker hostage for the circuit board. And there's another man missing. A friend of mine who is also involved. Jefferson Davis Warner."

"Those guys got Gobbles?" Felicia said. "I didn't know that. That's terrible. He's such a sweetie. I bet he's scared."

"Ray knows where he is," I told everybody. "Don't you, Ray?"

282

"We had him on the boat with us. And then we moved him to the car," Ray said. "Rodriguez was keeping him close. He had him in the trunk."

"He's not on the boat, and he's not in the car," I said.

"Then I don't know where he is," Ray said. "You have to ask Rodriguez."

My phone buzzed, and I looked at the readout. Skippy.

"Sorry," Skippy said. "I went to a bunch of different sources, but no properties turned up. Has the dog pooped yet?"

"No."

"I got an actor lined up, and if you don't get too close, he could be Hooker. All he has to do is get in the car and follow the guy in front of him at parade speed. We might be okay as long as he doesn't have to talk. If he opens his mouth, I'm fucked."

The line went dead, and I put my phone back in my pocket. I was between a rock and a hard place. I wanted to give the circuit board to Suzanne and her kids. I really did. But more than that . . . I wanted Hooker safe.

"I know that circuit board belongs to you," I said to Suzanne, "but I can't sacrifice Hooker for it."

Ray had been sitting on the toilet lid, taking it all in. "If you cut me in, I can help," he said. "I can talk to Miranda. I can make a deal so everyone benefits . . . even Hooker."

"Eat dirt and die," Suzanne said. And she closed and locked the bathroom door.

We followed Suzanne out of the bedroom and into the kitchen.

"If I let him go, he'll kill me," Suzanne said. "Just like he killed Oscar. And I *know* he killed Oscar. I have spies everywhere, listening at doors, reading memos before they get shredded. Ray decided to stage a coup, and Rodriguez was the designated hit man. Rodriguez grabbed the wrong chip because he'd just drilled Oscar and his slut girlfriend, and he was running late. Rodriguez had Oscar packaged up and in the back of his car when he stopped off at the hotel to get the chip. Rodriguez was in a rush and not paying attention."

"What are you going to do with the guy in the bathroom?" Rosa wanted to know.

"I don't know," Suzanne said. "I brought him here because I was told Miranda was coming into town to personally pick up the prototype. I thought I might be able to get the chip ahead of Miranda and use it as leverage to keep Ray in line. After I had Ray here awhile, I realized nothing is going to keep Ray in line. Ray is insane. He feels no remorse for anything."

"Maybe he needs to get fitted with cement shoes and go for a swim," Rosa said.

"First thing, we need to find a way to get Hooker and not give up the circuit board," I said. "Then we'll worry about Ray."

"We could *force* them to give us Hooker," Felicia said. "Just go in there and shoot 'em up."

"How many men are with Hooker?" Suzanne asked.

"Miranda and two others, for sure," I said. "Rodriguez and Lucca have disappeared. They could be with Miranda, but most likely they're playing poker with Oscar."

"We could take them," Rosa said. "Four against three."

"I'm game," Suzanne said.

This was a ridiculous idea that scared the bejeezus out of me. It wasn't as if we were army rangers or something. We were a former Vegas showgirl, a cigar roller, a grandmother who sold fruit, and a mechanic who wasn't any good with guns.

"Any other ideas?" I asked.

Silence. No other ideas.

"Gee, it sounds like a good plan," I said, "but we can't do it because we don't know where they are." Thank God.

"I've got that covered," Suzanne said. "We let Ray lead us to them. Three of us leave and one stays behind to guard Ray. The one who stays behind opens the door to see if Ray's okay, and then she feels sorry for him, so she opens the handcuffs so he can have some stone crabs. And she lets Ray escape. Then we just follow Ray."

"I don't know," I said. "It sounds dangerous for the one who stays behind." In fact, it sounded *nuts*!

"Piece of cake," Felicia said. "I could do it. Look at me. I'm a grandma. He'll believe I would let him go. But you have to promise to come get me before you bust in on the bad guys. I don't want to miss anything."

Who *was* this woman? Did she moonlight as the Terminator?

Rosa was at the wheel of the Camry, Suzanne was riding shotgun beside her, and I was in the backseat with Beans. We were across the street from the condo building, waiting to get the call from Felicia telling us Ray had escaped. Felicia had now been alone with Ray for almost twenty minutes, and I was mentally cracking my knuckles, worried something had gone wrong.

The call came through just as Ray bolted through the front door and hailed a cab.

"Felicia says it worked perfect," Rosa said, following Ray's cab. "She said it took so long because he locked her in the bathroom. And then she thinks he ate some stone crabs. And she said he took her cell phone and he better not be making any calls to Mexico."

The cab went south on Collins, and we all knew the destination. Ray was going to the boat. He didn't know about the fire. He didn't know the boat had sailed. He wasn't sure if Rodriguez and Lucca were at large. He was probably calling them on Felicia's cell phone from the cab, not happy because they weren't answering. Hell, what do I know, maybe they *were* answering. Maybe they were with Hooker, or maybe they were hiding out in Orlando with Mickey Mouse.

The cab pulled into the lot and dropped Ray off. Rosa idled on the street, and I ran through the courtyard attached to Monty's so I could spy on Ray when he stepped onto the marina footpath.

I slipped into place, to the side of the building, just as Ray emerged from the lot and stood, staring at the empty space on the dock. He made a hand gesture that shouted *where the fuck did the boat go?* And he was

286

back on his phone. Angry. Punching numbers in. Talking to someone. He had his hand on his hip, head down, trying not to go entirely gonzo with the person on the other end. He picked his head up and looked around. Not in my direction. Too pissed off to see anything anyway. He paced up and down the walkway, talking. He disconnected and punched in another number. The conversation was much calmer this time, but I could see the rage simmering below the surface. Not talking to an underling, I thought. Maybe talking to Miranda. At least that was my hope, because now that we were committed to a plan, I wanted to get on with it.

It was early afternoon. Not a cloud in the sky. Slight breeze coming in off the ocean, ruffling the water and rustling in the palms. Cool enough to wear jeans but warm enough to wear a short-sleeved shirt. In other words, the weather was perfect. And Florida would have been paradise if only I wasn't wanted for questioning in multiple murders and if only Hooker wasn't being held hostage, and if only Beans didn't have a billion-dollar circuit board working its way through his intestines.

Ray looked at his watch and nodded. He looked in the direction of the parking lot. He did another nod, then he put the phone away. Someone was coming to pick him up, I thought. Be interesting to see if it was Rodriguez or Lucca.

Thirty minutes later, I was back in the Camry with Rosa and Suzanne and Beans. Ray was waiting at the lot entrance. The black BMW rolled past us and stopped curbside. Ray got in, and the car pulled off into traffic. Simon was driving. Rosa kept them in sight, and she swept past them when the BMW stopped in front of the Pearl. She made an illegal U-turn and parked half a block away, facing the hotel. The BMW flashers went on, and Simon got out and went into the lobby. Five minutes later, Felicia called and said her nephew reported the BMW. Ten minutes later, Simon came out with the luggage, got behind the wheel, and took off.

"They checked out," Rosa said. "I guess they didn't think a fancy-ass hotel was a good place to rough up a hostage."

I knew Rosa was just using the phrase as an expression, but the thought of Hooker getting roughed up made my stomach sick.

The BMW went north on Collins, turned onto Seventeenth Street, and took the Venetian Causeway. We were two cars back, watching carefully. The BMW turned into a residential neighborhood on Di Lido Island, wound its way to the northernmost point, and pulled into a gated driveway.

"Nice house," Rosa said, looking through the wrought-iron gate to the house beyond. "I bet they got Dobermans."

"This isn't going to be easy," Suzanne said. "We're going to have to scale a six-foot fence to get into this place. And we don't have any idea how many people are in the house."

We were parked down the street, debating our options, when my phone rang.

288

"This is Anthony Miranda," he said. "I know the location of the circuit board, and I see no reason to wait any longer for it. You have one hour to give me either the circuit board or the dog."

Ray was a big blabbermouth. "And if I don't make the one-hour delivery?"

"I start to cut your friend's fingers off his hand."

"That's disgusting."

"It's business," Miranda said. "Nothing personal. There's a small parking lot adjacent to a convenience store on the corner of Fifteenth Street and Alton Road. My representative will be there to collect my property. One hour."

"I expect to collect my property as well. I'm not handing anything over until Hooker's released."

"Hooker will be released when I take possession of the circuit board."

"And Gobbles?"

"And Gobbles."

I disconnected and looked at the ladies. "I have an hour to get the circuit board to Miranda. If I don't get the circuit board to him, he's going to start cutting Hooker's fingers off."

"Hard for him to drive without fingers," Rosa said.

"I have an idea," Suzanne said. "If we could get Beans to poop out the circuit board, we could disable it. Remove the battery and ruin the circuitry. Then we could give it to Miranda, and we will have fulfilled his demands without giving him the technology. Not our fault if the circuit board got damaged, right? I mean, it's been through a lot."

We all looked at Beans. He was panting and drooling. He lifted his ass off the seat a little and farted. We all jumped out of the car and fanned the air.

"Do you think that smelled like prunes?" Rosa wanted to know. "I think I might have caught a hint of prune."

We got back into the car and Rosa drove off Di Lido and took the causeway to Belle Island Park. She pulled up to a grassy area, and I got out with Beans and started walking him around.

"Do you have to poop?" I asked him. "Does Beansy have to poopie?"

He took a seven-minute tinkle, and he did a lot of drooling, but he didn't poop.

"It's not time yet," I told everyone. "He's not ready."

Suzanne checked her watch. "He has forty-five minutes."

Rosa drove to Suzanne's condo, and Suzanne ran in to get Felicia out of the bathroom. When they came out, they had more prunes.

"I borrowed them from my neighbor," Suzanne said. "She actually eats them. Can you imagine?"

"I don't know if that's such a good idea," I said. "He's already had a lot of prunes."

"Yes, but look how big he is," Felicia said. "He could take a lot of prunes. Maybe not the whole box this time. Maybe only half a box."

I fed Beans a couple prunes, and he started to whine and claw at the door.

"He's ready!" Felicia said. "Get him out. Get the bags."

290

"He needs grass," I told them. "He only goes on grass."

"Ocean Drive!" Suzanne shouted.

Rosa had the car in gear. "I've got it covered. Hang on. We're only a couple blocks away."

She rocketed down Collins, hung a left onto Ocean, and slid to a stop at the curb. We all got out and ran with Beans to the grassy stretch of park between the road and beach. Beans reached the grass and abruptly stopped and hunched. I had a plastic bag wrapped around my hand. I was set to catch. Felicia had Beans by the leash. Suzanne and Rosa had spare bags.

"I knew the prunes would work," Felicia said.

Beans put his head down, squinched his eyes closed, and a box and a half of prunes and God knows what else exploded from his back end in a gelatinous spray that shot out over a ten-foot radius.

We all jumped back bug-eyed.

"Maybe too many prunes," Rosa said.

Beans picked his head up and smiled. He was done. He felt fine. He pranced around a little at the end of his leash.

"Okay," I said. "Let's not panic. He's obviously empty. So the circuit board has to be here somewhere. Everybody look."

"It's too small," Suzanne said. "It would have been hard to find in . . . you know, a pile. It's going to be impossible to find in this grass."

"Maybe they'll only cut a couple fingers off," Rosa said. "As long as he's got his thumb, he could be okay."

"We have twenty-five minutes," Felicia said.

"We'll have to fake it," I told them. "Everyone look for dog poop. Lots of people walk their dogs here and not everyone cleans up. We'll fill a bag with whatever poop we can find. Then we'll give the bag to Miranda, and we'll tell him we didn't have time to look for the circuit board. And the more poop the better, so it takes a long time for Miranda to go through it. We need time to make a getaway with Hooker."

"I'm gonna need some Pepto-Bismol when I'm done here," Rosa said.

"Sorry," I said to Suzanne, "you'll have to replicate the circuit board. But at least your technology won't get stolen."

"What's this?" Simon wanted to know.

"Dog poop," I said, handing the bag over to him. "We didn't have time to look through it for the circuit board, but I'm sure it's in there. Beans is all cleaned out."

"No kidding. This is a gallon bag of dog shit. Jeez, you could at least have double bagged it."

"I was in a hurry. I didn't want Hooker to lose any fingers." I looked around. "Where's Hooker?"

"He's in the car with Fred. I'm going to have to call Miranda on this. I wasn't expecting a sack of shit."

"It was the best I could do on short notice," I said.

Simon and I were standing in the parking lot next to the Royal Palm Deli. Rosa was idling in the slot closest to the driveway. Suzanne and Felicia had Simon in their sights, giving him the squinty-eye, guns in hand, ready to "take him down" should I give the signal. An SUV with tinted windows idled at the other end of the lot. Hard to tell who was inside the SUV.

Simon studied me behind his dark glasses. "Just between you and me, if I hadn't left you at the bar last night, would I have gotten to nail you?"

"You don't expect me to tell you, do you?"

He looked at the gallon of dog poop. "I guess I know the answer."

Simon put the poop in the back of the SUV and flipped his cell phone open. He held a short conversation with someone at the other end, presumably Miranda, the phone was flipped closed, and Simon walked back to me.

"Miranda says we bring the bag and Hooker back to the house, and when we find the circuit board we'll let Hooker go."

"The deal was that we'd swap here. I want my poop back."

"Lady, I'd love to give you your *poop* back, but no can do. The boss wants the *poop*."

I trudged back to the Camry and got in next to Beans. "They're going to release Hooker when they find the circuit board."

The black SUV pulled away, and Rosa cranked the Camry over. "Okay, ladies," she said. "A girl's gotta do what a girl's gotta do."

"What does that mean?" I asked Rosa.

"It means we have to kick some ass and get Hooker out."

"That sounds good on paper," I said to Rosa. "But we're not exactly a SWAT team. I think it's time to bring in the police."

Suzanne was in the back with me, sitting on the other side of Beans. "Easy for you to say," Suzanne said. "You didn't just kidnap Ray Huevo. I'm in favor of us going in and solving the problem ourselves. I work out, and I can shoot, and I'm in the mood to do some damage," she said, selecting a gun from the pocket in front of her. "I'm putting my name on this Glock nine."

We drove to the house and Rosa sat at idle in front of the gate. The gate was closed and attached to a six-foot solid-stucco fence that encircled the property. From what we could see of the grounds, we would have to get over the fence and then cover some open grass before reaching the house. A small metal medallion attached to the front gate told us the property was protected by All Season Security.

"It would be better if we could do this in the dark," Rosa said.

I looked at the sky. The sun was low. Maybe an hour until sunset. Maybe a little more. An hour felt like a long time to leave Hooker in there with the finger chopper.

"It'll take them a while to go through a gallon of poop," Felicia said. "They gonna have to put it in a strainer little by little and power wash it."

We all made gagging sounds.

"I think we have until the next phone call," Suzanne said. "If they don't find the circuit board, they'll call. They don't know for certain that this was a setup."

CHAPTER
SIXTEEN

We were parked four houses down from the estate where they were holding Hooker hostage, the Camry tucked back into the driveway of an ungated and unoccupied house. We'd carefully watched the street for activity, but there'd been nothing to see. No cars coming or going. No one out for a stroll. We watched the sun set in a brilliant display of fluorescent orange and pink. We watched the sky change from dusk to dark.

"This is it," Rosa said. "Showtime."

We armed ourselves, got out of the Camry, and started walking down the street. Rosa, Felicia, Suzanne, and me. Beans was left behind, and he wasn't liking it. Beans was in the car, barking loud enough to raise the dead.

"You got to do something with doggie," Felicia said. "People gonna call the cops on us."

I went back to the car, opened the door, and Beans bounded out. I took the leash, and he pranced beside me. He was happy. He was going for a walk with everyone.

"When I die I want to come back as this doggie," Felicia said.

We stopped when we got to the gate. It was still closed and locked. Beyond the gate we could see the

BMW parked in the courtyard. The house was dark. Not a single light burning.

"Maybe they have black-out shades," Rosa said.

"Maybe they're watching a movie on television," Felicia said.

Maybe they're waiting for us, I thought.

Lights were also off in neighboring houses. This wasn't high season in Florida. Not a lot of the rich folks in residence. We walked off the road and chose a spot where the shadows were deep.

"We gonna have to *alley-oop* over the wall," Felicia said.

Rosa and I linked hands and gave Suzanne a boost up.

"Everything looks quiet inside the wall," Suzanne whispered. She straddled the wall and silently dropped out of sight.

Felicia was next to go.

"I can't reach," she said, one foot in our hands. "I have to climb on your shoulders. Hold still."

Felicia managed to get onto Rosa's shoulders, I got my hand under her ass and gave her a shove, and she went over the wall and landed on the other side with a thud.

Rosa and I looked at Beans. He was alert, watching us, watching the wall.

"I swear, he's waiting to go over," Rosa said.

"We need one of those bucket trucks the phone company uses."

"If we can get Felicia over the wall, we can get *him* over the wall," Rosa said.

We stood him up on his hind legs with his two front paws against the wall, and we got our hands under his big dog butt.

"*Heave*," Rosa said.

We both gave a grunt and got Beans about three feet off the ground.

"Christ," Rosa said, "it's like lifting a hundred-and-fifty-pound sandbag."

"Here, doggie," Felicia whispered from the other side of the wall. "Nice Beansy."

"Come to Aunt Sue," Suzanne cooed. "Come on. You can do it. Come to Aunt Suzy Woozy!"

"On the count of three," Rosa said. "One, two, *three!*"

We took a deep breath and hefted Beans up another foot and a half. Somehow he got a back paw on Rosa's chest and pushed himself high enough to get his two front feet dug into the top of the wall. I got my head under his rear end, and when I stood straight he went over. There was a gasp and a thud and then there was silence.

"Is Beans okay?" I whispered.

"Yeah, he's fine," Suzanne said. "He landed on Felicia. It might take her a minute to catch her breath."

Rosa went up next, with a lot more blind determination than grace. She straddled the wall, turned onto her stomach, we locked hands and everyone pulled me over.

We were all plastered against the wall. A swath of grass lay between us and the house. Maybe thirty feet deep. When we ran across the grass, we'd be exposed to view.

"There's no way around it," Suzanne said. "We have to make a run for it. When we get to the house, we'll be hidden again, and we can creep along and try to find a way in."

We got halfway across the grass, and all the outdoor lights flashed on.

"We tripped the motion sensors," Suzanne said. "Don't anyone panic."

"They gonna let the Dobermans out next," Felicia said, running onto a patio. "I'm not waiting for that. I'm going in where it's safe."

She whacked a patio door with her gun butt, the glass shattered, she reached inside and opened the door, and the alarm system went off.

We all rushed into the house, Beans included. We fumbled our way through the house in the dark, guns drawn, going room by room. No reason to go slowly or quietly. The alarm was whining. The phone was ringing. No one was answering the phone. Undoubtedly the security company calling. Their next call would be to the police.

We crept into the kitchen, Beans gave an excited *woof*, and ran forward. Hard to hear much over the alarm, but there was the sound of something heavy crashing to the floor in front of us. Rosa flipped a switch, the kitchen came up like daylight, and we all gaped at Hooker. He was tied to a kitchen chair that Beans had tipped over. Beans was on top of him, giving him slurpeys, and Hooker was looking stunned.

I ran to Hooker and counted his fingers. Ten! *Yahoo!*

"Are you okay?" I asked him.

"Yeah, I just got the wind knocked out of me when Beans hit the chair."

298

"What about Gobbles?"

"He's in the house somewhere. I don't know what kind of condition he's in. He might be upstairs."

"I'll go look for him," Rosa said.

"Where is everybody else?" I asked Hooker.

"Gone."

"That's impossible. There's only one way in and one way out, and we were watching it."

"They left by boat," Hooker said. "Miranda and his two men. And Ray. And the dog shit. I guess Miranda didn't think he could get much more out of you or me, so he took Ray. If the chip's in the bag, everyone will be happy. If it isn't, I imagine Miranda will hold Ray hostage until he duplicates the technology. And if he can't duplicate the technology, I don't think things will look good for Ray."

Felicia was working on Hooker's ropes with a steak knife.

"How's it going?" Suzanne asked. "Is he almost cut loose? We need to get out of here before the police arrive. I don't want a mug shot with my hair looking like this."

Felicia made a last swipe with the knife, and Hooker wriggled free. He got to his feet and looked around. "Where's Beans?"

"He was here a minute ago," I said.

Hooker whistled, and Beans came into the kitchen dragging Rodriguez, who was obviously incredibly dead.

Felicia shook her finger at Beans. "You got to stop playing with the dead people."

Hooker found a box of crackers in a cupboard. "Here you go, guy," he said to Beans. "I'll trade you a cracker for the dead man."

I followed the drool smears down a hall to a powder room. The door was open, and I could see another body on the floor. I flipped the light on for a better look. It was Lucca. He was on his back, his black eye no longer seeming like much of a problem.

I know Rodriguez and Lucca weren't such nice guys. And I know they killed a bunch of people. Still, I felt bad they were dead. Okay, maybe not Lucca. I was a little glad Lucca was dead.

I closed the door on Lucca and returned to the kitchen where Hooker and Felicia were trying to get Rodriguez to sit at the table.

"How's this?" Felicia asked me. "You think this looks natural?"

"Yeah, if you don't count that he's been dead for two days, and you had to break both legs to get him to sit, plus his head is facing the wrong way. He looks like something out of the *Exorcist* movie." And then I saw the guns on the table. "I'm guessing those guns belong to Rodriguez and Lucca?"

"Simon laid the guns on the table when they brought Rodriguez and Lucca in," Hooker said. "And then everyone forgot about them. I'm hoping one of those guns was used to shoot Oscar."

Rodriguez started to list to one side, and Felicia propped him up on his elbow. "We put this guy here in case Officer Dummy is the first on the scene and can't figure it out."

300

We all froze at the sound of gunfire.

"Upstairs," Hooker said.

There was a loud crash, and then Rosa's voice. "It's okay," she yelled down. "I got Gobbles, and he's okay."

I went to the foot of the stairs. "What was the gunfire about?"

"I had to shoot the lock off the bathroom door," Rosa said. "I always wanted to do that." Rosa had Gobbles by the back of the shirt, holding him up like he was a baby kitten. "He's a little wobbly, but he don't got any holes in him he's not supposed to have. At least none I can see."

"I went outside with the garbage," Gobbles said, eyes glazed, semi-babbling. "It had the turkey carcass in it. It was a real good turkey, too. Nice and moist. Everybody said so. I made a real good Thanksgiving. Everybody left, and I was cleaning up, and next thing I was in the trunk of a car. And then they gave me some kind of shot, and everything was whirly, and I don't know where I was, and then I was back in the trunk. And when I was in the trunk, I saw Jesus. And the Virgin Mary. And Ozzie Osbourne."

"Must have been crowded in that trunk," Rosa said.

Rosa and I got Gobbles down the stairs and into the kitchen. We walked him to the middle of the room, and he spotted Rodriguez sitting at the table and totally wigged out.

"You!" Gobbles yelled at Rodriguez. "I didn't get any leftovers because of you. And leftovers are the best part. Everybody knows that. You don't fuckin' kidnap someone Thanksgiving night. I fuckin' wait all fuckin' year for

301

those leftovers. I hate you. I hate you!" He grabbed the gun from Rosa, and he shot Rodriguez in the knee.

Nothing happened. Rodriguez didn't jump, didn't bleed, didn't blink.

"You *do* know he's dead, right?" Hooker asked Gobbles.

"Yeah. I knew that."

"Feel better?"

"Yeah," Gobbles said. "But I surely would like a turkey sandwich."

I noticed a shoebox left on the table. Gucci. "Someone buys expensive shoes," I said.

Rosa picked the box up and looked inside. "Uh-oh."

Felicia, Hooker, Suzanne, and I looked over Rosa's shoulder. There were two cylinders attached to a small electronic component with a clock counting down. Two minutes left on the clock.

"Bomb!" we all yelled.

Hooker grabbed the box, ran outside, and heaved it toward the water. It hit the dock, went into a skid, and exploded. We were all knocked back, and half the windows blew out.

We didn't waste any time getting off the property. Too much trouble to alley-oop over the wall again. We ran to the water's edge, carefully stepped into the waist-high water, scooted around the protruding stucco wall, and dragged our soaked selves onto the bank on the other side.

The white light from headlights and blue emergency strobes raced down the street and stopped in front of the gated house while we tiptoed across the backs of yards. We got to the Camry, squeezed six wet people and a big wet dog into the car, and Rosa drove off, down the street then across the causeway, toward South Beach.

I had so much leftover terror my teeth were chattering and I was shaking.

"D-d-do you think it will work?" I asked Hooker. "D-d-do you think they'll connect Rodriguez and Lucca with the m-m-murders?"

Hooker had his arms locked around me. "There will be a lot of unanswered questions," he said, "but I'm hoping we left the murder weapon in the kitchen. I don't see where the police can dispute a murder weapon loaded with fingerprints."

"Guess we know why they weren't worried about leaving you behind," Rosa said to Hooker. "They were going to blow you up."

"That charge was left in the kitchen, next to the gas cooktop," Hooker said. "I'm guessing it would have blown *everything* up and probably burned the place down."

I woke up in the little bed in Felicia's house. Beans was on the floor, still sound asleep. Hooker was on top of me, wide awake, his hand on my breast.

"Your hand is on my breast again," I said.

"And?"

"You might want to move it lower."

He slid his hand down a couple inches. "Here?"

"Lower."

The hand went to just below my hip. "Here?"

303

"Yeah. Now a little to the right."

"Darlin'!"

Okay, big surprise. I was going to succumb to his charms . . . again. And I'd probably regret it . . . again. But I wouldn't regret it short term. Short term was going to be *good*. And who knows, maybe it would work out for us this time. And if it didn't, I'd be smart enough to keep the key to the golf cart.

An hour later we were still in bed, and Hooker's cell phone rang.

"I hear on the news that the police found the Huevo murder weapon in the possession of two dead suspects," Skippy said. "It sounds like you're off the hook. Are you planning on showing up here anytime soon?"

"Do I have to?"

"We had the parade of cars this morning and your stunt double did a burnout on Forty-second Street and took out Spanky's car. Marty Smith got to him with a microphone before I could reach him, and it sounded like Marty was interviewing Loni Anderson. If you don't want rumors going around concerning your sexual affiliation, I think you should get your ass to New York."

"Did they say anything else about the dead suspects?" Hooker asked Skippy.

"They said the one guy had been chewed up by the swamp monster. Imagine that."

EPILOGUE

It was sixty degrees and sunny, it was mid-January, and it was the first day of three days of preseason testing at Daytona. Hooker'd rented a beachside house for himself and his crew, and I was included. We'd all left the beach house at seven-thirty and driven to the speedway where his crew had unloaded both triple-two Metro cars from the hauler, then rolled them across the blacktop and into their side-by-side garage bays.

Both cars were flat gray, only adorned by their numbers. No need to decorate the car up with sponsor logos for testing. Only a handful of fans would find their way to the grandstand, and there'd be no television audience. This was a work session to get the car ready to race.

Hooker's crew was on the car, adjusting the setup. Hooker and I were in front of his hauler, drinking coffee, enjoying the morning sun. Beans was back at the house, taking his morning nap.

The 69 car was three haulers down from us, and Dickie was in the hauler with Delores. Best not to know what they were doing.

Light flashed in my peripheral vision. The sort of blinding flash you get when you tip a mirror to the sun. I shielded my eyes and turned to the light and saw that it was Suzanne Huevo swinging her ass down the garage area, the sun reflecting off her diamonds. She was wearing a Huevo Industries shirt, tight designer jeans, and boots with four-inch stiletto heels. A doggie bag hung on her shoulder, and Itsy Poo's tiny head was stuck up, her black button eyes taking everything in.

"Yow," Hooker whispered.

I gave him the squinty eye.

"Just looking," he said. "A guy can look."

I waved to Suzanne, and she walked past the two Huevo haulers to come say hello.

"We heard rumors that you were in charge, but I didn't know if it was true," I said to Suzanne.

"I was second in line as executor. And since Ray still hasn't surfaced, I'm in charge until my sons come of age."

"No word about Ray?"

"Miranda's been in touch, making ransom noises. I told him he'd have to pay *me* to take Ray back. He also said the only thing they found in the bag of dog shit was dog shit. I voiced surprise over that. He then offered to market my product for me, and I declined."

"What happens if Ray returns?"

"I suppose he could fight me for executorship, but I've had a chance to go into his files and collect evidence against him. He'd been robbing the company for years. The charges against him would be embezzling, at the very least. And I'm not wasting any time setting safeguards in place to protect Huevo property. The new battery and the wireless technology are in negotiation with a reputable buyer. The process is far enough along that Miranda doesn't have an incentive to strong-arm me into partnership with him."

"Looks like you're going hands-on with the race-car side of Huevo," Hooker said.

"I'm hands-on with everything my kids own," Suzanne said. "I thought it would be good to stop around today and make my presence felt."

Hooker's mechanic was under the hood of the primary triple two. He revved the engine and the sound was deafening.

"Gotta go," Suzanne said when the engine cut back. "I need to talk to Dickie before he gets in the car today."

"Yeah," Hooker said on a whisper to me. "Shore him up so he's not too crushed when he loses because he's not running with traction control."

"About traction control," I said to Hooker. "It turned out the gizmo wasn't working at Homestead."

"Are you shitting me?"

"Spanky drove a great race."

"That is so depressing," Hooker said. "I'm going to need some serious cheering up when we get back to the house."

"And I suppose I'd be expected to help with the cheering up?"

Hooker smiled at me. "I could cheer myself up, but it's a lot nicer when we get cheered up together."

I smiled back at him. Something to look forward to. Getting cheered up with Hooker was one of my favorite things to do these days.

Suzanne had detoured to the garage area to speak to her crew chief. She stood with one hand on the dog bag, one hand at her side, her feet planted wide. She was very much the owner. Woman in charge. She finished her conversation, turned on her heel, and stalked off to the hauler to meet with Dickie.

"Something else to think about," I said to Hooker. "Here's the bad news. Any woman who can swing her ass like that in four-inch heels and has mother bear programmed into her hormone system will do whatever needs to be done to keep the cubs in pizza money. I wouldn't be surprised if she used her technology to keep cheating. It's virtually undetectable."

"Is there good news?" Hooker wanted to know.

"Felicia called me the day after we flew out of Miami. She was walking barefoot through her dining room and pricked her foot on something sharp in the carpet. Turned out it was the chip. Beans hadn't eaten it after all. I sent it to my pal Steven, and he backed his way through it and reproduced it for me. I just got it from FedEx yesterday. And not only do I have the duplicated technology, but I've come up with a way to improve on it. Because in our case, the driver would be controlling the technology, I can insert the remote into a man's sport watch, eliminating the need for the relay."

Hooker slid an arm around my shoulders and hugged me into him. "Darlin'!"